ASHLEY ANTHONY

...drinks a lot of tea in front of his spider plants.

Little Miss Morning Star

First published 2024 by Hot Tea Press

Paperback edition ISBN: 978-1-0685522-0-5
Hardback edition ISBN: 978-1-0685522-1-2
E-book edition ISBN: 978-1-0685522-2-9

LITTLE MISS
MORNING STAR

ASHLEY ANTHONY

The Devil has escaped hell, and she's a four-year-old girl.

DEBUT NOVEL

PROLOGUE

On the sixth hour of the sixth day of a scorching hot sixth month, Ms Makewell arrived at Little Woods Kindergarten earlier than she normally would. A feeling that there was something she should have been preparing for awoke her in the middle of the night. It was a voice in the back of her head that was not entirely her own, tormenting her on something she had forgotten or, worse, something she was not yet ready to know. As hard as Ms Makewell tried, she could not think what it was she was supposed to know, could not make out what the voice was trying to say, but she could not get back to sleep, and so hoping the voice was God's, Ms Makewell said a prayer and readied herself for the day ahead.

On this same sixth hour, on the same sixth day, on the very same scorching hot six month, the residents of Lakeville were disturbed by water that ran black like tar. They recoiled as taps muddied hands, showers stained bodies, and garden sprinklers blackened lawns that had been kept green in spite of a sun so hot it refused clouds into its pale blue skies. Stranger still was that every cross nailed to the walls of their homes had come loose, upturning into foreboding symbols that upset their Christian sensibilities more than the sludge spraying over their lawns ever could, and even when the minute ticked to seven and the stains were washed clean, the crosses, no matter how hard they tried, would not stay right.

When Ms Makewell heard these tales from the arriving parents and children, she looked at the cross on her kindergarten wall, and like in their stories, it was upside down. A nail had come loose, but when she did not know. It was only then that Ms Makewell realised the voice in her head might not belong to God but to something else, something evil. The Devil. Had she led it to her schoolhouse? Or was it inside of her, twisting her stomach in knots?

1

As all the children of Little Woods Kindergarten ran to their bags to collect their prized possessions for show-and-tell, Ms Makewell flipped the cross on the wall for the second time today. She tried not to see the upturned cross as a bad omen, but like all the people of Lakeville, Ms Makewell was deeply religious and had a hard time separating coincidence from superstition. Darkness was coming; she could feel it curdling in her stomach. Thankfully, Ms Makewell had a gaggle of children to distract her from her worries, children who had not yet grown to associate innocuous little things like a loose screw with evil.

Ms Makewell took her seat at the head of the circle as the children jostled for a space next to their best friends or the brightest toy that had caught their attention from bag to floor. She tried not to look at what objects the children had brought to show-and-tell as she enjoyed the surprise as much as they did. Still, there was no mistaking the flash of red from Charlie Shaw's fire engine or the blue of Kaylie May's police car. Two toys that always came accompanied by riveting stories of bravery and heroics.

"Are we all settled?" Ms Makewell asked before the expectant gazes turned to boredom.

"Yes, Ms Makewell," the children sang back.

"Now, who would like to tell us all about their item first?"

Hands stretched into the air as if reaching for the heavens might help them get picked. "Me, me, me," all the kindergarteners shouted to Ms Makewell, buzzing with anticipation as they waited to see who she would choose.

Ms Makewell looked around the circle. She didn't have a family of her own. No kids, no husband or partner, and parents who had passed too soon, now headstones in the ground, markers of their journey into the arms of God, and so it was the annually changing children of her kindergarten class that had become her family. She loved the kindergarteners with all her heart, even those with a predisposition for naughtiness. However, this year, Ms Makewell was blessed with a flock of angels without a bad bone in their body, which didn't make picking the first to begin their show-and-tell any easier.

As Ms Makewell closed her eyes to a squint, not tight enough to darken her watchful gaze but tight enough for all the excitable faces to blur, she pointed a soft finger to the oak beams above and moved her hand around the circle.

"I pick..." Ms Makewell said, swinging her arm back and forth as she enjoyed the sweet sounds of snickering children who couldn't hold back their excitement.

Ms Makewell recognised every laugh and could put a name to every joyful sound even with her eyes half closed, all except one. There was a laugh amongst the circle painted with a touch of mischief. A girlish giggle hidden behind the palm of a hand as if trying to conceal an act of devilry that they knew would get them in trouble. Ms Makewell attempted to settle her finger on the unknown laughter, but each time she thought she had found its owner, it flew like a wisp to the other side of the circle.

As Ms Makewell followed her finger back across the blurred, smiling faces of her children, chasing mischief that refused to be caught, a new sound stole her attention. Hissing, moving around the circle, counter to her pointing finger and the laughter she was trying to chase. Ms Makewell should have opened her eyes in terror, but the hissing was hypnotic, and it lulled her into an unnatural state of calm. The two sounds that should not have been amongst the circle, serpentine and sly, conjured images of a fiery inferno, a hellscape dashed black with ash, and it had Ms Makewell wondering, was it calm that kept her eyes shut or inevitability?

After six passes over the circle, Ms Makewell finally found the girl trying to evade her. "I pick you," she said, disappointed in herself for still not having a name to put to the laughter.

Ms Makewell opened her eyes, but there was no girl at the centre of the now silent circle, silent but for the hissing that had settled amongst them. Whether it was the lack of sleep, or the stories of suspected sin told by the children's parents, Ms Makewell looked not to the kindergarteners but to the cross hanging on the classroom wall. As soon as her eyes found it, the screw came loose, and her symbol of faith swung into the position of evil. The Devil was watching, and as if he sought to capitalise on her complacency, chaos erupted around her.

"Snake," the children screamed.

The tiny tot's terror brought Ms Makewell's attention to where it should have been all along, to a snake whose scales undulated through shades of yellow and green. It reared up on itself and glared at the children with eyes that roared in the infernal shades of hellfire and blood-rain. Its split tongue tasted the terror in the air, flicking out from its mouth every time one of the kindergarteners cried out in its direction. It was poised to strike, and Ms Makewell knew she had to act before it did.

Ms Makewell threw her chair back and jumped to her feet, "Stay calm, children," she said, hoping to placate a pinch of the panic around her. "Get behind me."

As the frantic children leapt to Ms Makewell's side, scurrying like field mice afraid of becoming prey, she noticed a demonic shadow cast over the snake. It was darker than the black slits that split its eyes in two, and the figure inspired more fear in Ms Makewell than the reptile itself. The shape was human, though the horns that curled at the tip gave it away as something else. It loomed over the broken circle of lost toys with unnatural darkness as if whatever cast it had dragged something from the pits of hell to shine at its back. Even the other shadows appeared to bend away from it as if they, too, were afraid of its origin.

"Get Kaylie May's mum," one of the children screamed.

"We need police," another said.

"Charlie, get your dad."

"Call the fire bribgade," another said, a pronunciation that went uncorrected by the fireman's son, who clung to Ms Makewell's leg, too scared to speak.

As Ms Makewell traced the shadow's edges, not daring to look up and see what it belonged to, her heart thumped against her chest. Each painful beat bubbled bile in her stomach that wanted to be thrown up, but she had to ignore it and focus for the sake of the children.

She held her arms out, again, on instinct, putting a shield

between the evil and the kindergarteners that had sought shelter behind her. "It's just a snake. It's nothing to fear," Ms Makewell said, her voice shaking so much that she could only pray to God that they believed her and that she could protect them from the snake and the evil that had sent it here.

Still too afraid to look up, unsure if the demonic shadow from Hell was a making of her imagination, Ms Makewell kept her eyes on the snake. She watched its movements for any sign it might strike. The erratic turns of its head, the baring of its fangs she hoped weren't poisonous, and its coiling body that had lost its yellow hues and now quivered hypnotically between unimaginable shades of garden green. All seemed like tells of the snake's vicious intent, but Ms Makewell was a teacher, not a zoologist. The truth was that she had no idea what to do because, in all her years of teaching, a snake had never once entered her classroom.

What was strange, however, was that as Ms Makewell watched the snake, she couldn't help but feel this was all for show. That the creature was no less deadly than the children at her back and that the erratic looks around the room were more akin to a child seeking approval for a job well done than that of a predator readying itself to kill. She was almost inclined to reach forward and give it a pat on the back or offer it kind words of affirmation to draw out a smile, but Ms Makewell knew that was a foolish thought, so she kept her place between the snake and the kindergarteners.

"Here's what we're going to do, children," Ms Makewell said.

Before a plan tacked itself onto the end of her sentence, the snake reared upwards and hissed so loudly that it caused another flurry of shrieks and screams from the kindergarteners.

Ms Makewell knew she had to do something. Fortunately, she had a plan now, at least the start of one. It involved the children running and her jumping on the snake and doing whatever she had to do so that the little ones could escape, but as she was about to launch into action, the demonic, blacker-than-black, horned shadow, accompanied by the same mischievous, girlish giggle that had caught her attention moments ago, moved towards them.

The curdling fear bubbling in her stomach rose, though not from the snake that appeared ready to lunge or the imagined evil at its back, but from the thought that she had made a mistake. That the shadow did not belong to a devil but to one of her kindergarteners and that the mysterious girl, whoever she might be, was skipping into the scaled arms of danger.

"Stop," Ms Makewell shouted, unable to do anything more than reach out, thanks to the children wrapped tightly around her legs.

The ominous shadow moved with the girl as she skipped towards the snake and the cowering children. In a defiant act of bravery, Ms Makewell finally looked up, and how foolish she felt when she saw that the shadow's devilish horns were nothing more than an oversized, long-tailed, black bow sitting on the head of a girl dressed in a beautiful, billowing prairie dress, so pristine and white that its angelic glow served only to make the bow and the shadow she cast appear darker.

"I'm Lucy, and this is Albert," the girl said, lifting the snake above her head with a strength that didn't match her dollish size.

The snake coiled its body around Lucy's arms, letting its tail trail over her shoulders and down her back into obscurity. Although the children were still audibly afraid, mummering panicked words at Ms Makewell's feet, the snake no longer appeared as the threat it once was. Ms Makewell wasn't sure whether it was because the snake was made softer in the hands of the little girl or because, as much as she couldn't believe it, the snake was smiling down at her.

"He is my snake and…" Lucy paused, looked up at her snake with a mischievous glint in her eyes, then back to Ms Makewell and the children with a smile so wide it fattened her cheeks, "he eats little girls and boys."

Albert, the snake, turned to the group of scared children and hissed his loudest hiss yet as if he and Lucy had spent all morning planning every bit of her speech. The children screamed, and the ones clinging to Ms Makewell's leg squeezed tighter, and yet, every twang of fear that had Ms Makewell imagining terrible things had washed away.

"It's a joke, children," Ms Makewell said.

She wanted to add, I think, to the end of the sentence but had to maintain authority on the situation lest the classroom descended further into chaos.

"No, it's not," Lucy said, then she giggled, unable to keep a straight face. "Actually, Albert likes to eat apples."

Lucy lowered Albert from above her head and picked a perfectly shaped, glossy, red apple from behind her back. As she did, Ms Makewell was sure she saw a shift in the girl's shadow. A slight stretch. A change in clarity. A darkening to the shadow already six shades blacker than any other in the room.

The children gasped as Lucy presented the apple to the group as if by magic. It looked fresh from the tree, picked at the peak of its season. An apple so temptingly ripe it had Ms Makewell leaning toward it. It was the most perfect apple

Ms Makewell had ever seen. Its skin shone red, sparkling as if it had been dipped in glitter. It bore no blemishes of green or yellow. Nor was there a single bruise upon its shapely curves. Even the divot at its top had been picked clean of its stalk, leaving nothing woody or indigestible behind. It had her salivating, and Ms Makewell wondered if it would be a sin to steal from a child or her hungry pet snake who may or may not have a taste for little girls and boys.

Before Ms Makewell could answer her question of sin and soul, Lucy held the apple out for her snake and dropped it into its mouth. As Albert swallowed the fruit, an orchid scent burst into the classroom that overpowered the residual terror in the air. The smell soothed the children, and they watched in awe as the round apple swell moved through the snake's body.

Ms Makewell took this moment of calm to bring some semblance of control back to her kindergarten class. "You see, children. Nothing to be afraid of," Ms Makewell said. "Albert is a good snake, isn't he, Lucy?"

"Albert is a really good snake." Lucy beamed.

"That's what I thought," Ms Makewell said, prising the little hands from around her legs. "Do you hear that, children? I think we can all sit down again."

The kindergarteners gave Lucy a wide berth as they returned to the circle, each taking their place in front of their abandoned toys and clutching them to their chest for safety. Ms Makewell picked up her chair, not taking her eyes off the snake as she sat back down at the head of the circle, though not before dashing to the upturned cross upon the wall and setting it right, because as sweet as this girl seemed Ms Makewell couldn't shake the feeling that the Devil was amongst them.

"So, your name is Lucy, is it?"

Lucy nodded.

"Are you new to Lakeville?"

"Yes," Lucy said again, rapidly nodding as she did. "I came up this morning."

"Well, we're all delighted to have you, Lucy," Ms Makewell said, sure she hadn't seen a new name added to the register. A register on the desk at the other end of the classroom sat beneath an apple that was not quite as delicious looking as the one just fed to the snake. "Why doesn't everyone say hello to Lucy?" Ms Makewell said, deciding not to risk a trip across the classroom.

The children sang hello to Lucy, though their song of greetings was out of tune and out of sync, thanks to the nerves warbling through their voices.

"We would all very much like to know more about you and Albert, Lucy," Ms Makewell said. "How about you tell us all a bit about yourself?"

Lucy's jaw dropped as she looked around the circle and back to Ms Makewell. The excitement to talk about herself was apparent, but what was not so obvious was the surprise in her eyes was only there because someone had cared enough to ask. Fortunately, Ms Makewell was a seasoned kindergarten teacher and as sad as it was to admit, she was well used to seeing these signs of neglect.

"Go on," Ms Makewell said, encouraging Lucy to open up to the group.

"I am Lucy. I am four eons old. I am an angel. I am the morning star. This is Albert. He is one-eon-old."

"Do you mean one-year-old, Lucy?"

"No," Lucy said matter-of-factly. "Albert is my best friend. He likes to slither. He likes to hiss. He likes—." Lucy scrunched her face up as she stopped to think. "He likes me. He is green. He is sometimes yellow. The garden was green. So, he was green. My hair is yellow. Now he is yellow."

Ms Makewell couldn't help but admire Lucy as she jumped from sentence to sentence, reeling off a list of facts, hoping to get her peers to like her and Albert. It was working slowly, thanks to the snake being a snake, but with every word Lucy spoke, the children in the circle sank more comfortably onto their bums.

It was easy to see how Lucy could win over a crowd. There was a gravity about her that had Ms Makewell and the children leaning forward to listen to her speak. However, it wasn't what she was saying that was drawing everyone closer, as, despite the magic and wonder that carried her voice, Lucy spoke very simply for someone her age, frequently cutting her sentences short and stumbling over words when she didn't know what was supposed to come next. No, the gravity about Lucy came from her presence, her very being.

Lucy was beautiful, perfect in every way, just like the apple, and as she rolled through another flurry of snake facts, it occurred to Ms Makewell that Lucy reflected everything good about Earth. Her hair was as yellow as the sun, her eyes as blue as the oceans and skies, her smile was as bright as daylight, and her shadow as dark as a night that led you deeply into dreams. As Ms Makewell listened to her speak, she wondered where God's green grass gained its representation in the person before her. Only when she began to question how Lucy could comfortably keep a snake twice her size in her arms without breaking a sweat did the full picture come into form. Lucy was tiny, small and weightless, like a feather or a falling leaf, and yet despite it, she was powerful and immense, like a gust of wind or a tree with more rings than Ms Makewell had years.

"Albert is the first snake," Lucy said, still talking with no one to stop her. "Don't be scared of him. Albert didn't trick Adam and Eve. That was me. The apples are for Albert. He likes apples."

Lucy's eyes jumped around the kindergartener's circle when she realised that she had repeated herself, a movement of anxiety mirrored in her snake. She had already told everyone that Albert likes to eat apples. It was the first thing she had told them. Now they would be bored and not want to listen to her anymore. Or worse, they would think she was silly and stupid and couldn't do anything right.

"I said that already," Lucy said. "Sorry. I start again. I fix it. I say it better."

"That's alright, Lucy," Ms Makewell said. "There's no need to feel nervous. I am sure Albert's love of apples is so important that you had to say it twice."

Afraid she had lost everyone's attention, Lucy nodded frantically and said, "He can eat them forever. And ever. And ever."

"Then Albert must still be quite hungry?"

"Albert is always hungry for apples," Lucy said, her voice brightening back up now Ms Makewell had successfully eased her nerves.

"How about I go get that apple from my desk?" Ms Makewell said, hoping for a chance to double-check the register for this mysterious girl's name. "Would Albert like that?"

"No," Lucy snapped. "Not that apple. Only this one."

Lucy miraculously pulled another glossy, red apple from behind her back, which caused another gasp of awe from the kindergarteners and another temporary shift in Lucy's shadow that only Ms Makewell noticed. Albert slithered down Lucy's arm to the apple in her other hand and opened his mouth wide enough for his fangs to safely pass over the circumference of the fruit without scratching her hand.

There was a glint of anticipation in Albert's fiery eyes and a glistening pool of saliva settling beneath his tongue as he waited for his juicy meal to be dropped into his mouth, but when a flash of inspiration struck Lucy, and she pulled the fruit out from his jaw, Albert reared up and hissed.

Ms Makewell and all the children snapped upright from their enraptured lean towards Lucy as the frustrated hiss reminded them that they were sharing their classroom with a snake and that this unknown child's show-and-tell was a potentially deadly animal and not an inanimate, plastic, or cuddly toy like all the other kindergarteners intended to present. Ms Makewell was about to shut it down and tell Lucy that they needed to call her parents so that they could come to collect Albert, but when Lucy silenced her snake with a hiss of her own, Ms Makewell realised that if there was anything to fear in the classroom, it was the Devil disguised as a girl. Who else but the fallen angel could ensnare them so easily? Maybe that was why she wore a bow, Ms Makewell thought, to hide horns which could only be seen in shadow.

"Naughty snake," Lucy said to Albert, who lowered his head apologetically. Lucy turned to the group and held the apple out to them. "Albert is a good snake. You want to feed Albert?"

There was no inflection in Lucy's voice, and it was unclear whether Lucy's request was a question or a demand, but neither mattered to the children. Thanks to the snake's hiss and Lucy's in return, everyone, Ms Makewell included, had fallen back into fear, so as Lucy walked towards them, snake in one hand, apple outstretched in the other, they all shuffled away.

Lucy sighed. "Now no one want feed you. Albert, why you hiss so mean?"

Albert slithered around Lucy's neck and hissed softly into her ear. Whatever the sound meant, it soothed Lucy's sadness, though only slightly.

"I'm your friend too, Albert," Lucy said reassuringly to her snake, who seemed as keen to make friends as his owner was.

It hurt Ms Makewell to see Lucy give up on making friends. She didn't like seeing how tightly coiled the snake was around her throat either. In hopes of solving both problems at once, Ms Makewell did what any good teacher would and offered to feed the snake.

"You feed Albert?"

Ms Makewell put her hand to her chest. "You can call me Ms Makewell," she said, not wanting Lucy or her class of four-year-olds to get into the habit of referring to her or other people as you, even if she was guilty of doing that to Lucy moments ago.

"Ms Makewell feed Albert?" Lucy asked again, still getting over the shock that anyone would dare put their hand near her hissing snake's mouth after what he had done.

"Yes, Lucy. I will feed Albert," Ms Makewell said, emphasising the words missing from Lucy's sentence in hopes that by hearing them, Lucy might learn how to craft longer and more complete sentences herself.

Lucy skipped twice and was upon Ms Makewell in the blink of an eye.

"Take it," Lucy said.

The request seemed innocuous, yet there was something about Lucy's words that made Ms Makewell nervous. Her hand trembled as she hovered just out of reach of the apple, which appeared giant and foreboding as it sat in the palm of Lucy's tiny hand. She couldn't explain why she paused, other than that in the gap between her fingers and the glistening red skin, possibility buzzed like electricity. The feeling churned in her stomach like the temptation to sin. It had her believe that if she picked the suspiciously ripe fruit from Lucy's hand, she would learn everything she shouldn't and that the world would swallow her whole because of it.

A glint in Lucy's eye suggested she knew exactly what Ms Makewell was thinking. "Take it," Lucy said again, though this time her bright and happy voice was twisted with an evil and reverberating malevolence which caused the room to spin.

All eyes were on Ms Makewell. Nervous eyes. Eyes that looked to her for guidance. Ms Makewell blinked away the dizziness, swallowed her trepidations, and picked the apple from Lucy's hand. The electricity disturbing the room flicked off, but not like a switch like a candle being blown out, and though the room ceased to spin, Ms Makewell couldn't help but feel like there was something terribly wrong within it. Was it Lucy or the snake? Could it be the apple miraculously plucked from a tree no one could see? Or was it something else? A thing worse than all three?

"How do I feed Albert?" Ms Makewell asked, determined to maintain her composure despite the thoughts that plagued her.

"Hold apple like this," Lucy said, pinching the air. "Then drop in mouth."

The gesture wasn't the same as how Lucy fed Albert. She

had altered the process to better suit someone not used to being close to sharp and pointed teeth like she was. It was a kindness which helped push away thoughts of the girl's demonic nature, though it did nothing to ease the guilt of ever having them.

As Albert slithered down Lucy's arm, Ms Makewell held the apple out as Lucy had shown her. He kept his tail coiled around her forearm and hovered his head and body between them. Unlike with Lucy, Albert didn't go straight for the apple, and instead, like a previously punished child, he looked nervously between Lucy and the object of his desires.

"Open mouth for apple," Lucy said, giving him permission. Then, if there were any doubts about Ms Makewell's goodness, Lucy added. "She not a grumpy bum. Not like them down there." However, Ms Makewell wasn't sure what that meant.

Albert licked the air, tasting for any sign that Ms Makewell wasn't as good as she seemed. When he was finished licking the flavours only a snake could taste, Albert turned back to Lucy and hissed. Lucy's eyes flicked up from the snake to Ms Makewell. Her sky-blue gaze was piercing, and if Lucy's innocence hadn't matched her mischief in equal parts, then the intensity of the sudden and glassy stare might have disturbed Ms Makewell. Not because it was pointed with such force at her but because she felt Lucy's gaze baring down on the part of her that she assumed was meant only for the eyes of God. Her soul.

Lucy's eyes flicked back to Albert, freeing Ms Makewell from judgment as quickly as she came upon it. "I think she is too," Lucy said. "Now open mouth for yummy apple."

Ms Makewell wanted to ask what Lucy and Albert had conferred. It made no sense that a girl and a snake could commune, but for as good as Ms Makewell could explain, she felt as if she had been weighed by the divine. Though it seemed just as fruitless to know one's judgement as it did to know when you were going to die, and so Ms Makewell didn't press Lucy for an answer. Instead, wanting to prove to the impressionable kindergarteners that the snake was safe, she dropped the apple into its open mouth and hoped that she had passed whatever test had been exacted upon her soul.

As the apple fell, the children twitched on their bums, eager to look at the new girl and her snake but also keeping themselves ready to run away screaming if all ended in disaster. When Albert's mouth closed, and the juicy red orb disappeared, the kindergarteners gasped in unison, and then all fell still as they watched another apple move through his body.

The silence of fascination was lost on Lucy, a girl Ms Makewell could see was more inclined to drama. Ms Makewell watched as she nervously shot glances around the circle, worried the kindergartener's silence meant boredom or indifference. It was only when they began to clap and crawl forward that Lucy's smile brightened her face again.

"I want to feed Albert," one of the kindergarteners said.

"Me too," said another.

"No, me," another said.

"Please, Ms Makewell," a few said together. "Can we feed the snake?"

Suddenly, all the children were bouncing on the spot with their hands in the air and their toys forgotten on the floor between their crossed legs. The fickleness of children never surprised Ms Makewell. It was actually what adhered her to them. She loved the moment-to-moment surprise their curiosity brought into her life, and she was always happy to be pulled along for the ride when it did.

Lucy and her snake looked between Ms Makewell and her eager classmates waiting for her approval to start handing out apples, apples she was sure Lucy would miraculously conjure despite having nowhere in her flowing, white dress to hide them.

"Is Albert still hungry, Lucy?" Ms Makewell asked.

"Albert is very, very hungry. Aren't you, Albert?"

The snake hissed at Ms Makewell with an adorable smile on his leaf-green face, and she took that as a sign he was indeed very, very hungry.

"How many apples is Albert hungry for, Lucy?"

Lucy repeated the question to her snake in a series of hisses that the other kindergarteners found amusing, and when he hissed back, she translated for the class.

"Six more apples."

There was a collective sigh from the circle as the kindergarteners realised not all of them would get to feed the new girl's snake.

"Now, now, children," Ms Makewell said. "Lucy is going to pick six of you to feed Albert, and I don't want any kafuffle if you're not picked. Do you all promise not to make a kafuffle?"

"Yes, Ms Makewell," the kindergarteners sang back, trying their hardest to be on their best behaviour.

"I am sure there will be plenty of opportunities to feed Albert in the future, but we don't want to make the poor guy too stuffed to slither now, do we?"

"No, Ms Makewell," the kindergarteners sang back, and although their song was a little dejected and sarcastic because being on their best behaviour was indeed hard, Ms

Makewell chose to ignore it, knowing they at least understood and accepted what she had asked of them.

Ms Makewell clapped her hands together softly so as to not scare the snake. "Good, let's feed Albert."

Lucy squealed in excitement, an ear-splitting pitch that made Ms Makewell feel silly for fearing loud noises might set the snake off. She spun with Albert on the spot, giddy to make new friends, and as she did, Ms Makewell and half the children sneezed.

"Bless us," Ms Makewell said, laughing with the children as they all twitched their noses to rid themselves of the sensation that something light and feathery had tickled them.

"Sorry," Lucy said, letting Albert down to the floor, where he slithered a protective circle around her feet.

Ms Makewell was confused at the group sneeze, why Lucy felt the need to apologise for it, and why she was now fiddling with the air behind her back as if tucking a tail between her legs. Confusion wasn't a feeling Ms Makewell was used to. She was an experienced teacher and prided herself on how intuitive she was when it came to the young ones, but as endearing as Lucy was, Ms Makewell couldn't shake the feeling that evil was here. That Lucy was that very evil, and a tail did indeed flick wildly behind her back. Unfortunately, with all that was going on, there wasn't much time to delve deeper into these thoughts of superstition and coincidence.

The kindergarteners had a new-found confidence after watching Ms Makewell feed Albert. As he circled inches away from their feet, they reached out to stroke his back, all giggling at the curious textures of his scales, surprised at the lack of slime on his silky-smooth skin. Ms Makewell often wondered if she should have gotten a class pet, though she would never have considered getting the children a snake, maybe snake food, gerbils, hamsters, a mouse, but never a snake. However, in this case, snake food meant apples, and she was sure an apple wouldn't make for an interesting pet.

Lucy finished tucking nothing between her legs, then shook her body from the waist up like a bird ruffling its feathers. "One," she said, her too-dark, horned shadow stretching as she picked an apple from nowhere and placed it at the crossed feet of a random child. "Two," she said, placing another apple two crossed feet away. "Three, six, five," she said, putting three more apples down.

"Three, four, five, Lucy," Ms Makewell said, stopping her before she could place the final apple down. "It goes, one, two, three, four, five, and then six is last."

Lucy squinted at Ms Makewell, then looked to the apples as she tried to remember the order she had counted up in and why Ms Makewell felt the need to correct her. As Lucy silently mouthed the numbers, practising the sequence over and over again before placing the last apple down, Ms Makewell enjoyed one of her few sins: pride in her ability to teach.

"One, two, three," Lucy said, pausing to look Ms Makewell directly in the eyes.

The silence as Ms Makewell waited for Lucy to count the last number was unsettling. Time appeared to stand still as the void of nothing said weighed on her body like gravity. It filled the space between them with an irritating static that warped the sounds of the children's laughter into a cackling chorus of hellsong, all whilst the cross squeaked against the wall behind her.

"Six...six...six," Lucy said, placing the final apple down with a wicked smile that sent the cross on the wall spinning.

Nausea rose in Ms Makewell's stomach as the cross spun deliriously fast, turning molten and infernal from the speed. She wanted to ignore it, to believe it wasn't real like she had done so many times today, but this time she couldn't. Evil was staring her in the eyes, and it took all her strength to force down the rancid feeling in her gut. To not throw up and send the children screaming once again.

As Lucy stared unblinkingly back at her, the room, the circle of children, and the spiralling snake started to spin with the cross. Sweat dripped down her temple, one burning drop at a time. It seared her skin, stung her eyes, and tasted like ash on her tongue. Then, as bile threatened to erupt from her stomach, Lucy burst into laughter and fell into a heap on the floor, sending a soothing and curious gust of wind across her skin.

The breeze blew away all feeling of sickness and sweat as if they had never been there at all, and as the room settled, Lucy began to sing.

"One apple, two apples, three apples, four. Five apples, six apples, for Albert on the floor."

As Lucy sang, with a delightful, cherub voice, she wibbled and wobbled on her back, grasping at the air as if wrapping herself in an invisible blanket. It was innocence in its purest form, and despite the upside-down cross on her wall, not spinning, just fallen, Ms Makewell felt awful for having considered Lucy's simple act of bible-infused mischief to be anything other than a young girl looking for attention. However, there was still an unanswered question lingering in the classroom. Who was Lucy, and where did she come from?

2

The plains of Hell were endless and silent. Even the wind made no sound as it reshaped stone into disfigured horrors once used to frighten forgotten souls. Reaching the edge of the plains was pointless. Even if a lost soul could walk the uncountable steps required to get there, the flames that bordered it like a moat, lighting the sky a horrible shade of red, were so hot it could scorch away the intangible as easily as it could the tangible. It was a place unfit for a child, where the only thing to do was play with rocks in the blooded ash, and yet this was where the two angel brothers had hoped to find their little sister, Lucy.

Michael's voice echoed back at him as he called into the emptiness. "Lucy, if you have gone into the nine circles, you will be in big trouble, young lady."

"Do you think it is still just the nine?" Haniel asked.

"Why would it not be?"

"Remember when it was just this? Limbo."

"I remember."

"Simpler times."

"Humans were never simple."

"I suppose you are right, Brother."

"I am sure there are still only nine circles, Haniel," Michael said, trying to keep a steady tone in his voice despite knowing his brother had been able to spot his wavering uncertainty since before the hands of time began ticking. "But when we find a demon in this damned inferno, we will be sure to ask."

Michael and Haniel walked aimlessly on, as in the plains of Hell, even without the heavy mist formed from the disquiet of lost souls, intention could only guide you so far. Limbo was not meant for straight lines. Nothing here was as simple as that. Though nothing in life or afterlife ever was. They supposed that was why so many ended up in Limbo after they died. At least they had done until it was emptied for Lucy to serve out her punishment. Still, navigating their way to another angel, albeit one as tricky as their little sister, shouldn't have been this hard. After all, Lucy was the brightest of the six hundred and sixty-six angel siblings.

"I do wish Father had not sent Lucy down here," Haniel said.

Michael tried not to speak ill of their father, though he had to agree with his brother on the matter. "It was extreme."

"You think?" Haniel said sarcastically.

"I am certain a circle of Hell is dedicated to wit like that."

"Sorry, Brother, my nerves have been on edge since—."

"We will find her, Haniel, do not fret. It is not like she could have got out."

Haniel looked nervously at his brother.

"Father built the play gates high," Michael said reassuringly.

"It has been a long time since we saw her. What if she has learnt?"

"Could you fly at four eons old, Haniel?"

"I do not remember, but I was also never locked in a cage away from my family with no one to talk to but a snake and a hellfire of demons, demons who, from the looks of things, are not looking after her as instructed."

Michael sighed. He couldn't argue with Haniel's logic. "She is far too young, Brother. I am sure she cannot even lift her wings."

"Just to be certain, I am going to patrol the play gates," Haniel said. "Check for any sign that she flew out. Hopefully, the winds have not yet blown away her tracks."

"Whilst you do that, I shall check the circles."

"If the Mother of Demons has let Lucy into the circles, there will be hell to pay."

"Was that a joke, Brother?"

"I am being serious, Michael. If Lucy is in the circles, I swear to our father I am bringing her back up to Heaven. This punishment has gone on long enough. Hell is no place for a child, least of all the morning star."

"Go check the play gates. I am sure, like you say, that Lucy is simply trying to fly her way out."

"I hope so," Haniel said. "Send me a prayer if you find her."

"And you, Brother."

Haniel unfurled the wings draped across his shoulders like a shawl. With a single flap, sending a blooded cloud of ash into the air, he bound into the empty above, lighting up the landscape like the sun that was missing, as though the plains of Hell stole his beating wings of sound, nothing could hide God's bright, white light emanating from them.

Alone, and his brother nothing more than a fading star in the distance, Michael turned aimlessly away. He walked until he came upon a cave of flames, flickering in and out of view like a mirage trying to convince you it hadn't always been there waiting to be found. Like all things in Limbo, the cave was silent, but all that ended when Michael stepped through it and into the circles of Hell.

3

Lucy followed Ms Makewell around the classroom like a lost lamb as she tidied up the destruction left in her wake. Ms Makewell had just finished putting away a box of multicoloured stacking blocks that Lucy had tumbled into, and still, there was so much left to do. Across the classroom were toppled chairs, scattered pots of pencils, bags pulled from their cubbies, and a cross on a wall that refused to stay right.

On closer inspection of the cross, there was no reason for it to be falling upside down, and yet Ms Makewell had lost track of how many times she had flipped it back into its saintly position. Every time she caught it swinging, that unsettling feeling of lurking evil returned, accompanied by a bout of nausea that bubbled in her stomach. Fortunately, Lucy was always close by, keeping her far too busy with mischief and mayhem for her to ruminate on the unsettling feelings creeping through her body.

In kindergarten, mess was the norm, but Lucy gave clumsy a new meaning. Even the other children had fallen victim to Lucy's path of chaos, tripping flat on their faces every time they strayed too close to her. Now, instead of being scattered across the classroom engaging in various activities of play, they huddled together for safety, pushing toy cars on the city print rug at the centre of the classroom, shielded by the half circle of tables bordering their behinds. Ms Makewell did have a lesson plan, but being so caught up in clutter, she'd had to abandon it and allow the children an extended play session whilst she saw to the mess. A decision that didn't receive a single defiant cry.

The clutter wasn't the only thing keeping Ms Makewell on her toes. Whenever she looked away from Lucy for more than six seconds, she was climbing up something, fumbling and stumbling across surfaces as she sought a path to higher heights, knocking everything to the floor as she went. At first, Ms Makewell had thought Lucy like a cat, climbing to the highest point in search of a place safe from the rabble of all below, but after one too many crashes back to the floor, Ms Makewell realised it was not a cat that Lucy reminded her of, but a baby bird. That Lucy sought not the highest point to watch everything from but to jump off and test her wings.

Ms Makewell found herself enamoured by Lucy's resilience as she watched her repeatedly forge paths up shelves and bookcases, only to be forced quickly into action as Lucy's clumsiness had her tripping over nothing and tumbling ungracefully to the floor. Thankfully, on most failed flights, Ms Makewell had been there to catch Lucy, but on those where she fell with a crippling thud, she had to take a moment to thank God that Lucy stood up without a tear in her eye and miraculously unharmed.

"What's this?" Lucy said as Ms Makewell lifted Lucy off a cabinet, placing her back on the floor before she found a spot to jump or fall from.

"That is our tomato timer for when we do activities," Ms

Makewell said, moving on to the mess at the cubbies. "It rings to tell us when to stop and do something new."

Lucy twisted the ticking tomato, then, unamused, tossed it onto the floor to be forgotten. "What's this?" Lucy said again, dashing towards another shiny thing that had caught her attention, knocking over the freshly packed box of stacking blocks as she stumbled past Ms Makewell.

"That's Johnny's lunch box," Ms Makewell said, laughing away the frustration of seeing her hard work undone without any awareness from Lucy. "Did your mum and dad not pack you lunch today?" Ms Makewell asked, hoping to get more information about Lucy's family.

"What's lunch?"

"Lunch is when we all sit together and eat our food," Ms Makewell said, hoping Lucy's question was as innocuous as her curiosity made it seem and not a sign of neglect. Lucy certainly didn't look underfed, and she didn't look fat either, but that could be because all of it had congregated in her cherub cheeks. Ms Makewell took the sticker-covered lunch box from Lucy and put it back where she had found it, trying not to be swayed by the rejection on Lucy's face as she had her trinket stolen from her tiny hands. "Lunch is in an hour, and I don't think Johnny would like you playing with his food, do you?"

Lucy sighed. "I want one."

The sparkling sadness in Lucy's eyes was too bright not to give in to, and so Ms Makewell reached to the highest cubby and pulled out a clear tub, inside of which sat a neatly wrapped sandwich and a breakfast bar. With her lingering nausea, Ms Makewell knew she couldn't stomach either today, so she crouched down to Lucy and handed over her lunch.

"How about you go and find yourself an empty cubby to put it in."

Without mischief making Lucy's mouth crooked, her smile was as pure as they came. Ms Makewell took a moment to enjoy it, but not too long a moment, as there was far too much to do.

As Lucy skipped off to find a place to put her borrowed lunch box, Ms Makewell checked over the other children, pushed chairs back under desks, and returned pens to their pots. She knew she would have to do this all again in five minutes, but it was good to stay on top of things. A kindergarten class could descend into chaos fast, especially now that she had a devil amidst her angels and one with, of all things, a pet snake.

The snake. Ms Makewell had forgotten entirely about the snake. She looked around the classroom, her head swivelling like an owl on the hunt. The children weren't screaming, which was a good sign, but there was always time for them to start doing so.

"Lucy," Ms Makewell said, spinning to face the cubbies where she had left her.

She was gone, but her borrowed lunch box was tucked neatly into the nameless sixth cubby on the bottom row. A glance left to the door, fortunately still shut tight, and right to the art station littered with crafts and cuttings, and Lucy was nowhere to be seen. Ms Makewell wanted to turn around again, but an unnerving presence loomed at her back. It was here again. Evil. The horned shadow, the mischievous giggle, and the sickness they forced upon her.

"What's this?" said a sweet and sinister voice.

Unable to slow her heart from racing, Ms Makewell screamed, and all the children looked up to catch her jumping away from Lucy as if she were the Devil herself. Even knowing Lucy's horned shadow was nothing more than an illusion created by an oversized bow, which was more cute than evil when you were brave enough to turn and look, it did nothing to temper the panic prickling goose pimples over her skin.

The nervous expressions on all the watching kindergartener's faces had Ms Makewell sick with guilt. She knew she shouldn't show fear for silly things around impressionable children. Still, there was something about the smirk on Lucy's face which gave Ms Makewell the impression that Lucy knew exactly what she was doing and that the bow was an accessory picked deliberately to cause unease.

"Lucy," Ms Makewell said, "Why must you jump out on me like that?"

"What's this?" Lucy asked again, her voice no longer sinister but light and inquisitive as she waved her newly found curio wildly around.

"That is a ruler," Ms Makewell said, stilling the clear stick Lucy flailed like a sword between them. "It's for measuring."

"Why?"

"Sometimes we need to know how long things are."

"What things?"

"Like you," Ms Makewell said, patting Lucy on the head. "Would you like me to see how tall you are? We can add you to our tall wall." Ms Makewell pointed to the wall beside the door, which had hundreds of multicoloured lines from all the children she had measured in her two decades as a kindergarten teacher.

"I am this tall," Lucy said, holding her hand in the air, cheekily tiptoeing to give herself a little extra height.

"That's very tall indeed," Ms Makewell said, a white lie,

as, even though Lucy was proving to be a handful, she was easily the smallest child in the classroom. "Where is Albert, Lucy?" Ms Makewell asked, returning to the question that worried her before Lucy's demonic shadow had sent her screaming.

"Here."

Lucy flicked her wavey, yellow hair over her shoulder, and Albert lunged forward and hissed. Ms Makewell wanted to jump and scream again, especially knowing she had just patted Lucy on the head right where her snake was hiding, but she held her fear between tight lips and stood her ground, putting on a brave face for the still-staring children, because making friends was hard enough without giving them more reasons to exclude one another. Though Ms Makewell had to admit, it was a little scary, as how Albert hid in Lucy's hair was yet another mystery about Lucy she could not solve.

"How do you measure?" Lucy asked.

Albert slithered back into Lucy's yellow hair, and all the children went back about their business rolling cars on the carpet as Ms Makewell explained the numbers and notches of the thirty-centimetre ruler to Lucy. It was clear by the scrunched-up pout on Lucy's face that the numbers went far too high for her to remember, but she never stopped listening, nor did the sense of awe leave her face whilst she tried extremely hard to understand. Ms Makewell wasn't sure how many more times she could feel silly for allowing herself to be deceived by superstition, but there was nothing evil about the girl before her. There was a mystery here. Something that didn't sit well with Ms Makewell. However, it had nothing to do with the fear gurgling in her stomach. No, Ms Makewell's instincts as a teacher told her there was sadness here. Fortunately, whatever unspoken pain it was that Ms Makewell sensed in Lucy, it had done little to break her childhood spirit.

"I'm going to measure everything," Lucy sang, running off, falling flat on her face, then picking herself up only to fall over again.

Ms Makewell winced as she watched Lucy run and tumble without direction, but where any other child might have burst into crocodile tears and screamed, Lucy was always unphased and unhurt.

With something to keep Lucy busy, Ms Makewell returned to the task of putting her classroom in order. First, the crafts, then the forgotten toys, and the books returned to their shelves next. Then, when all that and more was set right, Ms Makewell put away the multicoloured stacking blocks for the second time today. However, this time, she pushed them safely into the corner far away from Lucy's wayward feet, where she should have placed them the first time.

Now that the classroom was tidy, Ms Makewell did her rounds with the other kindergarteners, making sure not to neglect a single one, even pushing a couple of toy cars around the carpet roads, joining in with the fun and games, all whilst doing her best to ignore the fact that Lucy had pulled the stacking blocks from the not-so-safe corner to measure each one individually. At least she was preoccupied, Ms Makewell thought, as it gave her a chance to chat with Sandy, who, was to no surprise, sat alone.

"Hello, Sandy," Ms Makewell said, joining the fuzzy, brown-haired girl and her stuffed rabbit cross-legged at the edge of the carpet. "What are you up to today?"

"Nothing," Sandy said, fiddling with her necklace, adorned with a simple, silver, and right-side-up cross.

"Do you not want to play cars with the other children."

"No."

"Are you still sad about Mr Fluffywuffy Bunnykins?"

"Mr Fluffywuffy Bunnykins the First," Sandy corrected.

"Of course, silly me, how could I forget," Ms Makewell said, pinching Mr Fluffywuffy Bunnykins the Second's stuffed ear, the not real replacement for her recently passed pet.

"It's okay." Sandy sighed. "She's pretty."

"Who's pretty, Sandy?"

"The new girl."

There was a strange look in Sandy's eyes. She was wide-eyed, but it went beyond wonder into something akin to reverence. "Do you mean Lucy?"

"Yeah," Sandy said, her voice floating as if daring her to feel happiness for the first time in weeks.

"Why don't you go play with her?"

"What about the snake."

"Albert is a good snake, remember?"

"I remember."

"Then why don't you go and say hello? I think you and Lucy could be friends?"

"Best friends?"

"Do you want Lucy to be your best friend?"

"Maybe."

"Then let's call her over?"

Sandy nodded, her gaze not leaving Lucy once, as if looking away or blinking might cause her to disappear.

"Lucy," Ms Makewell called, "would you come here for a second."

Wild excitement from hearing her name propelled Lucy into motion. "Ms Makewell, I have idea," Lucy exclaimed.

Lucy bound towards Ms Makewell and Sandy with her arms full of rulers that appeared to multiply with every chaotic step she took toward them. The multiplication was a curiosity that needed more attention to confirm its miraculous nature, but with Lucy hurtling towards them with no regard for anything in her path, Ms Makewell had to focus on the inevitable fall.

Chairs toppled as Lucy ran past them, toy cars were kicked flying, and children who had dared to step out from their protective circle tripped, just as Lucy always did, on seemingly nothing at all. Ms Makewell braced herself for impact, ignoring the falling cross in the corner of her eye and the nausea that its evil descent brought with it. As expected, Lucy tripped, the rulers were sent flying, and Lucy tumbled into Ms Makewell's open arms, but instead of jumping right back up, Lucy allowed herself to be hugged, as if that were her plan all along.

It was a peculiar sensation holding Lucy. Hugging her was like being wrapped in a blanket, one that was so cosy and inviting that it had Ms Makewell never wanting to get out from under it. Stranger still was how the niggling nausea that had been nagging her all day faded. Because, in Lucy's arms, it seemed there was only peace.

"Is everyone alright?" Ms Makewell called out to all the kindergarteners picking themselves up after Lucy's storm across the classroom. When they all nodded and headed, dazed and confused, back to the centre of the room, Ms Makewell returned her attention to Lucy.

"You must be more careful," Ms Makewell said, propping Lucy back up on her feet.

"Sorry. They get everywhere," Lucy said.

"Then at least learn to look where you are going," Ms Makewell said, assuming Lucy was referring to the children unfortunate enough to have stepped into her path and not an invisible thing only Lucy could see. "This is everyone's classroom, not just yours."

"Okay," Lucy said as she fiddled with nothing behind her back, just as she had during show-and-tell.

"I'd like you to meet someone, Lucy," Ms Makewell said.

"Who I meet?"

"This is Sandy, and I think you two could be very good friends."

"Hello," Sandy whispered, reverence still in her eyes, but now so overwhelmed by the sight of Lucy, she trembled and squeezed her stuffed rabbit tight to her chest.

"Hello, Sandy. I am Lucy. I am an angel. I am the morning star. This is Albert." Her pet snake popped his head out from behind her hair and hissed. "And he likes to eat—." Lucy paused and looked nervously at Ms Makewell, realising she was repeating herself again. She had said all of this during show-and-tell, but it was the only line Lucy had practised, and she really, really, really wanted to make friends.

Ms Makewell nodded in encouragement, but before Lucy could finish her introduction, Sandy spoke up to protect her scared and hopefully new best friend from further embarrassment. "And he likes to eat apples."

Lucy beamed an angelic smile and bounced toward Sandy. "He loves apples. Loves them lots. I have an idea. Want to help?" Lucy grabbed Sandy's hand and pulled her to her feet before she could say no. "First need to measure more things."

"I'll leave you two girls to it," Ms Makewell said, standing back up, swearing to return to her lesson plan before the lunch bell rang.

Slowly but surely, Ms Makewell put the classroom back as it belonged, and Lucy having finally found a friend to keep her distracted meant her hard work wasn't being undone moments later. The only thing that kept needing her repeated attention was the cross hanging on the wall. As she caught it mid-swing, nausea niggled at her again. Ms Makewell set the cross right, and instead of taking another lap around the classroom, she decided to take a moment to herself behind the relative comfort of her desk pushed too close to the wall because she wanted the kindergarteners to have as much space to run and play as the classroom could offer.

With her head buried in her hands, Ms Makewell tried to make sense of her morning. There was a new girl in class and one who had kept her on her toes like no other child had ever managed to do. The cross falling upside down or the room's spinning had nothing to do with Lucy. It was a coincidence. She was tired. That's all it was. Evil wasn't here; it was just a clumsy child and a cross that needed nailing to the wall. She looked over the register, keeping her finger trained on the names to keep them from blurring. It was as she thought. Lucy's name wasn't there. But if that was the case, then where did she come from? Hadn't Lucy said she had come up to Lakeville this morning? Up to Lakeville? Up from where?

As the word Hell teased its way into her thoughts, she heard the squeak of the cross behind her falling again. She brought her hand to her mouth as evil threatened to eject itself from her stomach. With the cross the wrong way up, she hoped God could hear her pray that she would spare the kindergarteners the pain of watching her throw up all over their classroom, but no matter how many times Ms Makewell repeated her prayer, the sickness rose. As the acid moved into her throat and she thought that all hope was lost, that evil had won, and God could not hear her, Ms

Makewell was given the strength to swallow the bile down.

With the nausea contained, Ms Makewell quietly thanked God as she got up to correct the cross on the wall, and then a new feeling of terror took over her. She didn't need to look at the clock to know she had allowed her watchful gaze to stray from the classroom for too long. Her teacher's instincts were more than enough to let her know something was amiss. Besides, any amount of time spent with your eyes closed was long enough for a naughty little girl to cause mischief.

"Sandy, Lucy, what are you two doing?" Ms Makewell called across the classroom, her tone not too poignant to be accusatory but enough to let them know she wanted their attention immediately.

"We're measuring Lucy's wings," Sandy said.

"Lucy has wings, does she?" Ms Makewell said, surprised that her instincts were wrong but relieved at the lack of chaos she found the girls engaging in at the centre of the room.

"I can't see them either, Ms Makewell," Sandy said. "I bet they're pretty."

"Maybe Lucy really is an angel?"

Lucy was deep in thought, likely, but hopefully not, plotting her next act of mischief, and didn't notice Sandy staring at her with fierce adoration. Sandy's eyes followed the space behind Lucy's back, where the other children might have been sitting had Lucy not taken over their space. When Sandy reached the last feather of Lucy's imagined wings, she gasped as a magical thought occurred to her. "I bet angel wings are too pretty for human people to see."

"That makes a lot of sense. I bet they are so bright and full of God's love that it would be like looking at the sun," Ms Makewell said, but she added, not wanting to miss a chance at turning this game of make-believe into a learning opportunity, "I wonder, can you tell me how long Lucy's wings are, Sandy?"

Sandy started to count the rulers when Lucy came out of her thoughtful gaze and instructed her to place one more ruler down. Sandy happily did as she was told and carefully placed one more ruler at the end of the neat line that began at Lucy's feet. "Six rulers long," Sandy said.

"Wow, those are some very long wings you have, Lucy. No wonder you are a clumsy little devil." Ms Makewell laughed at the idea that Lucy's clumsiness could be explained away by two long, invisible wings that she dragged behind her like a peacock. "Do either of you know how many centimetres that is?" Both the girls shook their heads but leant forwards, curiously waiting for Ms Makewell to tell them how long. "That's one hundred and eighty centimetres."

The girls looked at each other in astonishment as they tried to comprehend the sound of a number neither had heard before. Then, wanting to see if they could say it themselves, they repeated it aloud, neither realising how terribly wrong they got their pronunciations. Ms Makewell tried to correct them, but when the girls ignored her to have a whispered conversation, she decided she could risk leaving them to their secrecy, if only for a little longer.

As Ms Makewell announced to the kindergarteners that free play would be over soon and that they should start thinking about packing their toys away, there was a collective sigh. Still, they were good children, and Ms Makewell knew they would slowly but surely wrap up their games. Lucy and Sandy continued to whisper in secret, but as long as that was all they did, Ms Makewell felt it was safe to take a few more minutes to herself at her desk.

Her stomach was heavy despite how little she had eaten

today, and as she breathed the hot and muggy air through her hands, she didn't need to look behind her to know the cross was upside down again because the room only spun when it was. Ms Makewell wanted to believe the weather was causing her dizzy spells, not the upside-down cross, just a simple case of dehydration. Yet, superstition had her worried that it was something more because no matter how she tried to rationalise her day, she couldn't decide who to see first, a doctor or a priest.

The pitter-patter of tiny feet was rustling up a storm by the cubbies, and Lucy and Sandy's whispers had fallen prey to the rabble of rowdy children gathering with nothing to do. Ms Makewell knew she couldn't sit at her desk forever, that she had to pull her head out of her hands and get back on track with her lesson plan, but the room was still spinning, and the floor felt like it was sinking beneath her. She held tight to the desk and took a deep breath, but nothing steadied the room that shifted around her like sand. You can do this, she thought to herself, but she couldn't, and she was going to be sick. Then, as if deliberately set to trigger with her retching, the discarded tomato timer rang out across the classroom, the sharp, tinny, and offensive sound snapping her out of her dizzied daze.

"Lucy," Ms Makewell called, her teacher's instincts blaring like the timer, keenly aware something naughty was afoot.

"Ms Makewell, we measure perfect height," Lucy called out, though Ms Makewell couldn't tell from where.

Every child had gathered by the cubbies with their necks strained upwards as they cheered, goaded, and bounced in excitement. Ms Makewell followed their gaze up to Lucy, who stood atop a stairway of the multicoloured stacking blocks crafted precariously at the edge of the cubbies.

"Lucy, how did you get up there?" Ms Makewell shouted.

"Watch me fly," Lucy said, her whole body shaking in anticipation as she bent her knees, preparing to take flight.

"Don't you dare jump, Lucy."

Before the words had left Ms Makewell's mouth, Lucy leapt off the cubbies and stairway of stacking blocks and into the air above the excitable children below. A gust of wind blew across the room, knocking finger paintings and class photos from the walls. The stacking blocks smashed into pieces, and books and binders atop the cubbies were propelled into the walls at opposite sides of the room. Ignoring the chaos, Ms Makewell ripped across the classroom, leaping over her desk and all the stray toys between her and Lucy. Whether time slowed or Lucy had indeed flown for a second, Ms Makewell somehow managed to catch Lucy before she crashed into the children beneath her.

"Weeee," Lucy squealed. "I'm flying, I'm flying. Albert, Ms Makewell, Sandy, I'm flying."

Ms Makewell hated to put Lucy down mid-flight, especially with all the children screaming to be next, but as time caught up to her, so did the fear of what might have happened had she not managed to get to her before she hit the floor.

"Lucy," Ms Makewell snapped as she placed her carefully on the floor where she belonged. "You must stop climbing up onto everything."

The tone of excitement fell in an instant. The crowd of children hushed as they witnessed the very rare instance of Ms Makewell getting angry. Even Albert, who remained hidden in Lucy's yellow hair, couldn't be heard hissing in the silence.

"Why?" Lucy said, glaring up at Ms Makewell, her face

scrunched, and her hands balled into tiny fists as she readied herself for confrontation.

"Because I won't always be there to catch you."

"I fly," Lucy huffed.

"I'm serious, Lucy. Don't make me put you on the naughty step."

Lucy's glare became monstrous, and the already up-side-down cross upon the wall fell in a clatter to the floor. Even the cross around Sandy's neck, which had until now been immune to the evil in the room, snapped at the clasp. "I will fly," Lucy repeated, a heavy pause between each word as she stomped toward the closest desk and climbed onto its chair to better challenge Ms Makewell's threat of punishment.

God wasn't here. The crosses had fallen. Evil rose like bile. Ms Makewell was ready to put her foot down, but then she saw not just ferocity in Lucy's eyes but sadness. It flickered beneath her eyelids as she tried to brush away her tears. It spread down to her trembling lips and into her red, clenched fists. The terrible concoction of anger and upset formed an expression Ms Makewell had sadly seen before. An expression that could only be formed from the complexities of two clashing emotions yet to be fully understood by someone so young. It was a look worn so often by children who had spent more time on the naughty step than all their peers combined.

Ms Makewell had been a kindergarten teacher for twenty long and happy years, and she prided herself on her ability to see what each of her children needed, but she felt foolish now for not seeing Lucy's pain sooner. Here was a girl who was no stranger to punishment. A girl whose every act of mischief was a cry for attention. A girl from a broken home who needed to be held, lifted high and allowed to fly, not put down and shouted at. Still, Ms Makewell couldn't let Lucy keep climbing on top of things; it was dangerous for Lucy and everyone else, but shouting so rarely made children stop.

Crouching to Lucy's raised level upon the chair, Ms Makewell gently took Lucy's hand. "I don't want you to get hurt, Lucy."

Lucy's demeanour softened as she looked at their joined hands, but her temper tantrum was still not yet diffused, so she continued to speak back at Ms Makewell with deadly force. "I won't hurt. I want to fly. I want to fly now." Lucy stomped her feet, each thump dangerously wobbling the chair beneath her.

"It would be lovely if you could fly, but what about all these other children? What happens when you fall on top of them? I think they might get hurt. What do you think?"

"I don't know," Lucy said, puffing her long, blonde hair out her face as she tried to make sense of the calm trying to grow between her sadness and her anger.

"I think you're a very clever girl, Lucy. I think you do know."

"They get hurt."

"That's right. You might hurt them. You might hurt Sandy. And that would make me very sad. Do you want to make me sad?"

"No."

"I don't want you to get hurt either, Lucy. That would make me sad, too."

"I can't hurt."

"But if you did, I would be sad. So you have to promise me that you will be more careful in the future? No more jumping from high up?"

Ms Makewell could see the cogs turning behind Lucy's blue, tear-soaked eyes. Lucy didn't want to make anyone sad, least of all Sandy and herself. However, she also had no intention of being more careful, so Ms Makewell knew before the words left Lucy's mouth that they would be a lie and that she would have to work harder to keep one step ahead of her mischief.

"I promise I be more careful," Lucy sang to Ms Makewell, and, breaking her promise the moment she made it, she clambered over the back of the chair to reach for another shiny thing that caught her attention high up on the desk. "What's this?" Lucy asked, knocking a pot of stationary to the floor as she retrieved a red crayon from its contents.

Ms Makewell grimaced at the fresh destruction added to the already disastrous classroom. As she plopped Lucy back down on the floor, she tried to make sense of the sudden gust of wind that had thrown everything into the air when Lucy jumped from the cubbies. It was no doubt an act of God that she would never have an explanation for, and Ms Makewell accepted that, but what she would not accept was not knowing who this mysterious girl was and why, deep down, she was so sad. Fortunately, Lucy held in her hand the very tool with which Ms Makewell would finally get her answers.

"Children," Ms Makewell said, clapping her hands together, not needing to fight for the kindergartener's attention thanks to Lucy's failed flight and subsequent temper tantrum. "It's time for an activity.

1

As Michael stepped through the dripping flames and into the first circle of Hell, the silence of limbo was drowned out by the screams of the damned. It was louder here than Michael remembered. However, he hadn't been here for millennia, and even an angel's memories were susceptible to the corruptions of time.

Each echoing scream was carried by a personal note of pain, anguish, fear, sorrow, rage, and shame. It built into a crescendo of torment undeserving of forgiveness that would see it end. Michael had once been able to distinguish all the impenitent screams, but now there were countless sounds for which he had no name. He wondered if it was a sign that Hell had indeed changed in the millennia since he had been here. Were there more circles, as Haniel feared, or had he been in Heaven for so long that he had forgotten what the darker sides of humanity sounded like?

Michael prayed to his father that Lucy wasn't in the circles to hear the depraved screams of humanity. The plains above were certainly no place for a child, but the circles were nightmare-inducing. They proved monsters did exist, and, wings excluded, they looked exactly as she did.

"Lucy, are you in here?" Michael called out into the bowels of Hell, not wanting to take another step further if he didn't have to.

"My angel kin," an epicurean voice spoke from behind him, "what brings you down into the flames of his creation."

A red-skinned, stiletto-footed demon emerged from a flaming portal to greet Michael. Hellsong, the torturous yet magmatic verses of a demon choir, sang out from the flaming fissure. Though beautiful and cheery, the music induced unimaginable pain. It affected humans the most, but even for an angel without sin, the music was uncomfortable to listen to, enough so that it had Michael praying for its end.

Michael looked up and pleaded with the demon's brimstone eyes, and as he had done no wrong, she clicked her sharp and manicured fingers, the portal shut, the music was silenced, and all that was left between them were the screams of the damned.

When the pain of the music subsided, Michael asked, "Where is Lucy?"

"I am sure your little angel is up there somewhere."

"Do you mean to tell me you have not been watching her?"

The demon inspected the fine-pointed claws on her magma-washed hands, then huffed as she pushed past Michael. "This isn't a daycare, Angel."

"She is a child," Michael snapped, grabbing the demon and pulling her back to face him.

The demon didn't fight, only smiled, as if knowing the only reason Michael dared touch her was so that he wouldn't have to walk deeper into the fiery pits she called home. "We do have a job to do, Angel. For as much as these humans love to sin, they have a greater fondness for procreation. If you were to allow me more demons, I could devote more of my time to little Lucy. Give her the attention she so sorely craves."

"Are you telling me you have left her alone for millennia?"

"Should I take that as a no on the demon spawn?"

"Tell me where Lucy is," Michael commanded, throwing his voice out into the circles, hoping it would hide how the discomfort of her advances had brightened his cheeks.

"Of course not," the demon said, too wise and aware of Michael's anxieties to rise to his show of strength. "Even we know Hell is no place for a child. We did try to tell the creator that. And no," the demon said before Michael could ask her again. "We did not leave Lucy alone for millennia. We all love that little angel, but souls do not torture themselves."

"We have news on her father."

"Ready to apologise to the girl, is he?"

"Father left."

"Lucy will be devastated, but I cannot say I'm surprised. We all knew he would leave one day. Artists cannot help themselves. They need to create. It is who they are. I only wish I had not assured the girl that he would come back for her."

"In that regard, we are all guilty," Michael said.

"And yet it was she who was sent here."

"If Lucy is not in the circles—."

"She is not."

"Then it would be best I join my brother in his search and leave you to the damned."

"Give Lucy my love, will you."

Michael nodded to the demon and turned to leave, thankful that his search didn't take him deeper into the circles of Hell.

"Demon," Michael said, catching the torturer before she disappeared into the flames from which she came.

"Yes, Angel?"

"My brother was curious; how many circles are there now? It is still the nine, is it not?"

The demon raised her horned brow at Michael, a sympathetic expression that made him feel shame for not knowing. "The ways in which human sin astound even me."

"How many?"

"They spiral into oblivion and beyond. To count them would incite madness to angel and demon alike."

"I did not know."

"No, you did not," the demon said with a soft smile that Michael had forgotten could exist in Hell. "So please do consider my request for more demons. We really do need all the help we can get."

"It shall be taken under consideration," Michael said, this time finding no way to use anger and rage to hide his flushed cheeks. "But I must take my leave. My brother prays for me in the plains above."

"Michael," the demon said, a rare use of his name that had him nearly forget they were of two realms. "When you find the little devil, do let her down easy, will you? Though I would miss your little sister dearly, maybe it would be best if you took her back to Heaven now that he has gone. She does not deserve to be down here."

"All will be put right, I promise you." Michael unfurled his shawl of wings and bathed the demon in God's light. "Goodbye, Lilith," he said, making a silent vow to her and himself that he would not wait so long before his return and that he would do so before the countless circles became endless.

5

Ms Makewell had gathered the children together for a group drawing activity. It was not the lesson plan she intended for the day, but it was the perfect tool to get to know Lucy better. She had instructed everyone to draw their family in whatever colours they wanted, even if it was pink, green, or blue. This task would provide a lifetime of laughter for the parents, but, more importantly, Ms Makewell hoped it would shine a light on where the defiance in Lucy's eyes came from. Was it her family that caused it, or something else?

In Lucy's brief moments of pause, when she jumped from one thought to the next, Ms Makewell saw ageless wisdom shifting in her wandering eyes. It was a look worn by the tired and elderly, distant, as if sifting through everything they knew. It was a curious expression because the instant the pause was over, Lucy became a child again. One who knew far less than her wise expression let on.

It was odd. A child should never not know what a crayon was, yet every colour that Lucy picked up and scribbled with was met with unrestrained excitement. She and Sandy were in fits of laughter every time Lucy drew something. Lucy in awe of the colour, and Sandy in awe of Lucy. It was nice to have Lucy's ruckus contained in a single seat, and it was even nicer to see Sandy smiling again. Though the two of them had somehow managed to get hold of more crayons than Ms Makewell was sure she had given them to share.

"Are we finally drawing pictures of our families, you two?" Ms Makewell asked, sifting through their sheets of scattered paper scribbled on with chaos and colour.

"I have, Ms Makewell," Sandy said, waving her drawing in the air, eager for it to be seen.

With both girls sitting shoulder to shoulder, Ms Makewell crouched beside Lucy. She took the drawing from Sandy and counted five happy faces. A mum, a dad, Sandy in between them, Mr Fluffywuffy Bunnykins the Second, dangling in her hand, and what she assumed was Mr Fluffywuffy Bunnykins the First, hopping happily in a meadow of green clouds in the sky.

"What's Mr Fluffywuffy Bunnykins the First doing in the sky?"

"He's in rabbit Heaven."

"There's a rabbit Heaven?"

"Lucy says so." Sandy held tight to the cross on her necklace as happy tears lit up her eyes.

"Then I bet he is thrilled to be up there with all the other rabbits."

"I think he is. I bet he is hopping every day."

Ms Makewell passed the drawing back to Sandy. "It is an excellent drawing, Sandy. The proportions are lovely, and your colour choices are very accurate. Mr Fluffywuffy Bunnykins the First would be very proud of you."

"And Mr Fluffywuffy Bunnykins the Second?" Sandy asked, squeezing her stuffed pet so tight that Ms Makewell worried there would soon be a need for a Mr Fluffywuffy Bunnykins the Third.

"He's proud of you too, Sandy," Ms Makewell said, playfully pinching her stuffed rabbit on the nose.

Ms Makewell turned her attention to Lucy, who was frantically drawing on her sheet of paper with a thick yellow crayon grasped in her tiny fist. Her wonder of the colour appearing on the sheet of paper like magic was matched only by the intensity of her forceful scribbles as she smashed a sun into the top centre of her drawing. It was hard to look away from the expanding yellow aura, and Ms Makewell even worried that if she couldn't pull her gaze away, the drawn sun might blind her.

As the scribbled yellow expanded, blanketing all the figures flying on feathered wings beneath it, Ms Makewell could feel her sanity dancing on a knife's edge. She had to look away, but as hard as she fought, Ms Makewell couldn't do it. The blinding yellow light of the crayon scribbles was beautiful, mesmerising, heavenly. It was the beginning and the end. It was all things at once: past, present, and future. Then, as Ms Makewell's vision started to bleed white from exposure, Albert slithered over her arms and hissed, his return from across the circle of desks giving her the distraction she needed to break her trance.

"Thank you, Albert," Ms Makewell said, blinking away the stars flickering in her eyes.

A collection of crayons spilt out of Albert's mouth, and then he hissed again, letting Ms Makewell know he understood her and that he knew the agony of staring into the light.

"Do you two not have enough crayons?"

Lucy looked up from her drawing to Sandy, hunched her shoulders, and smiled mischievously. "Nope," they said together, failing to subdue a cackled giggle that gave away their plots and plans.

Ms Makewell squinted at them both and then to Albert, who made a U-turn and slithered off around the tables without looking back. Sandy was such a good little girl, never causing anything more than a ripple in the status quo. How easy it was to be corrupted, Ms Makewell thought. However, a little mischief wasn't anything she couldn't handle.

"Don't think I don't know what you two are up to," Ms Makewell said, letting the girls know they couldn't get anything past her. "Now, how about you show me your drawing, Lucy."

Lucy dropped the yellow crayon, now nothing more than a thumb-sized nub. "My family," she said, sliding the drawing across for her to see.

Every inch of the paper was covered in colour. Tall men with wings filled every space. The sun tried to pull her gaze towards it, but she had learnt her lesson and kept her eyes on the people below. Even with their peculiar proportions, with limbs that twisted like noodles, there was something majestic about Lucy's drawn family. Most looked like Lucy did, with two arms, two legs, a head, and two beautiful, white wings, but there were some whose shapes defied the laws of nature—monstrosities with warped bodies and the heads of beasts, things of nightmare sent to destroy. All were bright, but none were as blinding as the sun that watched over them. Though they still held a power over Ms Makewell that had her reluctant to look away.

"Who are all these people, Lucy?"

"My brothers."

"All of them?"

"Yes." Lucy shrugged, confused by the silly question because it was Ms Makewell who had asked her to draw them.

"How many brothers do you have?"

"Six hundred and sixty-five."

"Is that a lie, Lucy?"

"No. Need more paper. They don't fit."

"And where are your brothers now?"

"Heaven."

Ms Makewell gulped. It explained the wings, explained the hidden sadness. It explained a whole lot. She didn't want to ask her next question; she was afraid of the answer, but Ms Makewell knew she had to ask it. Her role as a kindergarten teacher required her to be there for the children, and she couldn't do that if she didn't ask the difficult questions.

"Are all of your brothers in Heaven, Lucy?"

"Mmhmm," Lucy said lightly, not weighed down by death's sadness.

"I am so very sorry, Lucy."

"Why?"

"You must miss them dearly."

"I miss them lots and lots."

"I imagine you do. But don't worry, if your brothers are in Heaven, then I am sure you will see them again one day."

"When I can fly. I visit."

"Wouldn't that be a nice idea," Ms Makewell said, taking a sneaky look behind Lucy's back for the supposed wings she dragged behind her.

"But I like Earth more. So, I stay. With you and Sandy."

"I'd like that, Lucy."

Lucy gasped. "Really?"

"Very much so," Ms Makewell said, her heart aching as Lucy smiled up at her with a grin so wide and cheek fattening it must have hurt. "And is this you?" Ms Makewell asked, pointing to a little rainbow girl drawn at the centre of her brothers in every colour Lucy had been able to get her hands on, which, thanks to Albert, was all of them.

"I can't fly yet. They hold me up," Lucy said, pointing to the two extra-long, wiggly, and massively out-of-proportion arms of the two brothers beside her.

"Your brothers are much older than you, Lucy," Ms Makewell said, stating the obvious as she wondered if Lucy was adopted.

There was a pause, and that distant look returned to Lucy's eyes, the one which suggested she knew more than she should. "I'm a mistake," she said, her voice quivering as her wide, cheek-hurting smile fell to a frown.

"I beg your pardon?"

"I am a mistake," Lucy huffed.

"And who told you that, might I ask?"

"Father said I made on accident."

"Your father told you this?"

Lucy shrugged. Her bottom lip trembled as she fiddled with the paper. "It's true. I'm mistake. A silly mistake."

"I don't think it's very nice to say that about yourself, Lucy. You are not a mistake. You are a beautiful, special little girl who I am delighted to have in my class."

"With pretty wings," Sandy added, pointing to the scribbled wings that drooped down Lucy's back instead of out to the sides as her brother's wings did.

Lucy sighed as if she had heard all of this before, and Ms Makewell knew that it would take much more than kind words to get her to believe it. "And what about your father or your mother? Did you draw them too?" Ms Makewell asked, doing her best to temper the jagged edges of her voice, disgusted at the fact her father had supposedly told

Lucy she was a mistake at the young age of four. A matter she would bring up with whoever picked her up at the end of the day.

Lucy pointed to the sun, and Ms Makewell, still afraid she might be blinded if she looked directly at it, squinted and tried to see if she had missed something behind its blinding rays. But she hadn't. It was just a sun. An intense, bright, rousing, mind-melting, and eye-scorching sun made of crushed crayon.

"Lucy doesn't have a mum. Her daddy is God," Sandy whispered, who, like Ms Makewell, couldn't look directly at the light burning above the disproportionate angels.

"Is he now," Ms Makewell said bluntly, blinking away the stars in her eyes again as she forced herself to look anywhere but Lucy's captivating drawing. "I'm sure it must seem that way sometimes."

Lucy scrunched her face up as she tried to make sense of what Ms Makewell was trying to say. "He is God," Lucy said, looking to Sandy like Ms Makewell was the silliest person alive for suggesting he wasn't.

Ms Makewell was starting to glean a clearer picture of what made Lucy the way she was. It was not strange for a child to develop coping mechanisms in the face of isolation and death. Still, the biblical references were slightly over the top and quite possibly out of her skill set. Unless Lucy was indeed an angel, not that her being one would make helping her any easier, but it would explain everything. At least, she thought it might.

"This is a wonderful drawing, Lucy," Ms Makewell said, laughing away the idea of her being an angel as she slid the drawing back to Lucy, chalking the ridiculous thought up to spending too much time around imaginative children.

"There's a fantastic use of colour here, and I think Albert will love to see how you added him in too," she said, pointing to a skewed green face tucked away behind a scribble of hair.

"I never forget Albert," Lucy said with a cheesy grin, her eyes not-so-discreetly flitting around the tables to check on the progress of his covert crayon-stealing operation.

Albert was returning to Lucy with his mouth stuffed full of crayons. Ms Makewell shook her head at him disapprovingly as she saw the other kindergarteners looking around, confused as to where all their pinks, blues, and greens had disappeared to. She had given Lucy's snake too much reign, Ms Makewell thought. It was time to end that and restore order in her classroom, but first, she had to set the children another task to keep them from leaving their seats.

"Lucy," Ms Makewell asked in a hushed voice so that her next question would not cause any embarrassment, "do you know how to write?"

"I write good," Lucy said, her brilliant blue eyes twinkling like a sun-drenched ocean as she looked proudly up at Ms Makewell. "I know every word."

"You know every word, do you?"

"Yes," she said with a hiss.

"Do you know what a dodecahedron is?"

"Funny round square," Lucy said, crossing her arms and nodding a single, confident nod.

"Very good," Ms Makewell said, taking a mental note to go over all the different shapes with Lucy later. "Class," she clapped, getting everyone's attention. "If we have all finished drawing a picture of our families, what I want you to do now is write a short sentence on the back that tells me a bit about them. It can be anything you want. What makes you happy," she said with a smile. "What makes your heart all warm and fuzzy," she said, holding herself in a deep, loving embrace. "And it can even be something that makes you grumpy and sad," she said, finishing with a comical frown that made all the children laugh. "Does everyone understand?"

"Yes, Ms Makewell," everyone sang back, including Lucy, who was blatantly hiding all Albert's collected crayons in the ruffles of her prairie dress.

"Brilliant. We will all get together when the ticking tomato rings to read what we have written. I look forward to hearing what you all have to say about your families."

Ms Makewell turned the ticking tomato for ten minutes, set it down on her desk, and then set about looking for a solution to the problem of the freely roaming snake.

*   *   *

Ms Makewell was reluctant to make a mess when she had spent so much time tidying, but she wouldn't have lasted as long as she had as a kindergarten teacher if she hadn't been able to embrace the inevitable. From atop the cupboard, which housed all of her lesson plans, carefully crafted over the years to make education fun, she grabbed a clear box filled with nick-nacks and mementoes and emptied it into the bottom drawer of her desk.

Carefully and quietly, to avoid arousing suspicion from Lucy or her snake, Ms Makewell cut holes into the lid. When she was sure the makeshift vivarium had enough breathing holes, she snuck over to the last table in the half circle and patiently waited for Albert to reach her.

"It's over, Albert," Ms Makewell said, gaining a curious look from the kindergarteners, who were unaware their crayons were being stolen. "I know what you and Lucy are up to, and I think it's time you get in the box. We can't have a snake slithering around a classroom filled with four-year-olds. What would the parents say? Now empty your mouth and get in."

Ms Makewell hadn't thought Albert would listen to her and had half expected to have to fight him into the box using what little she could remember from the various nature documentaries of handsome, snake-wrangling Australian men. Instead, all she got was a look of concern as he slithered into the open box, leaving a collection of crayons behind him.

"I don't know why you're looking at me like that, Albert. You're a snake. No, what you are, Albert, is a stealing snake. A slithering, stealing snake," Ms Makewell said, hissing her s's just as Lucy did when speaking to him. "Nothing's going to happen. Lucy is a big girl. She can handle a few hours without you wrapped around her neck." Albert hissed. "I don't have to explain myself to a snake," Ms Makewell said, placing the box on her desk, unsure whether she was conversing with Albert or herself. "You can have my apple in case you get hungry."

Albert turned his nose at the apple, and Ms Makewell rolled her eyes at the derision. "It's just like any other apple," she lied, clearly seeing that her bruise-covered, yellow-blemished, dimpled and divoted apple was far from the miraculous and perfect fruit that Lucy plucked from nowhere. "It will be fine," Ms Makewell said, readdressing the concern in Albert's fiery, flitting eyes one last time.

As Ms Makewell snapped the lid into place, she wondered if she had made the right decision. Was the concern in Albert's face warranted, or was she making something out of nothing, the same way she had been doing all day with the upside-down cross and the accompanying nausea? The thought caused her to check the wall for a sign that evil was here, and for the first time today, the cross was right side up. If that wasn't a good sign, she didn't know what was.

The ticking tomato timer rang, and Ms Makewell did not jump out of her skin. The class was as it should be. Lucy was not clambering or climbing, and everyone's bums were firmly planted in their seats where she had left them.

"Everything will be fine," she said again, more to herself than Albert, who continued to look at her with the same unblinking expression of concern.

Ms Makewell took her spot in front of the children and, one by one, listened to everything they had to say about their families. Charlie Shaw spoke about his hero father and how he wanted to be a fireman like him. Kaylie May spoke about her mother, a police officer, and how she once stopped a robber from stealing her neighbour's TV. A girl called Emily spoke of a new baby in her family and how she was afraid she might be forgotten because of it. Ms Makewell assured her that her parents have so much love in their hearts it would be impossible for them to forget about her. A boy called Nathaniel talked about riding bikes, and another boy talked about going to big school and how he thought it seemed scary. Ms Makewell told him there was nothing to be afraid of and that he would make more friends than he could count on one hand, but it was a long way away and, for now, he should enjoy his time in kindergarten and learn as much as he could whilst he was here. Sandy shared a memory of Mr Fluffywuffy Bunnykins the First, which was nice for everyone to hear as it had been many weeks since she had spoken in front of the class so bravely and joyfully. Everyone clapped for her, Lucy the loudest, and it made Sandy smile, knowing that everyone supported her even though she had decided to sit alone a lot lately.

During all the children's speeches, Ms Makewell keenly watched Lucy, ensuring she wasn't up to no good. Fortunately, she sat quietly and listened intently to the other kindergartener's stories. The lives of her classmates were as exciting to her as the colours of her stolen crayons. Between each message read, Lucy scrambled on her seat, reaching for the heavens, hoping to get picked next to speak. Ms Makewell hated turning Lucy down, especially when she had page after page of writing to read, but having given Lucy so much attention today, Ms Makewell didn't want the other children to feel ignored. But there was a balance to be had. Ignoring a child desperate for attention would do no one any good, least of all Lucy, someone that Ms Makewell now knew had suffered great loss. So, when she had heard over half the kindergartener's messages, she decided it was finally time to give Lucy her moment in the sun.

Lucy squealed in excitement, elated to finally be picked. As she fumbled with her papers, trying to put them in order, Ms Makewell noticed that whatever Lucy had written was not in English nor any other recognisable language.

"You have written a lot, Lucy?" Ms Makewell said, looking over her glasses to get a better view of Lucy's scribblings.

"I write good. I write a book once."

"You did, did you? A whole book?"

"Yes. My bible. But Mr Pope locked it away."

"The Pope locked your book away?" Ms Makewell said, entertaining the idea that Lucy knew the Pope.

"Yes." Lucy slammed the papers down and crossed her arms. "I want my bible back, Mr Poop."

Lucy stuck out her tongue and blew a raspberry at the word poop, sending the entire class into hysterics, all amazed at her wit for connecting the words pope and poop together.

"Lucy, you cannot say that," Ms Makewell said, shocked at the blasphemy being uttered about their Holy Father.

"Poop, poop, poop, poop, poop," Lucy said again, this time accompanied by a couple of her most encourageable classmates.

Ms Makewell wanted to reprimand Lucy for speaking ill of their spiritual leader, but Lucy had caught her smiling at her cheeky comment, so it was far too late for that. Instead, she raised her eyebrow and moved the ruckus along.

"Very clever, Lucy, but how about you read us something about your family instead of being a rude little girl?"

"Yes, Ms Makewell," Lucy sang, sniggering as she looked to her new friends for approval of a joke well said.

With the joke over, bar a few giggles and whispers of poo, Lucy grabbed her writings and flicked them out as if she were a newsreader addressing an audience of thousands. She licked her lips and patted the sheets down, but as soon as she started speaking, chaos erupted across the classroom once again.

"I don't like it," one child shouted, put off by the evil sounds pouring out Lucy's mouth.

"It hurts my ears."

"DEMON!" all the children screamed.

Ms Makewell didn't want to admit it, but it pained her to hear whatever language Lucy was speaking. She couldn't quite explain why that was, only that listening to it made her so sad it ached.

"Lucy," Ms Makewell said, raising her hand to put an abrupt end to the agonising tongues in which she spoke, "what language is that?"

Lucy looked around at the terror in everyone's eyes, and even Sandy held onto her cross like it was the last line of defence against evil. Ms Makewell had expected Lucy to pout at her new friend's attempt at banishment; instead, a toothy, maleficent grin spread across her face.

"All of them," Lucy said, the cross on the wall flipping with the cock of her head.

Doing her best to ignore the vile intrusion of nausea that accompanied the swinging cross, Ms Makewell walked over to Lucy and looked over her writings. She couldn't believe it. Lucy had written page after page of writing in languages old and new, forgotten and never known, at least, as far as Ms Makewell could tell. There was French, German, both Chinese and Japanese, though if Ms Makewell was being honest, she wasn't sure which was which. There were glyphs, symbols, shapes, and scripts, no letter or word following another of the same language, each written in a different colour, no two shades touching. It was impossible and amazing, and as she attempted to read it, Ms Makewell began to understand the painful sadness she felt when hearing it aloud.

There was an unquenchable desire to understand, one she knew deep down she could never satisfy. Worse, there was a feeling that, a long time ago, an ancestor had once spoken it with ease and that, for whatever reason, she had lost the ability to do so herself. It was a truth that made Ms Makewell want to cry.

"Why not pick one language instead?" Ms Makewell asked, hating how narrow-minded the request sounded.

Lucy climbed on the table, snatched her papers back, and slumped into her chair. "You try reach God. Not my fault."

"I never said it was," Ms Makewell said, confused as to what she was defending herself for. "Sorry, what do you mean, reach God?"

"Wasn't me that time. You built tower on own."

"What tower?"

"Babel."

"The tower of Babel?" Ms Makewell asked.

Lucy grumbled as she reordered her writings, putting her last blank page at the top. "Fine, I just write in English," Lucy said aggressively, repulsion contorting her face as if the idea of conforming to a single language made her sick. "Albert, green, please," she said," holding her hand out expectantly for her pet snake.

"Lucy, I noticed you and Albert were—."

"Green, please, Albert," Lucy said again, ignoring Ms Makewell so that she could quickly translate all her hard work into one boring language.

"Lucy, could you please listen to me for a second?"

"Albert, where you?"

"I thought it best that—."

"Albert?"

Ms Makewell couldn't get a word in, and Lucy's voice began to take on a warble of anxiety with every utterance of her snake's name. Ms Makewell was losing control, and she knew it.

"Albert?" Lucy said again, looking frantically from side to side, scanning the tables for her pet snake. Lucy looked up at Ms Makewell like a saviour. "Where Albert?" she asked.

A string of guilt snapped in Ms Makewell's stomach for not being honest with Lucy sooner. "I've made a home for Albert, Lucy, but he is right over there on my desk, nice and safe, watching over us all," she said, pointing behind herself to Albert in his plastic cage.

Lucy fell silent, and all the kindergarteners shuffled back in their seats, sensing what was coming before even Ms Makewell did. She pulled her waiting hand close to her chest, realising that Albert wasn't coming to give her a crayon, and looked past Ms Makewell to see him curled up in his plastic cage, face pressed against the surface, trying to get as close to her as he could. As Lucy looked back up at Ms Makewell, she began to shake in her seat, and it was then that Ms Makewell realised she had made a mistake and that, despite what she had said to Albert, all wasn't going to be well.

Lucy's eyes flitted around the room, looking for an escape, and when she caught eyes with the children around her, she looked at them no longer as potential friends but as the strangers they were. Each time her eyes turned back to Ms Makewell, they grew wetter. She looked upon her as if she had been betrayed, and then that betrayal turned to confusion, turned to fear, turned to anger, turned to fear again.

"Lucy, it's alright," Ms Makewell said, foolishly hoping she could undo her mistake before it was too late. "Albert is just over there. How about we go get him out together," Ms Makewell said, offering a gentle hand to Lucy.

Lucy looked at Ms Makewell's hand with hatred and hope, and with every conflicting emotion fighting for her attention, they collapsed in on themselves, too young to know what to do with them. Then, with the only warning Lucy could give, balled-up fists and a face scrunched up so tight it turned her red, she screamed.

The sound that erupted from Lucy's mouth was piercing, and Ms Makewell was sure it could be heard from the clouds of Heaven above and the pits of Hell below. Tears drenched her face as she shook in her chair, and between screams, she would shout for Albert, only for his name to be cut off by another ear-splitting wail.

The children put their hands to their ears, and some even joined her in tears. It didn't happen often, but Ms Makewell froze as guilt and heartache consumed her. Fortunately, Sandy was there to help. She reached out for Lucy, but being only four herself, four and three-quarters if you asked her, Sandy was unsure how best to console Lucy's grief. Her hand trembled just out of reach of the supposed wings on Lucy's back, hoping the proximity alone would be enough to calm her, but eventually, even that small gesture was too much for Sandy to deal with, so she grabbed her stuffed rabbit and squeezed it tight, and began crying along with Lucy, unable to stand watching her new best friend scream.

As Ms Makewell watched the class descend into chaos, a bird crashed into the window, and then another, and then another, and when the sixth bird crashed into the glass with a crack, the upside-down cross on the wall fell. Every sign pointed to evil, but how could a girl in so much pain be anything other than pure? Ms Makewell squashed the corruption rising in her stomach, held back the spell of dizziness that had her wanting to hold onto the floor, and with a quick prayer to he who watched from above, she summoned the strength to do what any good kindergarten teacher would do, be there for her children.

Ms Makewell ran to her desk, unclipped the lid of Albert's makeshift cage, and expertly lifted him out as if she had done this many times before. As she carried him to Lucy, Ms Makewell and the snake shared fleeting glances, not ones that said, I told you so, but ones that said, we need to help her, and she needs us. Ms Makewell didn't need to understand why Lucy needed Albert. Not yet. Some children held onto blankets for comfort, others stuffed rabbits. Lucy had a snake, and it was Ms Makewell's job to get him back to her.

"I'm sorry for taking Albert away without telling you, Lucy," Ms Makewell said, placing Albert on the desk in front of her.

Albert rushed up Lucy's arm, but it wasn't until he was coiled around her neck with his tail concealed behind her did she stop screaming. Fear still lingered in her crying eyes, but wrapped up in Albert's comforting embrace, her whirlpool of emotions slowly began to settle into something more manageable for a little girl.

"I promise I won't take Albert away from you again, but you can't let him slither around the classroom causing mischief, do you understand?"

Lucy snuggled her head into Albert's, then pressed her lips tight together, refusing to speak as she frowned at Ms Makewell. She looked at her, not with true hate but a child's hate born from misunderstanding. Not that it hurt any less knowing that. Making children cry was not Ms Makewell's job. Making them smile was.

"I don't like you being sad, Lucy," Ms Makewell said, slowly placing her hand on Lucy's, careful not to make any sudden movements lest she think she was trying to take Albert from her again. "Do you think you could ever forgive me?"

"No," Lucy huffed, quickly shutting her mouth as she remembered she wasn't speaking to Ms Makewell.

"Even if I apologise to Albert, too?"

Lucy shook her head and sniffled up her tears as she squeezed back on Ms Makewell's hand.

"I'm going to apologise to Albert anyway. I think he de-serves one," Ms Makewell said, turning her hand so Lucy could hold onto her fingers more comfortably. "I'm sorry for putting you in a box, Albert. That was very mean of me. I promise I won't do that again."

Lucy didn't let up her grip on Ms Makewell's hand as Albert hissed into her ear. "What did Albert say?" Ms Makewell asked, rummaging in her pocket with her free hand for a clean handkerchief that was kept ready for a crying child who might need it. "Does he forgive me?"

Lucy shook her head as Ms Makewell dabbed away her tears. "Are you lying?" Ms Makewell asked, sensing she might be.

Lucy nodded as Ms Makewell caught the last falling tear in her handkerchief.

"I thought so. I'm so very glad to hear that Albert forgives me. Do you think you might be able to forgive me too?"

Still not speaking to Ms Makewell, Lucy shrugged, but Ms Makewell knew that she had been forgiven and that Lucy was trying to control the situation in the only way she knew how - with her silence. It might take a few minutes for her to open back up, maybe even an hour or two, because happiness couldn't be rushed, but Ms Makewell was willing to wait however long it took.

"How about this," Ms Makewell said. "Why don't you finish reading to the class? I know how excited you were to read all that you wrote, and I'd like to hear it too."

Lucy shook her head, still overwhelmed by fear and the threat of more tears yet to come.

"It's okay if you don't want to speak anymore," Ms Makewell said, assuring Lucy she didn't have to do anything she wasn't comfortable with. Then, reminding Lucy that the other children were nothing to fear, she said, "Do you want to listen to what all your new friends have written instead?"

Lucy glanced around the room at the other children, then quickly looked back to Ms Makewell and nodded.

"I knew you were a brave little girl. You and Albert can listen with me."

Ms Makewell moved to stand up, but as she did, Lucy tightened her grip on her hand.

"Do you think I could have my hand back?"

Lucy violently shook her head, and without any effort, she pulled Ms Makewell to her knees.

"Then I will sit here with you whilst we listen together."

Ms Makewell got comfortable at the front of Lucy's desk, and a small smile crept onto Lucy's face. However, when Lucy realised it was there, she forced it back into a frown as she remembered she was supposed to be angry.

It was always hard watching a child struggle with their emotions. Seeing them go through the motions to get to the other side was a labour. Fortunately, it was a labour of love because Ms Makewell knew that if she did her job right, by the end of the year, all her children would better understand the existential feelings that frustrated them.

Perched in front of Lucy, Ms Makewell restarted the class activity, but thanks to all the drama, instead of focusing on the children and their speeches, she was entirely distracted. From the feathered imprints staining the now cracked windows to the multicoloured drawings of an angel family, Ms Makewell realised that the activity set to learn about Lucy had only created more questions, one of which made no sense at all. It was a biblical question. A question that had Ms Makewell wanting to reach behind Lucy's back and feel for what couldn't possibly be there. Wings.

6

Michael flew down to his brother, who paced outside the play gates of Hell. The golden bars, wisps of twinkling starlight, made up of the very thing that kept souls inside their mortal shells, towered high into the skyless above. If it wasn't a cage designed to keep an angel locked away from her family and the other realms, then Michael might have thought the play gates beautiful, but it was a cage, so the sight of it only caused disdain and revulsion.

"Have you found her, Brother?" Michael asked, shawling his wings as he landed gracefully by Haniel's side.

Haniel didn't look up as he spoke, the fury of failure painted on his face. "Keep your sister out of trouble, Father said."

"Did our little sister learn to fly?"

"She did not need to," Haniel snapped, his panic digging deep furrows into his brow. "The play gates are wide open," he said, gesturing wildly to a gaping wound cut through the bars.

"But how?" Michael asked, the impossibility of it being the only explanation for not having spotted the opening himself. "Father made sure they were Lucy-proofed."

"I should never have let Father put her down here. This is

all my fault. I am a terrible brother. Lucy must hate me."

"Let us not start this again, Haniel. We shoulder the blame together. All of us brothers do. Now, what is required of us is to be better. Besides, I suspect as we speak, Lucy is awaiting our return to Heaven."

"Do you really believe Lucy took the stairway to Heaven to see the brothers who allowed Father to banish her to Hell, alone, for millennia?"

"There is that cutting wit again, Brother," Michael said, no friend to the dry tone of his brother's recent bout of self-flagellation. "I asked Lilith about the circles, and she said there were more than would be sane to count, so I do expect there to be a circle for that obnoxious mockery spewing from your mouth."

"Do not tell me the demons allowed her down there?" Haniel rubbed the ache in his temples as he attempted to hold back a wretched feeling of guilt that wanted to rise from his stomach, take the form of something vile and twisted, and drag him down into the circles where he felt he belonged. "The terror. The horror. The pain. So much pain. What have we done?"

Michael grasped his brother by the shoulders and pulled him to a stop before him. "Calm yourself, Haniel. Stop your pacing. Even Lilith knows not to let a child into the circles. Now, breathe."

Michael matched his brother's erratic breathing, then when he was sure Haniel was focused on him and not the guilt eating him from within, he gradually slowed his breaths, guiding his brother back to peace.

"We will find our little sister, Haniel, and we will make everything right."

"I suppose we should return to Heaven then. If she is

waiting."

"Yes, I believe so."

As they looked up through the skyless above into the next realm and Heaven above that, the angel brothers opened their wings in unison, bathing the plains of Hell in God's light, ready to fly home. Then, as they were about to take off, a terrible scream filled with all the emotions a child could not yet understand overwhelmed the unnatural silence of limbo. It cracked the wind-carved horrors of bloodied rock, threw ash into the air, and fuelled the fires that roared at the never-reached edges of the lost land.

Michael pulled his gaze back from Heaven and focused on the scream. "Little sister is on Earth."

"Of course she is," Haniel replied, shaking his head, feeling foolish for not realising sooner. "Lucy always did love Father's garden."

With a single flap, the angel brothers soared over the play gates towards their sister's realm-piercing screams. When Lucy fell silent, the echo of her torment repeated behind them for what, to a lost soul, would have felt like an eternity, but, eventually, the unnatural silence of Limbo collapsed in on Lucy's pain, reclaiming the plains for itself.

7

Lucy eventually let go of Ms Makewell's hand after their classroom activity had ended. She had even started talking again to both Ms Makewell and the other children. Lucy was back to her lively self, running around causing chaos and mischief as if the unfortunate incident with her pet snake had never occurred. Though, now, whenever there was a lull with no one paying her attention, Lucy ran back to Ms Makewell's side and forced her hand back into her comforting grip. And that was where she was now.

"Where everyone going?" Lucy asked, looking around the playground as parents or their minders collected their children after a long day of work.

"Everyone is going home. Do you not have anyone coming to pick you up?" Ms Makewell asked, anxiously looking at her clipboard full of Lucy's drawings of angelic brothers.

"I'm not going home. I'm staying."

"You are, are you?" Ms Makewell said, triple checking the register as best she could with one hand, and as she had already confirmed six times over, Lucy was not on her list. "And where will you sleep when you get tired?"

Lucy hummed in thought, pouting as she looked for a

suitable spot to lay her head. "There," she said, pointing to the lonely tree that shaded the small patch of grass growing in from the field beyond the gated playground.

"Good old Mr Willow. I'm sure he would keep you nice and cosy all night long, but wouldn't you be much happier in a bed?"

Lucy shrugged, and Ms Makewell hoped it was not a sign that her story was more tragic than it already seemed. She tried not to think about it, to not let her mind run amok with thoughts of neglect and abuse, of a home where Lucy didn't even have a bed to sleep in. These thoughts would remain locked away, at least until she had seen Lucy's carers. If they ever showed up to collect her.

From across the playground, Sandy darted towards Lucy and Ms Makewell, with Mr Fluffywuffy Bunnykins the Second flailing by his stuffed feet behind her. When she was six jumps away, she leapt through the air, bouncing on invisible hopscotch squares before landing flat on her feet in front of them. The act of joy had her parents smiling from afar, glad to see their daughter was running and laughing once again, and best of all, towards a new friend.

"Bye," Sandy said, giving Lucy one last hug before she left.

"Bye," Lucy replied, her voice soft, sad, and slow, as she realised that her first human best friend was leaving.

As Sandy wrapped her arms around Lucy, she scoured her back for her supposed angel wings, and, for a second, it looked as if her hands landed on something invisible with a thousand feathery layers for her fingers to weave their way between, but, then, her hands sank through the air, landing on Lucy's back, leaving only faith to tell her that the wings were there, somewhere, safely out of sight. Ms Makewell still had the urge to check for Lucy's wings, but when Lucy's hand wasn't grasping her own, she couldn't bring herself to reach and find out.

"Bye, Albert," Sandy said.

Albert poked his head out from Lucy's hair and hissed goodbye. His scales were golden and yellow, and then, in a flush of happiness, he shifted momentarily into shades of verdant green as he allowed himself to be seen. Sandy's parents, now in each other's arms as they watched their little girl from afar, turned to each other in shock as they saw the flash of colour emerge from Lucy's golden hair. Ms Makewell was sure she saw them mouth the word snake to one another, a line of questioning she knew she would have to prepare for tomorrow morning when all the rightfully concerned parents confronted her about the new girl and her peculiar pet. Yet another thing she would tuck away in the back of her mind until she met whoever Lucy belonged to.

Ms Makewell said her goodbyes and sent Sandy on her way. As she skipped off, Lucy slipped her hand from Ms Makewell's grasp and followed after her, forcing Ms Makewell to give chase before she escaped out the open school gates. Like every other time Lucy had been stopped doing what she wanted, she puffed and pouted, but within minutes, her tantrum was forgotten, and she bounced back into babbling curious questions that Ms Makewell did her very best to answer.

With the playground empty, Ms Makewell looked up and down the street for Lucy's carers one last time. When none appeared from around the corner or through the alley across the way, she pulled on the jangling chain of keys secured to her waist and locked her and Lucy inside together.

As the heavy gate lock clicked into place, Lucy stiffened at Ms Makewell's side, and her eyes darted across the playground as she looked for an exit. Ms Makewell tried, as she had been doing all day, not to let her imagination run wild, but when you feel a child trembling in fear through the palms of their sweating hands, it is hard not to think the worst.

"Lucy," Ms Makewell said, crouching in front of her, gently squeezing her hand, using her presence to draw her focus onto her and away from all the possible escape routes out of the locked playground. "Why are you afraid?"

"Lock me in. I didn't do anything."

"I locked the gate to keep us safe."

"From who?"

"Bad people who want to come inside and steal all of our toys."

"I'm not afraid of bad people."

"You aren't?" Ms Makewell said, brightening her voice with feigned shock.

"Nope," Lucy said, her cheeks plump with pride as she shook her head.

"You must be very brave then, but I want to keep the gate locked anyway. It will make me feel much safer knowing that no one can get in here and get our toys. Is that alright with you?"

"Okay. But we go out whenever want?"

"Whenever you want to leave, we can leave together."

"Now?"

"No, not now, but soon, I promise."

Ms Makewell hated lying to Lucy, and she knew she would have to come up with another clever excuse for why they had to stay behind the locked gate alone without any other children to play with, but that too could wait because, for now, her thoughts were solely on the phone call she knew she had to make to social services.

As they walked back to the classroom, Ms Makewell silently prayed that the stories Lucy had told her weren't true, that Lucy did have a family, and this was all one big misunderstanding. And then, just in case, she prayed that if Lucy did indeed have no one and that her brothers were in Heaven and her father was gone, that someone kind and loving would adopt her before she got lost in a broken system. Ms Makewell also prayed for herself, asking to see Lucy again, wherever she ended up, and, despite how often her mind had wandered there, Ms Makewell prayed that Lucy wasn't the evil causing her stomach to twist itself in knots.

Bringing her prayer to a close with a silent amen, a gust of wind blew at her back, and Lucy pulled her to a stop as she twisted to face it.

"I do not know what stories Lucy has been telling you, but I can assure you that only most of them are true."

Ms Makewell turned with Lucy to face the deep and powerful voice that, despite the air it commanded, reverberated with warmth so comforting that it wrapped her up like a hug.

Stood before her, in the previously empty playground, was not one man but two. The tallest, broadest men she had ever seen, illuminated by the setting sun like Heaven sent angels. Their size should have been intimidating; they should have incited fear into her heart, but instead, all she felt in their presence was peace.

"Who are you," Ms Makewell said, reminding herself there was a child at her side to protect and that this was no time to succumb to their pious beauty, "and what are you doing in my playground?"

"Brothers," Lucy squealed, leaping away from Ms Makewell

into the shadows of the towering men.

"Brothers?" Ms Makewell asked, cautiously eyeing the man on her right as Lucy wailed at her supposed brother to make her fly.

"Yes, we are her brothers," the man on the left said. "Why, what has our little sister been saying about us?"

"I was led to believe you were dead?"

The man chortled a single, booming laugh. "What did she say exactly? It's not like Lucy to lie like that."

"She said you were in Heaven. She even drew this," Ms Makewell said, flicking Lucy's colourful drawing of her angel-winged family from her clipboard and presenting it before the man who had so far said nothing to ease her concerns surrounding Lucy.

"This is impressive," the man said, "Haniel, look how good Lucy has got at drawing wings."

Haniel plopped his wailing little sister back on the floor. "Wow, Lucy, this is amazing. I do think you have made my chin a little pointy, though. I have more of a dimple, see," Haniel said, placing a finger into the concave of his chin.

"Fly me. Fly me. Fly me," Lucy said, ignoring the compliments and critiques of her artwork, her mind set on only one thing.

"Lucy, how about you go play with Albert whilst I have a quick chat with your brothers," Ms Makewell said, crouching down to Lucy, hoping to send her away for a bit of privacy so that she may speak some stern words not meant for the curious ears of a child.

"I want to fly," Lucy snapped, blowing her cheeks out as she readied herself for a tantrum.

"You need to learn to be patient, Lucy. You will fly after I have had a chat with your brothers," Ms Makewell said, then she looked up to the two imposing men who, for all their beauty, appeared oblivious to the tantrum boiling in the balls of Lucy's fists. "Won't she?"

"Yes, yes, of course, we will fly after, Lucy," Haniel said, Ms Makewell's short tone causing him to jump into action.

Lucy huffed hot air and scrunched her dress to her body, ruining the shape of its ruffles as she stomped her feet. "I don't believe you. Fly now. Fly now."

"I promise we will fly," Haniel said, following Ms Makewell's lead and crouching to Lucy's eye level. "As high as you want. All the way to the clouds and back. But right now, Ms Makewell wants to talk to us, and I think Albert wants to play."

Haniel tickled the snake's yellow nose through its hiding curtain of long, golden hair and received a lick in return, a welcoming sniff for a familiar face. Whether it was Haniel's calm demeanour or the reacquainting of two of Lucy's favourite people, Lucy released her dress from her fists and fluffed it back into shape with a playful twist of the hips.

"Albert, fly," Lucy said, pulling her snake out from her hair and lifting him effortlessly above her head as she ran off around the playground.

For a second, Ms Makewell remained crouched and watched Lucy play. The sight of joy running free was a simple pleasure she was never in short supply of as a kindergarten teacher. When she'd had her fill and was sure Lucy was preoccupied and out of earshot, Ms Makewell stood up, dragging Haniel, the brother who had remained crouched with her, up too.

"I think she likes you," Haniel said.

Refusing to be derailed, Ms Makewell ignored Lucy's brother's attempt at idle chit-chat. "If you are Haniel, what should I call you?" Ms Makewell said to the brother, who had remained stiff as a board during the entire interaction with Lucy.

"I am Michael."

"Michael and Haniel," Ms Makewell confirmed.

"Correct."

"How angelic."

"Very," Michael said, a soft and stoic smile forming on his closed lips.

Ms Makewell shook her head. "And your surnames? Because I do not see a Lucy on this register. In fact, I see no new names, and I would have been informed if a new child had meant to be joining my kindergarten class."

"No surname," Michael said. "But I believe I see her name on your register. Just there."

Michael reached over and pointed to a spot six names from the bottom. As he did, there was a shift in the sunlight at his back, and, for a moment, his shadow darkened, just as Lucy's shadow did whenever something miraculous occurred around her. Ms Makewell looked down to where his finger lay, and despite having rechecked the register time and time again, there, where it shouldn't have been, was Lucy's name.

"And her surname," Ms Makewell demanded again, whipping the clipboard away from his intruding fingertip.

"It is just Lucy."

"You mistake me for someone who likes playing games," Ms Makewell said, addressing both the brothers even though it was Michael who appeared to be taking charge of the conversation. "I assure you both that the only games I play are with the children. Now, I would like to know the girl's surname."

"We do not possess your human family names."

"Then what am I to put down here?" Ms Makewell said, pulling a red marker from her pocket and tapping it impatiently against the board.

"I suppose you would call her the morning star.

"Lucy Morningstar."

"No, no, no," Haniel interjected, swishing his hand at the clipboard as Ms Makewell attempted to scribble the surname for Lucy. "She is the morning star," Haniel said, emphasising the word 'the.' "You would not call Jesus, Jesus Sonofgod, would you?"

Michael laughed the same booming chortle as before. "I do not approve of my brother's sarcastic tone, and this is the third time I have told him so today, but he is right. That is ridiculous."

"Haniel," Ms Makewell said, pointing to the brother on the right. "Michael," she said, pointing to the brother on the left. "And Lucy, the morning star," she said, nodding to Lucy, who was running circles around the willow tree with Albert still held above her head. "I get it. You're messing with me. You are both angels, and your sister is—."

"The Devil," Lucy said, leaping impossibly out from behind Ms Makewell with her already too-familiar evil, toothy grin.

"Lucy," Ms Makewell screeched, looking back and forth between the willow tree and Lucy, wondering how she had moved so fast. "What did I tell you about jumping out on me like that?"

"Don't do it," Lucy said, giggling as she ran away, proud of herself for disrupting the adult's serious conversation.

"Just ignore her," the brothers said together, timed perfectly as if having said those three words many times before.

Ms Makewell pushed her round Windsor glasses back to the bridge of her nose and eyed the brothers sternly. Her patience was wearing thin, and not because she felt like her questions weren't being answered or that they were mocking her religion as if it were a joke, but because of the ease and nonchalance with which they told her to ignore their little sister. Fortunately, their indifferent outburst led her neatly into her following line of questioning.

"Lucy's parents," Ms Makewell said. "Are they in her life?"

"Parent, singular," Michael said. "And no, our father has not been present in Lucy's life for some time."

"But when he was, did he ignore her?"

"Ignored is a strong accusation," Michael said, his warm bass tone faltering as if the insult had been directed at him.

"He sent her to Hell, Brother," Haniel said. "I think that goes well beyond ignoring her."

Michael sighed as he grappled with the sad truth of Haniel's statement, a sign he wasn't as devoid of emotion as he clearly wanted to present himself to be. "Haniel is right."

"And where were we when he did? Not with our little sister, that is where," Haniel said.

"I know, I know. Can we not do this again, Brother?"

"Is it true," Ms Makewell said, butting back in before the brothers spiralled into self-pity, "that your father told Lucy she was a mistake?"

"Despite the common belief, our father has made many mistakes," Michael said.

"Do you remember the dinosaurs," Haniel said, shaking his head at the memory of such ridiculous creatures.

"Leaving their remains here did cause quite the stir," Michael added.

"I never did understand why Father did not simply think the dinosaurs out of existence. Truly a tragic way to go."

"I believe, Haniel, that we have established many times

today that Father had a penchant for drama when it regarded his mistakes."

Haniel grumbled, casting a sad eye towards Lucy, who was still happily running circles around the playground with Albert lifted high above her head.

Not wanting to think about what had been done to Lucy, Haniel returned to tales of their father's ridiculous creations. "Octopi," Haniel exclaimed.

Michael boomed with laughter, startling Ms Makewell straight as she tried to follow the strange conversation unfolding before her. "Octopuses?" she asked.

"They never were meant to get to Earth," Michael said. "Though I suppose that is what happens when you give a creature nine brains."

"I don't know what either of you are talking about, but I suggest we return to what matters most. Your sister's wellbeing."

"Our apologies, Mary," Michael said.

Ms Makewell eyed Michael suspiciously, sure she hadn't given either of these angelic men her name. "It is Ms Makewell," she snapped, demanding control over the situation just as she would with her children when they disrespected her.

"Yes, Ma'am," the brothers said together.

With the boisterous behaviour calmed, Ms Makewell continued her line of questioning. "It is true, then, that your father told Lucy she was a mistake?"

"Sadly, this may be Father's greatest failure."

Ms Makewell sighed as she started to glean a clearer picture of Lucy's childhood. "Lucy wrote this," she said, slipping Lucy's multi-language prose from her clipboard and presenting it to the brothers. "Alas, I cannot read it."

"She has always been a wordsmith," Haniel said as he took the paper, keen to see what his little sister had chosen to commit to writing.

Ms Makewell was glad to see a glint of interest for their sister in at least one of the brother's eyes, but as he read through the multicoloured scripture, his curiosity fell to sadness.

"What does it say?" Ms Makewell asked.

"I love my brothers. I haven't seen my brothers in a long time. It makes me sad they never come see me. We used to play in the sky. I want to play in the sky. Hell hath no sky to play," Haniel said, the sadness in his voice lifting only for the final sentence, amused by his sister's use of the word 'hath.'

Haniel looked to Lucy, who had settled on the grass outside the willow tree's shade. Albert slithered a yellow circle around her head like a halo, looking up to the sky every time she pointed to the clouds and laughed at their funny shapes. Ms Makewell recognised the guilt weighing on Haniel and knew that whether they meant to or not, the brothers had a hand in their sister's neglect.

"I have spent only a day with Lucy, and I can already see she is starved for attention, and 'just ignoring her,' as you both put it, will only cause irreparable damage. So, I suggest you both start paying her some mind."

"We understand," Michael said.

"I do hope so. Because a little girl's best friend should not be a snake."

"You did not try to take Albert away from her, did you?" Haniel asked, nervously looking around for Ms Makewell didn't know what.

"I did."

The brother's grimaced then turned to one another, realisation raising their heavy-set brows. "That explains the scream," Haniel said to his brother, then, turning back to Ms Makewell, he added, "I wouldn't have done that."

"You humans have a word for pets like him." Michael mused for a second, but unable to finish his thought, he turned to Haniel. "What would they call Albert?"

"An emotional support animal," Haniel said.

"That's right," Michael continued. "Even God could not take him away from her."

"A fact I would have liked to have known at the start of the day. That, amongst many other things," Ms Makewell said.

"Our deepest apologies again, Ms Makewell," Michael said. "If we had known our sister had escaped Hell's play gates, we would have been here sooner."

It was odd, Ms Makewell thought. She could hear the way Lucy's brothers spoke of Heaven, Hell, and the almighty father, God, but it was not like that of a pastor or a fellow believer but like someone without faith. She wanted to reprimand them, to accuse and chastise them for mocking her religion, but something was stopping her. Something was keeping her from acknowledging the curiosity in her heart. It was the same thing that kept her hand from Lucy's back to feel for wings that couldn't possibly be there, the same thing that had her not want to taste the miracle apples meant for Albert, and the same thing that pained her when hearing Lucy speak every language at once. Faith.

"We are not like your conventional family," Haniel continued. "I have lately been drawn to the conclusion that we may not be a very good one either, at least not to Lucy. Father was absent. Distracted. Another child was not part of his grand plan. There were no others her age, and we were kept busy, so Lucy spent much time down here alone in the garden. Albert was all she had. I wonder sometimes if we should have demanded more of our father. Demanded more of ourselves."

"Lucy is a sweet girl. Bright, spirited, curious, and despite all you have told me of her hardships, filled with boundless joy," Ms Makewell said, offering a slither of optimism before she laid down the law, "but I suggest you both start showing Lucy the love she deserves. I do not wish to call social services, but if I feel as if her needs are not being met, if she is being mistreated in any way at all, I will be forced to take action."

"I can assure you, Ms Makewell," Haniel said, placing his hands together as if in prayer, "Lucy is our highest priority. Our shortcomings over the millennia will be rectified as if the Creator himself commanded it."

"You will do it because it is the right thing to do," Ms Makewell said "Because you love your little sister, and you can't think of any better way to spend your time."

"It is all we want."

Ms Makewell looked from Haniel to Michael over the rims of her glasses, demanding his assurances with a stern gaze. "She will have our divine attention," he said, joining his hands together in prayer like his brother.

"Good," Ms Makewell said, and satisfied with what she had learnt so far, she called out to Lucy, ushering her back to them.

As Lucy ran across the playground, Ms Makewell saw both of Lucy's brothers' love for her. It was not presented in the same way, but it was undeniably there. As they watched her run with Albert, screaming, 'fly, fly, fly,' all the way towards them, Michael hid his smile in the corners of his mouth as he maintained a level of seriousness that Ms Makewell could now see was nothing more than a façade. It didn't need to be broken, so long as Lucy could see beneath it. The other brother, Haniel, was not so reserved. His love for Lucy was unashamed, and like his little sister, when he smiled, his cheeks plumped and reddened like a cherub waiting to loose his arrow. It was endearing and did a lot to settle the nerves Ms Makewell had about Lucy's home life. Though, unlike her, neither of the brothers seemed ready for what was about to happen.

Preparing herself for Lucy's inevitable fall, Ms Makewell crouched down and opened her arms wide, and when Lucy did indeed stumble on nothing, she embraced her in an unsuspecting hug.

Lucy giggled with glee as Ms Makewell held her, a joyous sound, which caused Michael's façade to crack a little more, the corners of his mouth threatening to plump his cheeks as it did for his two siblings. Ms Makewell did not want to let Lucy go, and Lucy squeezed tighter, not wanting to be let go either, but it was home time, and with another day filled with rambunctious children fast approaching, there was much to prepare for.

As Ms Makewell released Lucy from their hug, she realised her hands had been resting on Lucy's back where a pair of angel wings should have been. Ms Makewell forced a smile to hide her disappointment, not wanting Lucy to think a frown or sad eyes were because of a wrong she had committed, but as Ms Makewell tried to shift her face, she realised that there was no disappointment to hide. Angel or not, Lucy was a special girl.

"It was really lovely to meet you, Lucy," Ms Makewell said. "And Albert?"

"And Albert, too," Ms Makewell said, tickling Lucy's hair,

not knowing where in her golden veil her snake was hiding. "I can't wait to see you both again tomorrow, bright and early, for another day of learning and fun."

"What we learn tomorrow?" Lucy asked.

"I'm not quite sure yet, but I was thinking we might go for a walk."

"Outside?" Lucy whispered, her sky-blue gaze flitting across the playground to the world beyond as if it were a place kept out of her reach for far too long.

"Of course. Fresh air, green grass, fields of flowers, and singing birds with all your new friends. How does that sound?"

Lucy looked up at her brothers, her face lit up. Then, before seeing the nervous look in their eyes, she turned back to Ms Makewell and nodded frantically, practically shaking as she looked forward to another day of kindergarten.

"Walk. Walk. Yes. We walk outside," Lucy said, her words charged with a buzz of electricity.

"A walk outside it is."

Ms Makewell stood up and said her goodbyes to Lucy and her brothers. As Lucy threw herself around her legs, she saw trepidation in her brother's eyes and knew from their sorrowed gaze that this would be their last hug good-bye. Lucy would not be coming back. Instead, her brothers would take her far away to a place she could not follow. Ms Makewell wanted to put it down to a teacher's intuition, but something greater was feeding her this knowledge. She wanted to ask a final question of Lucy's brothers, to find out if what she suspected was true, but faith continued to keep her from asking these questions.

When Lucy released Ms Makewell's leg and allowed her to return to the kindergarten schoolhouse, she heard Lucy begging her brothers to let her fly again. Ms Makewell knew by the mischievous giggle that one of Lucy's brothers had lifted her into the air. She suspected it was Haniel, the more emotionally open of the two, who had finally complied with Lucy's berating. As another peculiar gust of wind hit Ms Makewell, she looked back to see the joy on Lucy's face one last time, but instead of seeing two towering, Heaven sent men and a girl so perfect it made the world spin, Ms Makewell was alone, staring at an empty playground, clutching her nausea poisoned stomach, and left wondering if they had ever existed at all.

8

As the angel siblings soared away from Little Woods Kindergarten, leaving Ms Makewell to shrink into a lonely, confused smudge, Lucy pointed out every natural wonder the landscape had to offer.

"Field," Lucy said, pointing to a stretch of empty grass behind the kindergarten. "Water," she said, pointing down to a lake a short walk away from that. "Trees," she said, pointing beyond the town to a small patch of woodland that had been allowed to grow as long as it kept its distance from the expanding rows of houses. "Where all trees go?" Lucy asked Haniel, who held her tight in his oaken arms. "Used to be loads, loads more."

"Humans need places to live."

"Why?"

Michael slowed his flight ahead of Haniel to assist in the answering of questions. "Humans are fragile. They get cold, do not like the rain, and they need somewhere to store all the things that they like to collect."

"Why?"

"It's how Father made them," Haniel answered.

"Why?"

Haniel and Michael rolled their eyes together and ignored their sister's incessant questioning, never knowing how to appease her when she got like this. Lucy's mouth opened to repeat her question of why, but before she let her words out, she paused, and her brothers looked at each other in amazement, assuming that her millennia in Hell had been enough time for her to grow out of one of her more annoying habits.

"Where we going?" Lucy asked, fidgeting as she was flown above the greying blanket of clouds.

"We are taking you back to Heaven," Haniel said, nodding at Michael, demanding his agreement that they were not taking Lucy back to Hell.

"It is time for you to come home, Lucy," Michael said. "Time for us to be a family again."

"No. I want stay here."

"You cannot stay on Earth, Lucy. It is too dangerous."

"No. I stay in garden. I good now."

"I'm sorry, Lucy," Haniel said. "You can come back when you are older."

"Want to stay. Want friends."

Haniel had expected this reaction from Lucy and wondered if he should have lied to her until they had at least breached the boundary of this realm. Unfortunately, or fortunately, depending on your perspective, whilst Lucy had mastered the art of deception in the name of mischief, it was not in an angel's DNA to lie, so Haniel wouldn't have known where to start.

It was not that Lucy didn't like Heaven, only that she had always preferred life down in the garden. Neither Haniel nor his brothers ever understood why Lucy felt this way, especially when Heaven was the crown on their father's creation, but he supposed it had something to do with her conception. Lucy was the miracle that was never meant to be. The spark that had given life to their father's final work of art. Lucy was the reason Earth existed, and it was the reason she existed, too, but Lucy had proven time and time again that she was much too powerful and far too young to be left wandering outside the celestial realms unattended. With their father gone, his garden, Earth, couldn't handle another act of accidental cataclysm.

"Stay still, or I might drop you," Haniel said, struggling to keep Lucy and her oversized wings contained in his arms as she fought to be free.

"No, no, no," Lucy wailed, tears already pouring rivers over her chubby cheeks. "I'm good. I promise. I'm good."

Haniel hated himself for forcing Lucy to a place she did not want to be. He couldn't help but think he was doing exactly what his father had done to her millennia ago, the same thing he had scolded him for doing.

As his little sister struggled in his grip, the greying clouds below darkened to an ominous ashen-black as if feeling her turmoil. With a crackle of jagged electricity, the clouds joined in with Lucy's screams and growled at the angels, demanding they return their miracle into its blue and green arms.

"Lucy," Michael said, his voice stern and demanding. "Either you sit still and come back with us to Heaven, or we will take you straight back to Hell."

Haniel cast Michael a deathly glare, but before his disapproval caught his brother's attention, Lucy's wings burst open in a flash of blinding light as she screamed in terror at the idea of being sent back down and abandoned in the lonely pits of Hell.

The angel brothers watched with open mouths, stunned as Lucy soared away from them. With her wings spread wide for the first time in her life, starlight sprinkled out like trapped dust, motes on the wind, a miracle trail for all the world to see. Each fluttering feather was pure and white, brighter even than their own, and her heavenly light cut through the blackened cumulonimbus clouds, parting the heavy canopy of thunder and lightning like Moses parted the seas.

It was true; stories about this day were already being written, and this would be the first act in the latest gospel dedicated to God because whilst Michael and Haniel stared down in disbelief, pride swelling in their hearts as they watched their little sister's first graceful fall from the sky, all below who happened to look up at just the right time to just the right spot in the crackling, rain-filled sky, were born again in the dazzling light of the morning star.

"Did you know she could do that?" Michael asked.

"I did not."

9

It was good that nothing from the mortal realm could cause an angel physical harm because although Lucy's first descent was graceful, her landing was as clumsy as ever. Haniel and Michael flew down to the child angel-shaped imprint in the once lush garden where Lucy had landed face first, belly flat, arms, legs, and wings splayed out. It was a sight that would indeed become the talk of the town and a source of religious contention across the world once the angelic image had been spread beyond the grapevine.

As the angel brothers wrapped their wings around their bodies like a shawl, they looked nervously up to the blackened sky, neither daring to speak what they feared.

"Where do you think she has gone?" Haniel asked, wiping the biblical downpour from his brow.

"Over there." Michael pointed to a trail of knocked-over bins and post-boxes that led towards an alleyway crammed between two homes. "Do not fret, Brother. Lucy will not be far. She may have opened her wings, but she still cannot fly."

Michael moved to follow the path of carnage, but before he could lead the charge, Haniel grabbed him by the shoulder, determined to settle something before they returned Lucy into their care. "We are not taking our little sister back to Hell," Haniel said.

"I know, Brother. I am sorry. I had not meant for her to escape."

"There should be nothing for her to escape from. She is our little sister and should not be running from us in fear."

"Then what would you have us do? You know Lucy will not return to Heaven without putting up a fight."

"Father told us to keep Lucy out of trouble, and that is what we shall do."

"You cannot mean for us to stay on Earth?"

"Yes, Brother. If Lucy wishes to stay, then we shall stay. Now come. Let us find the little devil before she ruins any more of these human's precious lawns."

Lucy was as fast as Haniel and Michael remembered her to be from back when they used to play hide and seek together before their father cast her into Hell. In her panic, Lucy had not only knocked over the bins and post-boxes, littering the ground with waste and unread mail, but had crashed through picket fences, freshly shaped topiaries, and bushes of rose, peony, and dahlia. Not a single home had gone unscathed, though this unfathomable destruction was not surprising, considering the one who had caused it couldn't walk two feet without stumbling on her oversized wings. Fortunately, it was nothing that Michael couldn't put right with a quick prayer.

As Haniel led the way forward, charting a path to Lucy through the suburbs, Michael's attempts to return the streets to their former state of meticulous care were hindered by his concern for the ever-blackening sky.

The thick blanket of clouds roared at the angels who had thought themselves wise for threatening its morning star with another era locked behind the play gates of Hell. The roads ran with unnerving rivers of rain, bubbling above drains as they became clogged with windswept leaves and runaway mail; solitary trees bowed, groaning and moaning as unexpected summer winds battered them, and shutters flapped and slapped against windows, causing a racket that tried to compete with the booming thunder that echoed after each bright strike of lightning that split across the sky. It was apparent that Haniel was sharing the same concerns as Michael about the downpour, but as he stopped to voice them, the bright, playful sounds of laughter caught his attention.

"This way, Brother," Haniel said, darting through an open gate that led onto yet another winding path between two houses.

Michael gave chase, no longer following or fixing the clumsy trail of destruction their little sister had left for them, but the joyous sounds of whimsy and wonder that sang out through the storm. The path between the houses was fenced high, and with the rain coming down heavy, it was impossible to see when and where they would come out, but when the path finally did open up, they found Lucy running circles around a solitary set of swings bordered by conifers of juniper and pine which turned this waterlogged park into a secluded and secret garden.

"There she is," Haniel said, his strong voice barely a whisper in the face of the tremendous winds.

Lucy's wings were crooked and misshapen as she struggled to tuck her oversized appendages behind her back. Though nothing from this realm could stain them, and they glowed with heavenly perfection, her white dress was not under the same protection from the mud and rain. From neck to hem, Lucy was covered in a thick caking of mud that grew thicker with every trip and stumble into the drowned grass.

"Brother, she is doing it again," Michael shouted, his serious demeanour eroded as panic took over. He had seen this before, but his father had been there to set things right. Now that he was gone, the sky falling would be his failure to bear.

Instead of jumping into action to save Earth from the obvious, impending cataclysm, Haniel stopped at the park's edge and watched Lucy with a smile as she bounced from puddle to puddle, singing songs he only now remembered teaching her.

"Rain, rain, come again, come again, again, again," Lucy sang, bouncing from puddle to puddle as she felt the cool drenching of rain for the first time since her escape from the burning pits of Hell.

"Haniel, Brother, you must grab Lucy," Michael continued, his panic rising as he watched the world disappear beneath the rising water. "Take her back to Heaven or Hell. Anywhere but here. You do that, and I will find another Noah. There is no time to waste. The floods are coming. We have failed."

Haniel wrapped his arm around his brother and pulled him close to his side. "Calm yourself. We have not yet failed, and this will be no flood. It is simply one of the garden's natural meteorological events."

"How can you be sure?"

"Let your worries fall away and listen, and you will see that the only miracle at play is our little sister's laughter."

Michael put his hands together in prayer and listened for all that could be heard beyond the senses. It took a moment for his fears and emotions to fall to the wayside, but when they did, he knew that his brother was right. No miracle had been performed, and the only sounds that he could hear were the usual aches and pains of a world left to fend for itself. As he parted his hands, the world rushed back into focus, but the fear that had stopped him from enjoying the miracle before him was gone.

"It really is his most beautiful creation," Haniel said as he felt his brother return to the present.

"Earth?"

"No. Her smile."

Michael nodded in agreement. "Maybe you are right, Brother. We could stay for a short while."

"I would like that."

"But we will have to be careful. We cannot have her destroying the garden again."

"Father tasked us with keeping her out of trouble, and that is what we shall do."

"Then we are agreed," Michael said, unfurling his wings.

Haniel stepped forward to give his brother an inch of space to take flight. "Where are you going?" he asked, casting Michael a cursory glance before turning his attention back to Lucy.

"If we are to stay, then we will be needing one of these human-made homes of wood and stone."

"Do try and find us one that has not been soaked through."

"I will do my best, Brother, but you know as well as I do that they put little care into their most used creations. Nothing a quick miracle cannot fix, mind."

Michael took flight, carving a path through the thundering clouds. When his light faded into the distance, Haniel called out to Lucy, "Guess who is staying on Earth?"

Lucy stopped splashing and looked up like a deer caught in headlights as he approached her. Haniel hated how scared his little sister looked and how her wings twitched as she realised that, still unable to fly, she had nowhere to run, but he swore to himself that this would be the last time that he ever saw that look of terror on her round, mud-covered face again. From now on, they would be happy.

"We are staying," Michael roared, jumping into the biggest, wettest, muddiest puddle he could find, sending Lucy into a fit of laughter as a wave of sludge rained down on her head.

10

Haniel and Michael massaged their eyes as they stepped into the kindergarten schoolhouse and were met with the bustling sounds of rowdy, well-rested children. It had been a tiring night trying to get Lucy to contain her excitement long enough to be put down to sleep; it had taken even longer to set themselves down. After a lengthy debate about how they would keep Lucy out of trouble during their stay on Earth, they finally nodded off. Sadly, they didn't have a chance to dream before Lucy was awake and running around their new home like a wild animal again.

They could barely believe that they were letting Lucy come back to kindergarten, let alone stay on Earth, but when their sister bound towards her new best friend Sandy, who was waving at her from the cubby wall, they knew it was going to be worth the hardships inevitably coming their way.

"I go now," Lucy said, cheeks fat as she waved goodbye.

"One second, Lucy," Haniel said.

Before Lucy threw herself across the classroom, Haniel pulled her back toward him to check over his little sister one last time before he let her go. He fluffed her prairie dress that had been cleaned of mud from yesterday's afterschool antics with the power of miracle. He adjusted the strap on her new black satchel that hung over her shoulder, picked to match the giant black bow tied neatly in her hair. Haniel then double-checked inside to ensure her lunch had been packed. Not that an angel needed to eat, but he knew Lucy would feel left out if she didn't have something to put in her cubby with the other children.

"We need to go over the rules one last time before we leave," Haniel said.

"Why?"

Michael folded his arms and sighed. "Do not start with this again, Lucy."

"Why?"

"What is rule number one?" Haniel said, ignoring Lucy's questions of why, questions she had been asking all morning.

"Don't scare people with Albert," Lucy said.

"Very good."

"But why?"

"Rule number two?"

"No run away. Stay with adults."

"Very good."

"But why?" Lucy said again, rolling her head to the ceiling, tired of all the rules she didn't understand.

"And what about the final and most important rule?" Haniel asked.

Lucy remained silent as she looked into the rafters as if having seen something scuttering along the beams that no one else could see. Haniel was ready to repeat the question, knowing that if she didn't answer this last rule promptly, Michael might attempt to ferry her back to Hell, but before he had to worry about such things, Lucy huffed, hung her head in defeat at the rule that made the least bit of sense to her, and said, "No true miracles."

"Good girl," Haniel said, playfully flicking Lucy's chin up in an effort to return the smile to her face. "Only lesser miracles for now, okay?" Haniel said, having decided with his brother that getting Lucy to stop performing miracles altogether would be an impossible rule for her to follow. However, as long as she kept her miracles simple, they could at least avoid an early apocalypse.

"Whyyy?" Lucy said again, elongating the word until she ran out of breath to speak it.

"Because we said so, that is why," Michael said, watching sternly from above. "If you want to stay on Earth, then those are the rules you must follow."

Lucy took a deep breath, not stopping until she was shaking and her chest puffed all the way out. "Whyyyyyyyyyy," she wailed.

Although all the children were busy making enough noise of their own to pick up on Lucy's frustration, Ms Makewell was astutely aware of the kerfuffle taking place in the doorway to her classroom.

"He definitely doesn't eat children, only apples," Ms Makewell said to yet another concerned parent who had been told tales, tall and small, about Lucy's snake.

"Apples?" the parent said.

"I was surprised too, but it is true."

"That doesn't sound right. I thought snakes ate mice and rats," the parent paused, then said, whispering so as not to cause a commotion, "and children."

"Not this snake. Not Albert."

"Albert? What a peculiar name for the most sinful of creatures."

"I saw him eat a whole bushel. It was quite the sight," Ms

Makewell said. "I assure you that despite the stories, Lucy's snake is completely harmless and certainly not a sinner."

"Could you not put it in a box or something?"

"I tried that, and it resulted in one very loud and very sad, screaming child."

The parent grumbled, but remembering another story her chatty child had told her, she relaxed her tone and said, "I heard the girl's entire family are in Heaven." The parent placed a hand on her heart as she looked to the fortunately upright cross on the wall, then up to the rafters in the ceiling and beyond. "Who looks after the poor thing now?"

"Lucy has her brothers," Ms Makewell said, drawing the parent's attention to the two giant men trying their hardest to keep their little sister under control.

The parent's jaw dropped as Ms Makewell's had when she first caught sight of the two angelic men. They were handsome beyond words, and their chiselled silhouettes seemed to be perpetually outlined by a halo of light, but it wasn't these things that stunned all who looked upon them. It was the comfort and peace in which their presence radiated. They induced a state of being that could only be achieved when kneeling in prayer, and knowing that they existed in this confusing world had your worries drift away.

"I am sure the snake is fine," the parent said, her voice a whisper as her gaze lingered on the two men and their perfect little sister who put the entire world to shame with their beauty.

Seemingly appeased and distracted by the faith-affirming family of three, Ms Makewell walked over to Lucy, who continued to bleat 'why' at her baggy-eyed brothers.

"Please stop asking why, Lucy," Haniel said.

"Why?"

"We do not need another Dark Age, Brother," Michael said. "How did we stop her last time?"

"If I could remember that, then we would not be having this conversation, would we?" Haniel said, furrowing his brow as he racked his brain for a way to quiet his little sister's incessant questioning.

"Why, why, why, why, why, why, why?"

"Because we said so. Those are the rules, and you must follow them."

"But whyyyy?"

"Good morning, Lucy," Ms Makewell said, strained as she forced herself not to laugh at the brother's misfortune. "I am happy to see you again."

"Why?"

"Because I think you are a very lovely girl."

"Why?"

"Because you are a cheeky little devil with a big heart and an even bigger bow," Ms Makewell said, admiring the giant, black, satin loops that had, when they first met, gave her a terrible fright.

Lucy pulled at the long-tailed strings of her bow, unravelling it from her hair with a flick of the wrist. "For you," Lucy said, handing Ms Makewell the obsidian ribbon.

"Thank you, Lucy, but I think it looks better in—." Ms Makewell paused as she saw that despite Lucy waving her ribbon before her, another was miraculously tied into the back of her long, blonde hair. "Thank you," Ms Makewell said again, blinking the confusion from her eyes as she took her present and tied it to the hoop on her clipboard.

"How are you both?" Ms Makewell asked the brothers as Lucy ran off giggling.

"I have not been this tired since the genesis," Michael said.

"How do you do this every day?"

"With love," Ms Makewell said, faithfully ignoring Michael's curious biblical testaments.

"How did you do that?" Haniel asked.

"How did I do what?"

"Get Lucy to stop asking why," Haniel said. "You would not believe how long she was at it last time."

"Isn't the curious mind of a child brilliant," Ms Makewell said, wincing as Lucy barrelled across the classroom and tripped on nothing as she always did, crashing face-first into the cubbies. She was going to leave the brothers to check if she needed a plaster or two, but when Lucy got up without a scratch and showed no sign of needing medical attention, Ms Makewell returned her attention to the brothers. "Have you tried answering her questions until she has been satisfied?"

Haniel looked to his brother and shrugged, feeling silly for not having thought of that sooner, but Michael, with his serious demeanour and still folded arms, appeared dismissive of such a notion.

"I do not think she would understand all the answers," Michael said.

"That's funny. I often find it is we adults who fail to fully grasp the complexities of life."

"How so?" Haniel asked, allowing himself to be curious for his and his brother's sake.

"No one knows everything. So much of this world will forever remain a confusing mess of unanswered questions. Even the obvious can remain hidden behind a question only a child might think to ask." The brothers raised their brows unconvinced, but it was an expression Ms Makewell was used to after suggesting to a parent that their child might be able to teach them something. "Some homework for the two brothers who want to give their little sister the attention she deserves," Ms Makewell said, bringing a serious tone back into her voice as a reminder to the brothers that she was watching them closely for any sign that they were neglecting their little sister. "To the best of your ability, you will answer all of Lucy's questions. Become teachers, not gatekeepers, and, who knows, you might learn something yourselves in the process."

"We shall heed your advice," Michael said.

"Yes, you shall heed it," Ms Makewell jested, smirking as she peered over her glasses, amused at how Michael tried to hide his awe behind a shield of seriousness.

Ready to begin the day, Ms Makewell spun on her heels and flipped through her clipboard to the class register as she took in the wonderful sight of her kindergarten class filled with happy faces and the sounds of laughter and love.

"The day ends at three p.m. Be prompt," Ms Makewell said to the brothers before leaving them in the doorway.

Haniel and Michael nodded politely to the last of the parents filtering out of the schoolhouse, each looking up at them with gaping mouths and eyes wide with reverence. They were familiar expressions, the same, no matter the era. However, there was no point in acknowledging them, as the parents wouldn't either. They would never ask if they were angels because most preferred to believe. Most preferred to hold tight to their faith and allow truth to find them when their stories on Earth, God's bountiful garden, were over.

As they looked around the classroom, all the children gawked at Lucy with the same curious amour, none more so than her newly anointed best friend, Sandy, who had Lucy whispering, their father knows what, into her ear.

"Goodbye, Lucy," Haniel called out. "We will pick you up at the end of the day."

Lucy stopped whispering to Sandy and waved goodbye to her brothers before quickly turning back to her, not bothering to hide the mischievous glint twinkling in her eyes.

"She is up to something," Haniel said.

Michael looked at his brother as if he were stating the obvious. "Lucy is always up to something."

"I hope we are doing the right thing leaving her here."

"Do not doubt yourself now, Brother," Michael said. "Besides, what is the worst that could happen?"

"I don't know. An eleventh plague?"

"Yes, I believe that was what I said before you spent all night convincing me to allow this madness, but I am sure her teacher is more than capable of handling a plague or two. Now come, Haniel, let us leave before either of us changes our mind and Lucy decides the punishment for such treason is a swarm of locusts."

11

Because Ms Makewell was well aware of the learning levels of all her students, she devoted most of the morning's attention to Lucy so she could better understand her needs in the classroom. After a job well done during literacy and numeracy, without theatrics or interruptions, she allowed the children to start recess early whilst she reflected on all she had learnt about her budding new student.

Lucy's numeracy skills were below that of her peers, but nothing to be worried about, nothing that couldn't be improved. Regarding her literacy skills, Lucy's writing was years above her age and far exceeded anything she had ever witnessed for someone so young. When forced to stick to a single language that Ms Makewell could understand, she found that Lucy could write in long, flowing sentences, not always with perfect grammar, but with a wide vocabulary and an ability to form complex thoughts beyond what was expected of her, but although her literacy skills were good, so good that it had Ms Makewell believing there might be some truth to Lucy's claims of having written her own bible, her speech skills left much to be desired.

Lucy spoke fast and simply, not bothering to think about

what she wanted to say before she said it, often skipping words to reach the end of her sentences before someone interrupted her or, as it seemed Lucy feared, gave up listening, which seemed odd because, whether Lucy noticed it or not, she was enthralling. Everything she said and did put Ms Makewell and the children under a spell, and no one, so long as Lucy wasn't trying to scare them, would ever not listen to her.

Ms Makewell supposed Lucy's lacking speech skills was due to, as her brothers claimed, the many years she had spent alone. Isolation was the biggest killer of education in the young. However, Ms Makewell was not yet so worried that she felt there was any cause for concern. Some children fell behind, others fell a little further, but for now, she was confident that, with enough time, she could put Lucy on the right track.

Looking around the freshly reorganised room to maximise space for Lucy and her clumsy feet, Ms Makewell was happy to see less clutter needed tidying away. Having sacrificed her desk space further by cramming it into the corner of the room and then bringing all the tables together as opposed to bordering the classroom in a circle, she had made a nice open space between the cubbies and the activity areas for all the children to run and play without fear of being accidentally tackled to the ground by a rogue and alleged angel. Yet, despite how pleased Ms Makewell was with the state of her classroom, something unsettled her, and it wasn't just the cross that had once again flipped upside down.

With her hand on her stomach, ignoring the bubble of nausea the symbol of evil caused her, Ms Makewell counted the heads darting around the classroom. She counted them twice and then a third time. Someone was missing from her schoolhouse, and she wasn't about to give herself a pat on the back for guessing who. Lucy was gone and, no doubt, up to no good, but where was she, and what did she have planned?

"Sandy, where is Lucy?" Ms Makewell asked.

"I don't know," Sandy said with a long voice of feigned innocence as she kept her eyes down, refusing to look away from the tea party she was having with Mr Fluffywuffy Bunnykins the Second and the other teddies she had collected from the soft play area.

Ms Makewell squinted through her glasses at Sandy, letting her know she knew she was up to something, before turning her attention back to the classroom. As she looked around, Ms Makewell realised Lucy wasn't just missing, but things were out of place. First, she noticed a chair dragged to the edge of the cubbies, right where it shouldn't be. On top of the cubbies, placed vertically below a shelf that would have otherwise been out of reach, was Albert's makeshift vivarium. The shelf, once filled with books a little too complicated for the children to read themselves, had been knocked clean. The now empty shelf led to another, but this one had kept its books upon it, though each one had been turned on its side, stacked suspiciously into steps that led up to the cupboard in the corner of the room.

The trail continued over wonky picture frames and crumpled blinds, up to another shelf where a bright red plank, plucked from the indoor see-saw, lay precariously balanced as a bridge to the rafters crisscrossing through the roof. The path that led high above the classroom was impossible for any of Ms Makewell's children to have made, yet she had no doubt about who she would find at the end of it.

Ms Makewell screamed as she saw Lucy tiptoeing along

the thick beam that divided the classroom in two. "How did you—. What are you—. Lucy," Ms Makewell said, trying her hardest not to panic as she rushed across the classroom to the space beneath her.

"I learn to fly," Lucy said.

"Not this again," Ms Makewell said, following below Lucy with her arms held out, ready for the inevitable fall.

"You can do it, Lucy," Sandy shouted, causing the other children to erupt into cheers as they goaded her into jumping.

"Jump, Lucy, jump," another child shouted.

"Did you all do this?" Ms Makewell asked, panicking as she meandered through the crowd of children who had gathered at her feet to witness a miracle. "Did you help Lucy climb into the ceiling?"

"Fly like an angel."

"Fly, Lucy, fly," they all began to sing.

Lucy wobbled on the beam, raising her hands to address the children like a prophet. "I soar from clouds. Wings open wide. Now I flap, fly, into sky."

"Don't you dare jump, Lucy," Ms Makewell said, not entirely sure how she was going to get Lucy down from the ceiling if she didn't.

"It time," Lucy said, spreading her arms like wings. "Witness the morning star's first flight."

The children cheered louder, some even taking to their knees in prayer. The kindergarten was a rapturous roar of rambunctious ramblings, but then all fell silent as Lucy leapt without further warning from the rafters above.

A whistle of wind whipped down from shadow-banishing wings that no one could see. For a second, it seemed as if Lucy hovered in the air, held aloft by the children's gasps.

As the other children called to the heavenly father, speaking the names of angels they had heard recited by the local pastor in Sunday School, Lucy closed her eyes and smiled as she tried her hardest to flap her wings. For a moment, even Ms Makewell thought that some invisible force beyond her comprehension might carry Lucy away, but then, as she had expected, Lucy fell.

"I flying," Lucy said, laughing as she made a fool out of gravity, shaking with joy and unable to open her eyes from the excitement of finally spreading her wings like a big angel could. "Mortal friends. Witness the miracle. I am angel. The morning star. The bright light of Father."

"You are not flying, Lucy, and you are not an angel. You are just a very naughty girl who is trying to scare me half to death."

"I am. I am angel. Watch me flap."

"Open your eyes, Lucy."

Lucy opened her eyes and found she was not soaring above God's creations but had landed gracefully into Ms Makewell's open arms. At first, she appeared dejected, but then the thrill of the fall renewed her energy, and she began clambering up Ms Makewell's body, determined to regain her perch in the rafters.

"Again. Again. Again," Lucy said.

"Again. Again. Again," the other kindergarteners sang with her.

"Lucy will not be jumping again," Ms Makewell said, trying to get a handle on Lucy as she crawled over her shoulder. "But how about we all go for a lunchtime walk?" Ms Makewell asked, hoping fresh air might steal away some of the children's excess energy. "It looks like the sun has worked almost as hard as my kindergarteners and dried up yesterday's thunderous storm."

"Outside," the children cheered, quickly forgetting about Lucy's attempt at flight now that the wide world was promised to them.

As the children ran to the cubbies to collect their bags, Ms Makewell took a feathery slap to the face as Lucy forced herself out of her arms. With a hefty thud, Lucy fell face flat on the floor, but before Ms Makewell could compose herself to check if she was okay, Lucy got up as she always did, unphased and unhurt, and ran after the other children to join in with the frenzied tussle for their bags and their lunches tucked inside.

Ms Makewell touched her cheek, where the sensation of being tickled by feathers still tingled. She wondered if all Lucy's biblical ramblings could be real because as she walked around the classroom, taking apart the pathway Lucy and her fellow miscreants had built to the rafters, she was overcome by a lightheaded feeling of weightlessness as if the feathery touch was a blessing from above.

As Ms Makewell grappled with these dizzying thoughts, the children ran around her, lining themselves up by the door as she had taught them to do before one of their excursions outside the safety of the classroom. When they were ready, even Lucy, who stood hand-in-hand with Sandy, Ms Makewell set the upside-down cross back to its holy position. Happy the classroom was in order, she put her hands together and thanked her ever-listening God for bringing her a new child to nurture and mould, but as she silently prayed Lucy's name, the cross fell, and, with its descent, evil forced a rancid wave of bile into her throat.

12

In the evenings, the field behind the kindergarten was used by various sports clubs, but during the kindergarten hours, it was mostly empty. Bordered by hedges with a small opening in the far corner, it was easy to keep an eye on all the children as they played their made-up games that were too fluid and ever-changing for Ms Makewell to grasp. Whilst she usually wished there were more trees than old willow, who remained locked behind the kindergarten gates, with Lucy insistent on jumping from great heights, Ms Makewell was glad for once that this was nothing but a vast open space where everyone had no choice but to keep their feet planted firmly on the ground. Still, she thought it might be a good idea to get the parents' permission to take their children on a short trip to the lake at the end of the week. It would be nice to allow the kindergarteners to see a place where nature had been allowed the freedom to thrive.

Lucy played with the other children for a while, but with her attention drawn to the flowers in the grass and the birds in the sky, she had peeled off into solitude to commune with her oldest friend, nature. With her back to Ms Makewell, Lucy had chosen to sit at the centre of the field in the middle of a circle of daisies growing in a patch of particularly lush grass. From afar, it seemed like Lucy was a part of the flowers, the skirt of her white prairie dress blending in with the delicate petals. Curiouser still, the illusion appeared to spread every time Ms Makewell blinked.

It looked like, for once, Lucy wasn't doing much of anything, and in her stillness, the sun had found her. Its shafts of light lit her up as if Heaven were attempting to keep her tethered to the realm she claimed to be from. She was as beautiful as ever. However, even in Lucy's heavenly beauty, there seemed to be a sadness weighing down on her shoulders.

Hating to see one of her children alone and upset, Ms Makewell moved to join Lucy in her circle of daisies, but then Sandy, accompanied as always by her stuffed rabbit, came barrelling toward her new best friend. Seeing as it was good practice to let the children solve their problems first, to learn to alleviate each other's sadness through companionship and compassion, Ms Makewell wandered to a patch of daisies of her own and thought about where she might acquire fishing nets for their hopeful trip to the lake.

*   *   *

"Are you talking to that bird?" Sandy asked, stopping at the edge of the circle of daisies in fear of frightening the copper-chested chaffinch perched on Lucy's knee. "Can you talk to animals?" she added, too excited to wait for an answer to her first question.

"I talk to everything," Lucy replied before returning to her tweeting, which, to Sandy, sounded bright and cheerful, even if Lucy wasn't smiling.

"Is that bird sad?" Sandy asked, not needing to step forwards into the daisies because more had bloomed around her, swallowing her sandaled feet whole.

Lucy nodded. "There no trees here. No branch to make nest."

"What about the bushes?"

"This one wants tree," Lucy said, the chaffinch hopping onto Lucy's pointed finger.

"I have a tree in my garden," Sandy said, cautiously stepping closer to Lucy and her bird friend. "They could come home with me."

As Sandy sat down in front of her newest but already bestest friend in the world, Lucy tweeted something to the chaffinch. Whilst Sandy waited for Lucy to finish whistling, she gave Albert a quick tickle to the chin as he slithered through the grass to greet her. When Lucy's birdsong had ended, there was a mischievous glint in her eye, and despite only knowing her for two whole days, Sandy knew Lucy was about to do something that she knew she shouldn't.

"Are you going to be naughty?" Sandy asked, covering her stuffed rabbit's ears so he couldn't tattle on their plans.

"I make trees here. For all the birds."

"That sounds nice, not naughty."

"Brothers say no miracles."

"Why?" Sandy asked.

"I don't know." Lucy shrugged. "They like silly rules."

"Rules are silly," Sandy agreed. "Sometimes I think adults want us to be sad."

"Or they forget how be happy," Lucy said.

"How do you forget how to be happy?"

"Too many rules."

"That makes sense. You are very smart," Sandy said, nodding in agreement with Lucy's angelic wisdom. "How are you going to make trees? Do you make a wish? Like blowing out candles on a birthday cake?"

"What's a birthday cake?" Lucy asked.

"It's a cake, but for your birthday. It has jam. Frosting. Sometimes chocolate. I had a rabbit cake once. I know it not a real rabbit, but I think Mr Fluffywuffy Bunnykins the First didn't like me eating his friend. So, I said to Mum and Dad, 'no more rabbit cakes, please.' And now my favourite cake is a caterpillar."

Lucy gasped, shocked by how much she and Sandy had in common. "I like caterpillars too," she said.

"That's why we are best friends."

"Best friends," Lucy agreed, nodding happily. "We will plant this," Lucy said, miraculously plucking one of Albert's apples from thin air. "Trees will grow."

"Wow, that's amazing. Let's dig," Sandy said. "Tell Mr or Mrs Bird we will have new home soon."

"Mrs bird," Lucy said before relaying Sandy's message to the chaffinch with a chorus of tweets.

Lucy and Sandy dug a hole with their hands at the centre of the field. As they did, the chaffinch hopped excitedly around them, occasionally taking a perch on Albert's verdant green head as he slithered a protective circle around the two girls. Knowing they needed to safely bury the apple before Ms Makewell came to spy on them, Lucy and Sandy scrambled to dig the hole as quickly as possible. Albert could sense Lucy and Sandy trying not to giggle as their act of naughtiness tingled in their bellies like fluttering butterflies, and so, being the good snake that he was, he kept a watchful eye out for anyone looking to stop their mischief. Fortunately, everyone was far too busy running around, even Ms Makewell, who appeared to have finally understood enough rules of the kindergartener's made-up game to join in.

When Lucy and Sandy had finished digging, and the earth had stained their nails brown and green, Sandy and Albert looked not so discreetly over to Ms Makewell whilst Lucy looked up to Heaven. When they were sure no one was coming to stop them, Lucy snatched up the apple and dropped it in the freshly dug hole.

"Quick. Cover up," Lucy said.

The girls swiped the dirt back into the hole, filling it far faster than they had dug it, two pairs of dirty hands flailing together, working in tandem until there was only a mound of rich-scented, freshly turned earth between them. But that wasn't enough to hide the naughtiness they knew no one could notice, so when Lucy started patting the ground flat, Sandy did, too. Then, when Lucy wiped away excess clumps of dirt and tossed away stones once buried deep, Sandy copied that also, and when Lucy ripped up grass to hide their buried apple, Sandy did the same.

When the only sign of their mischief was the dirt beneath their nails, Lucy nodded, satisfied with the preparations, but there was one last thing to do. Pray.

Big miracles were usually tricky. Lucy's had always gone wrong, and then she got told off for performing them, which wasn't fair because she was an angel too, and if she wanted to do miracles, then why shouldn't she? Why else would she have her father's power in her wings if not to do good things with it? Fortunately, this miracle was going to be easy. The Eden apples were one of the holiest of artefacts, and all Lucy had to do was put her hands together and ask for the apple to grow, and it would oblige her without a fight because that was its purpose. And so, eyes open, hands together, Lucy asked the seeds to break free of their shells, spread beneath the earth, and provide for all life so that life may provide for it in return.

"Nothing's happening," Sandy said.

"I feel it," Lucy said, sensing a ripple of change beneath the earth that was imperceptible to all but the microscopic creatures making way for the spreading life force.

Sandy tilted her head as she tried to listen for a faint whisper of change, but to her disappointment, she heard nothing. Still, she was faithful and believed wholly in Lucy's angelic abilities, so she put her stuffed rabbit's ear to the ground instead, hoping at least he would get to hear the change instead.

"Few days. Lots of trees. Promise," Lucy said in English first, then repeating herself in tweet for the chaffinch.

The tiny twittering bird sang a beautiful song, flying in circles around the girls as a sign of thanks. Sandy had never heard wings flap so loudly or seen a bird fly so close. It seemed impossible for it to stay above the ground, but every time it dove down, it beat its wings and lifted itself higher. It was the most amazing thing Sandy had ever seen, except for Lucy, whose heavenly beauty Sandy had not yet learned enough words to describe.

Watching the bird fly made Sandy wonder, was this what Lucy would look like when she learnt how to lift her wings, or would her flight be as invisible to her as the feathered appendages at her back? Sandy clasped her cross necklace and prayed that she would see Lucy fly one day, but if she didn't, that would be okay, too. Sandy was just happy to have a friend.

As the bird tweeted its final goodbyes, Lucy worried about

what her brothers might do to her if they found out what she had done. Would they take her to Heaven, away from Sandy, Ms Makewell, and kindergarten, which she really, really liked, or would they throw her back behind the play gates of Hell, punishing her with loneliness just as their father had done?

Lucy was too scared to think about what fate awaited her, but she did want to know she wasn't alone in her persecution, so she asked Sandy, "What silly rules you have?"

"Lots of rules," Sandy said. "Eat all my vegetables. No dessert for breakfast. And the worst rule," Sandy paused to pick Mr Fluffywuffy Bunnykins the Second up from the ground, who had, until now, been happily listening for the changes happening beneath the ground, "no more bunnies," she said, sniffling as she squeezed her stuffed rabbit tight, wishing it would come to life in her arms.

"That's a silly rule," Lucy exclaimed, flailing her arms, frustrated at all the commandments big people liked to make. "Adults are silly."

"They are silly," Sandy said. "We still have rabbit house. He could live there. He could hop in our garden. Hop in my bedroom. Hop wherever he likes."

"Why no rabbit?" Lucy asked, but Sandy only shrugged in response.

Lucy understood this lack of understanding better than most. Lucy had always been told what to do and what not to do, but she had never been told why. No miracles. Don't let Albert scare people. Go to Hell. Don't leave. Stay out the way. Be a good angel. What even was a good angel, Lucy wondered. She was sure she was one. She did nice things. It wasn't her fault that no one wanted to play with her at the beginning, nor was it her fault that no one wanted to help her make the garden better for everything that lived here. And it definitely wasn't her fault she was a mistake. Lucy was a good angel. She was sure of it. And she was going to prove it by making her new friend smile.

Sandy's eyes were scrunched shut as she tried her hardest not to cry. Not because crying was wrong or because it had made some people not want to talk to her anymore, but because it made her tired. Sandy was sure she had cried a whole river for her pet rabbit, but now all she wanted was to smile when she thought of him. But even though Lucy had told her there was a place in Heaven for rabbits to hop about, Sandy couldn't help but get sad when she thought of how much she missed him and how badly she wanted to have a new fluffy friend to remember him by.

As Sandy felt like everything was going to end, that all of her sad emotions might come crashing out of her, she felt herself bathed in a warm light, and then, when it subsided, something started to wiggle in her arms. At first, Sandy didn't dare open her eyes, but then Lucy said, "I make you rabbit," and she knew what the wiggling meant. Her prayers had finally been answered. Lucy had listened when no one else would.

Sandy opened her eyes, and the world and the cuddly grey mass in her arms was a waterlogged smudge. She wiped the tears from her eyes and looked down to see that the stuffed Mr Fluffywuffy Bunnykins the Second was gone, and in his place was a real Mr Fluffywuffy Bunnykins the Second, a living, breathing, tail twitching, nose wiggling, ears flopping Mr Fluffywuffy Bunnykins the Second, who looked up at her with dazzling black jewels for eyes.

"A rabbit. A real life rabbit," Sandy said, squealing as she smushed her miraculous pet into her face to give it hundreds and thousands of nose kisses, just like she used to do with Mr Fluffywuffy Bunnykins the First.

The rabbit, born from a teddy, was already enamoured with his new owner and wiggled his nose against Sandy's. He was as soft as her previous pet, and his fur was the same wonderful shade of grey, which, in the right light, shimmered metallic and blue. Sandy knew Mr Fluffywuffy Bunnykins the Second wasn't her original rabbit, as Mr Fluffywuffy Bunnykins the First had a white spot on his left paw, whilst this one had a white spot on his right paw, but she already loved him just the same. He wasn't a replacement, just a new friend, a new friend like Lucy. One who would help turn her sadness into smiles.

"Thank you, Lucy," Sandy said. "You are my angel."

With a happy bird and a happy human, Lucy was sure she was a good angel. What did her brothers know about miracles? Not as much as she did, Lucy thought. Miracles made everything better, even if her brothers couldn't see that. Lucy was a good angel, and so she would break their silly rules all day long. Besides, soon, she would be able to fly like a big angel, and then no one would be able to trap her all alone in Hell ever, ever again.

13

It was the end of the week, and Ms Makewell was glad to have gotten permission from all the parents to take their children on a trip to the lake. She was happy to be out, and not just for the children's sake but for her own. The kindergarten schoolhouse was starting to unsettle her. Ms Makewell was sure an evil lurked in the cramped confines of the four walls where she had usually found solace. Between the cross never staying upright and the constant mess that she had once accounted to Lucy's clumsiness but now believed to be the act of something unholy and demonic, she was having a hard time keeping her mind focused on her kindergarteners and not the nausea that had made a home in the depths of her stomach. A day outside, surrounded by God's creation, was exactly what the doctor ordered, or at least it would have been had she not decided to see Lakeville's local pastor instead.

The pastor was a good man and had listened to her confessions without judgment since she was a child. His wise words for her this time were of acceptance. He reminded her how easy it was to conflate good and evil when both concepts were as intangible as our souls. That she should not feel guilt for suspecting a child of being the Devil, the bringer of evil and end of days, when so often the greatest tests of our faith were our young.

After sharing a few minutes of laughter, reminiscing about all the tearaways that Ms Makewell had guided into respectable young adults, the pastor reminded her that the mind was powerful and, like the Devil, could lie to us. Sometimes, a dark thought could take such a strong hold of us that it would bleed out into reality and infect everyone we know and love, and because of this, she should take care not to let her thoughts of evil spiral like the Devil wants them to, and if she should find herself struggling, she should remember that God's love and light would always be there for her, even in the laughter of a little girl who may, for all she knew, be the angel she claimed to be. They laughed again as old friends did and imagined a world where angels walked amongst them. With a final act of assurance, the pastor agreed that if, by his next service, she still felt evil lurking within her schoolhouse, he would bless her humble sanctuary once again, as he had done when it was first erected, long before Ms Makewell was even born.

"Another fishy. Another fishy," Lucy said, running over to Ms Makewell with a bucket full of tiny fish, the only one of her kindergarteners so far to have caught anything.

"That's amazing, Lucy," Ms Makewell said. "How many do you have now?"

Lucy peered into her bucket. "Six grey fishies, six yellow fishies, and six silver fishies."

Six, six, six, Ms Makewell thought, the fresh air doing nothing to alleviate the terror she felt from hearing such an evil number. Ms Makewell swallowed her fear into her nauseated stomach and forced an awkward smile onto her face. "That's impressive, Lucy, but I think you should try and catch one more fish, don't you?" Ms Makewell said, hoping another fish in the bucket might prevent evil from rising out from the bowels of Hell and onto God's green earth. Assuming it wasn't already here, stood before her, disguised as a golden-haired girl.

"Nope," Lucy said, twisting her head and glaring up at Ms Makewell with a sinister smile that made the world spin. "Six, six, six, is enough fishies." Then Lucy stood up straight, her smile beamed, her eyes brightened, and she said, "I help everyone catch fishies now," and then ran away giggling, taking extra special care with her steps, afraid of dropping the fish plucked from their home.

Ms Makewell wobbled as she took a deep breath to calm her vertigo and steady the world pulsing before her. She tried to remind herself of what the pastor had said, that the mind could lie like the Devil, that she should try not to let it infect her reality and that she should focus on God's light wherever she could find it, but with nothing making any sense, and her breathing doing nothing to quell the shifting lake, Ms Makewell was struggling to heed her pastor's advice.

Trying a new tact, Ms Makewell removed her wellies and socks and pressed her bare feet into the soft dirt, connecting herself physically with the world her almighty lord created. As she wiggled her toes in the mud, the lake slowed its spinning, yet everything remained out of focus. She walked to the lake's edge and allowed the cool water to soothe her rising temperature, but still, something curdled in her stomach. Bunching up her trousers, Ms Makewell waded deeper, and when the lake rose above her thighs, she closed her eyes and listened to the singing songbirds, the whispering winds, and tying it all together like the composer of a choir, Lucy's laughter as she tried to help the other children add fish to their buckets. Was this what the pastor meant about finding God's light in a child who may or may not be the angel she claimed to be?

Not wanting her eyes shut for too long because she needed to ensure she paid keen attention to the kindergarteners, Ms Makewell counted down from ten. Ten, nine, all her fears pooled in her stomach. Eight, seven, her anxieties sank to her toes. Six, five, the water carried her worries away. Four, three, she asked for forgiveness, Lucy was not the Devil, evil incarnate. Two, God's light warmed her heart. One, everything fell silent. No laughter, no wind, no birdsong. The world carried away, nothing left but herself.

Then, through the peaceful emptiness, the kindergartener's conversations weaved their way back into her conscience.

"Why no fish."

"Ms Makewell said they be louds."

"Is all the fish gone, Lucy?"

"Maybe they dead?"

"I don't want fishies to be dead."

"Fishies where are you? Where are you fishies?"

"Lucy, are the fishies in Heaven? Do dead fishies go to Heaven?"

Ms Makewell opened her eyes and looked down at her feet. There once had been a time when fish would flock to her toes to check out her curious worm-like appendages, but the lake now appeared empty. The occasional fish could be seen in the murky depths, and even the odd water strider zipping across the surface, but with so little activity, it was a surprise Lucy had managed to catch the fish she had. However, was it really so hard to believe that Lucy's magnetic personality was as attractive to the fish as it was to her peers?

The world had changed a lot in Ms Makewell's time, and it continued to do far faster than she could keep track of. It seemed each year that another area where she had once taken the children berry picking, bug hunting, or cloud watching had been replaced with houses. How long would it be before the new builds intruded on this sanctuary? Or was it already too late?

If Lucy were an angel, would she have the power to revitalise the lake? Could she bring back the life that had once made this secluded spot a place of magic and wonder? Ms Makewell drifted into a trance as she watched Lucy run between the other children's empty buckets. Like on the first day they met, Lucy wore the same expression of ageless wisdom that grew sadder with each empty bucket she peered into. It looked to Ms Makewell as if Lucy were thinking the same thing she was, that there used to be so much life here, but how could she, a four-year-old child, remember anything of a time when buildings of wood and stone didn't dominate the landscape? But the look of contemplation was clearly there. It put a stomp in her step, a wobble in her chin, and a twist in her smile as she found herself caught between the memory of a better time and the one that she was living in now.

The world needed a miracle, Ms Makewell thought. Earth wasn't just for humans. It belonged to all living things. Then, as if hearing her prayers, Lucy put her hands together, intent on making a change. The sun parted the clouds, and its light beamed down upon Lucy as she walked through the crowd of kindergarteners who had gathered together to sing. It all seemed like a dream, and Ms Makewell knew that this heavenly sight would fade if she blinked, so she strained to keep her eyes open, even when her voice got added to the choir.

The dream continued as Lucy walked to the water's edge and did not stop. With her eyes closed, but for the one she kept half open, Lucy walked across the lake's surface without sinking. The water rippled from her cherub feet and the invisible wings on her back. It was the miracle of miracles. Proof of the divine. An act performed by the saviour of human sin. The choir grew louder, the sun's light grew brighter, and then, without meaning to, Ms Makewell blinked, and the screams of her children came flooding in.

The kindergarteners ran in all directions, fleeing from fish that flew towards their empty buckets. There were more fish than Ms Makewell could count, more than she had ever seen, more than what this lake could reasonably contain, fish of all shapes and sizes, fish shimmering with vibrant colour that didn't belong, and fish she was sure should not exist. They leapt into the air, flipping and flapping, slapping children across the backs of their heads as they fled to the safety of dry land. It was chaos, and Lucy was at the centre of it all, not walking on water but knee-deep, fervently clapping, spinning, and splashing as she egged the fish on.

Ms Makewell's teacher's instincts kicked in, as they always did when the screaming started. She leapt through the water towards the children who had been scared still and gave them the push they needed to get them running to the shore. As Ms Makewell went to shout for Lucy, a fish slapped her in the mouth, sending her stumbling backwards into the lake with a splash. The kindergarteners, who had found safety where the fish could not reach, switched from screams to laughter as they watched their teacher fumble on all fours.

It was chaos. Ms Makewell could hardly see through the flurry of fins, but when she finally spotted two more of her children panicking together as a barrage of clownfish assaulted them, she crawled through the water toward them. When she had them both tucked between her arms, she pushed up against the storm of tropical fish and looked for other kindergarteners who needed her help, but she had done her job, and the only one left to save was Lucy.

"Get out of the water," Ms Makewell shouted to Lucy, wondering if she had room for a third child in her arms.

"Fly, fly fishies," Lucy sang back, the least bit concerned by the cyclone of fish jumping around her. "Lots of happy fishies. Buckets full of fishies. Fishies, fishies, fishies."

"Can you please get out of the water," Ms Makewell said, trailing off and sighing as she realised the futility of getting Lucy to do anything she was told.

There was no room for three in her arms, so Ms Makewell darted to safety, dropped the children off with the others, and made a run for Lucy. She ducked, weaved, dodged, and dived, and as she was about to gather Lucy up, a flurry of fish flew towards her face, sending her down into the tumultuous lake, causing everyone and Lucy to laugh and point as she floundered with the fish.

At least the children were enjoying themselves, Ms Makewell thought as she picked herself up for the second time today.

14

It had been a long day, and all but Lucy had been picked up because, apparently, angels were terrible at keeping track of time. She had gained a few bruises in her falls into the lake, and her clothes were soaked through, but fortunately, like she had asked the kindergarteners to, Ms Makewell had brought a change of clothes. Unfortunately, her hair was still wet, and the cold, damp, resting in a bun on the top of her head was giving her a chill. As she coughed into her arm, flipping the cross upright for the umpteenth time today, the schoolhouse spun, only settling when a deep, comforting, and already familiar voice reached to her from the doorway.

"I would leave it," Haniel said.

"You are late again." Ms Makewell pointed to the clock, over half an hour past pick-up time.

Haniel apologised, as he had done every day this week, and said, "She will only keep flipping it."

"Lucy is doing this?" Ms Makewell asked sceptically.

"She likes to mess with you Christian folk."

"I knew it," Ms Makewell said.

Ms Makewell didn't really know it, but she looked at Lucy

hiding beneath the table and squinted at her as if she did, letting her know she was on to all of her naughty antics. Lucy peered up at her with her tight-lipped, fat-cheeked, mischievous grin and quietly giggled before scarpering out of sight in a flash of gold and white.

"I am sorry if she has been causing you trouble," Haniel said. "Lucy has always been quite the handful."

"It's nothing to worry about. I wouldn't have lasted this long as a kindergarten teacher if I couldn't handle a little devilry."

Ms Makewell wondered if she should tell Haniel of the miracle she had witnessed at the lake or of the visions and vertigo she had been experiencing, but deciding it would be best to keep all of it to herself, she smiled and moved on. Ms Makewell didn't know whether faith or fear kept the truth tucked away inside, but for now, updating Haniel on his little sister's development in her first week seemed more prudent.

"After a week with your little sister, I can safely say that Lucy is an exceptionally bright girl. A little behind her peers but nothing that can't be remedied with attention and structure."

"Is there anything I should be doing with her at home?"

"Be with her. Enjoy each other's company. Relish in her inquisitive mind."

"That I can do."

Happy with Haniel's attitude towards his little sister's future, Ms Makewell dropped the stern, commanding voice and relaxed, allowing herself to be seen as more than just a teacher, but as a friend.

"Will I be seeing you both on Sunday? Your brother, too?"

"I thought humans did not go to school on the weeks end?"

"No, but we humans do go to church."

"I believe that would not be a good idea at all."

"And why might that be?" Ms Makewell asked. "No, wait, let me guess," she added quickly. "Lucy likes to mess with us Christian folk."

"Exactly."

Ms Makewell held on to her stomach. Even though she now knew it was Lucy tormenting her, she couldn't shake the feeling something was wrong. "If I can handle Lucy for a whole week, then I am sure the pastor and his parishioners can cope for an hour or two."

"Trust me. Lucy will cause a stir. I am sure of it."

"The pastor does a good reading. I think even Lucy might be able to sit through one of them."

"Oh no, Lucy does not like the stories."

"Stories?"

"In her defence, most of what has been written is way off."

Ms Makewell gasped at the blasphemy. "Excuse me?"

"The messages tend to be true, but the presentation, not so much."

"Church isn't just about God and his teachings, or these 'way off' stories as you put it, but about community and togetherness. It will do Lucy good to get out of the house and be around adults as well as children."

"I will have to discuss it with Michael."

"I'm sure he'll agree it is in Lucy's best interest. And naturally, the church is filled with crosses. So, if you could get her to stop playing with them, I'm sure the pastor would appreciate it."

"I cannot make any promises," Haniel said, turning Ms Makewell's gaze to the once again upside-down cross.

"How?" Ms Makewell said, looking around the classroom

for Lucy but only hearing her evil laughter moving around the room as if she were hiding behind the walls. Defeated, she took the cross off the wall and held her stomach tight as insidious forces swelled out from the pores of the schoolhouse and into her belly. "I think I need to see the pastor again," Ms Makewell said.

Haniel looked at Ms Makewell with a piercing, all-knowing gaze. She felt his eyes on her soul, but instead of running, hiding herself away from his judgment, she let him in. What did he see beneath the surface that she couldn't see herself? Was she a good person? Was she worth the time taken to be judged? His gaze softened; her soul exposed.

"I believe it would be far wiser for you to see a doctor instead."

"I'm sure it is nothing," Ms Makewell said, trying her best not to sound concerned by the revelation. "Besides, I doubt I'll be able to get an appointment on such short notice. You know how it is these days. The doctors are rushed off their feet. Everyone is ill with something."

"I believe Doctor Richards has time to see one last patient before the day's end," Haniel said, miraculously plucking a doctor's note from the air in the same way Lucy retrieved Albert's apples.

Haniel placed the note and his hand in Ms Makewell's. His touch was warm, and his gaze burned with undying love. The room brightened as his eternal life alleviated the aches and pains in her body, drying the last of the damp in her coiled bun, all giving her mind the space to realise what had been bothering her all along. If the Devil was here, it was not in the schoolhouse or the little girl who made everyone laugh, smile, and sometimes scream. No, the evil was living inside her, taking her apart from within.

"We will see you Sunday," Haniel promised.

"Yes, Sunday. I will see you Sunday," Ms Makewell said, keeping hold of Haniel's hand as she did, too afraid to let go as her mind raced through the questions she did not want to ask.

What had Haniel seen? What darkness corrupted her? Could he make it go away? Would he? Had she done enough with her life to deserve a miracle? If only she were brave enough to believe.

15

Haniel and Michael lurked on the other side of the street as the parishioners filed into the church two by two. There were a lot of familiar faces from kindergarten, and Haniel had to hold tight to Lucy's hand to stop her from running across the busy road to say hello, but he knew he couldn't keep his little sister here forever. Lucy was itching to get inside and bounced on the spot as if she had to go to the loo, not that angels needed to do such things. Eventually, she would break free, and then all of Hell would break loose.

"I have a bad feeling about this," Michael said.

"It will be fine," Haniel said. "You will be good, won't you, Lucy."

"I be good," Lucy said brightly before dropping her blonde brows and smiling sinisterly. "I promise."

"You see, Brother. Lucy promises to be good."

"You cannot possibly believe her. Look at that face. She is already plotting something."

"Of course I don't believe her," Haniel whispered harshly to Michael. "But we cannot keep her locked up. Besides, was it not you who reminded me that Lucy was always up to something?"

"It was," Michael said, shaking his head, hating hearing his own words spoken back to him. "But what would you suppose we do with her when she starts acting up."

"We do as we were told. Keep our little sister out of trouble."

"Very well, Brother. Then let us get this over with."

Lucy in hand, the three angels crossed the road to the church. Everyone had now found their way inside, but even with the heavy doors shut, the soft murmur of voices could be heard from within. It was packed, and that only made the brothers more nervous. As they reached the double doors, Lucy slipped her hand from Haniel's and hid behind his leg. He assumed that if she, too, were nervous to be around so many people, then maybe his little sister might not get up to quite as much mischief as previously thought. Thinking the same thing, Michael pushed both doors open with a confidence he immediately regretted.

As the doors swung open, sunlight beamed down on Michael and Haniel from the stained-glass window at the end of the aisle; the choir erupted into a chorus of angelic vocals, and the bells high in the tower rang despite no one beneath them to pull their strings. All eyes turned onto them, and everyone gasped at their beauty. The parishioners knew what they were but could not admit it to themselves or each other. No one ever could. They stared longingly at them, their presence in the multi-hued light a testament to everything they believed in. Then, the sunlight died, the choir silenced, and the bells fell still. Lucy leapt out from behind Haniel's legs and roared like a child possessed, her terrifying voice lighting every unlit candle with a violent pillar of flames that cast ghastly shadows on the ornamental gargoyles and the sorrowed faces of Christ. The choir resumed singing, but their angelic tones were now deep and demonic. The organs played a single, loud, and foreboding note that shook the towering stone walls around them more than the bells ever could. And, as expected, every cross not chiselled permanently into the brickwork fell wrong, and with their descent into the ungodly position, another gasp was stolen from the parishioner's already open mouths.

The only thing quelling the onlooker's screams was that, despite Lucy's devilry, she was an angel, too. Her innate charisma had everyone enamoured with her, and it would take a lifetime of trickery and misdeeds to convince humanity she was more than a mischievous child. That being said, Haniel didn't want to risk the second coming of the anti-Christ, so he swiped his little sister up into his arms and carried her down the aisle.

As Lucy crawled to comfort in Haniel's grasp, she giggled and let her miracles of mischief end, silencing the organ, releasing the choir, blowing out the candles, and allowing the sun to return to its usual place in the sky where it could light the church with its diffused, morning glow. The crosses, however, remained upside down, causing those who had noticed them to fidget in their pews.

"You promised you would be good," Haniel said, but having never really believed her lie, he let himself smile, not wanting to hide the joy he derived from hearing his little sister laugh.

"I told you this would be a bad idea," Michael said.

Haniel rolled his eyes. "I am sure it will be fine, Brother."

"Let us find our seats before she does something truly terrible."

A thin red carpet that barely muffled their footsteps on the cold, grey stone led them down the aisle. The church was a magnificent building that, if not marred by age, might not have looked out of place in Heaven. There hadn't always been structures in the clouds above, but as soon as the human souls poured in, so did the rise of their churches, crafted out of God's light in hopes of bringing themselves nearer to him. The irony being, of course, that they had never been closer. But love for the creator was powerful, and sometimes love made you do crazy things.

"Ms Makewell," Lucy said, reaching over Haniel's shoulder. "Sit with Ms Makewell."

Whilst most eyes in the church still lingered on the three of them, Ms Makewell's gaze hung low as if her mind were elsewhere. She had squeezed herself onto the edge of her pew, and it wasn't until Lucy screeched her name that she looked up and waved. Sadly, something terrible preoccupied her mind, so dark and consuming that not even Lucy's excitable greeting could put anything other than a forced smile upon her face.

"There is no space to sit over there, Lucy."

"Sit," Lucy pleaded, her happy voice wavering as she was carried further away from her favourite, and only, teacher.

"We will see Ms Makewell after mass. Why don't you give her a wave?"

Lucy perked up at the promise of seeing Ms Makewell later and waved whilst wailing hello, over and over, until the echoes of her made her smile real.

"Here," Michael said, pointing towards a space between two families.

The hall fell silent as the pastor entered the podium from a hidden door in the corner of the church. He was an elderly man, but he moved quickly for his age. When he found his place behind the lectern, he watched with a gentle smile as the three angels struggled to reach their seats.

The gap between the pews was tight, and Haniel was forced to apologise as he knocked the knobbly knees of the parishioners too enraptured by his angelic beauty to give him more room. As he shuffled forward, Lucy's struggling caused her wings to fall onto the heads of those on the pews in front, and when a flurry of sneezes erupted from their feather-tickled noses, Haniel spun Lucy and her oversized wings away, only to accidentally slap an old, white-haired lady in the face with them instead.

As Haniel witnessed the light of the morning star stun the elderly lady with a glimpse of Heaven above, he snapped at his brother, who was fumbling uselessly behind him.

"Michael."

"What?"

"A little help."

"I told you this was a bad idea."

"Could you please just get a hold of Lucy's wings?"

The people who could hear the brother's agitated conversation looked up at them with wide eyes and open mouths, surer than ever that they were in the presence of the divine. Everyone else, however, held their lips tight as they questioned whether it would be unholy to laugh at two burley men struggling to keep themselves from being felled by a girl a fraction of their size.

The pastor's kindly smile grew wider as he watched the newest members of his flock fail to contain the miniature force of nature because, oblivious to her cumbersome wings, Lucy only exacerbated her brothers' struggles as she caught sight of Sandy at the back of the hall. As she clambered over Haniel's face to get her best friend's attention, jabbing her feet into his chest and pulling on his ears to reach higher,

her flowing prairie dress obscured his vision. Blinded by the white ruffles, Haniel stumbled on a stray foot of an awed parishioner. He wobbled, he wibbled, and Lucy giggled, but as he was about to fall, Michael, who, to all watching, appeared to be holding onto nothing but air, caught his brother and guided both him and their little sister's wings down into the pew.

The pastor chuckled to himself, and as he did, his flock let go of their nerves and laughed along too. "I may be an old man, but I am not so stubborn to admit when I am wrong." He wheezed as he laughed at an old joke made a thousand times. "Maybe we do need extra space between the pews, after all." The pastor wiped a single tear from each of his wrinkled eyes and then placed a hand on the good book waiting for him on the lectern. "Now that our newest residents of Lakeville have taken their seats let us all join our hands together for morning prayer."

Lucy shuffled in Haniel's lap and watched everyone put their hands together. Her eyes widened as an idea struck her, but before she could put her hands together, Haniel slapped them down, knowing exactly what sort of mischief she was up to.

"No miracles."

"But priest man said."

Lucy raised her hands above Haniel's, but before she could clap them together in prayer, Haniel slid his hands between them. "I do not care what he said."

"Priest man says do prayer. I do prayer."

"If the priest told you to jump off a cliff, would you do it?"

"Yes."

"Oh right, you have wings," Haniel said, slapping his little sister's hands apart again.

Michael shook his head at his siblings as they caused a kerfuffle while everyone around them tried to silently pray to their father. The pastor had his hands together too, but with one eye open and a smile creeping onto his weathered face, Michael knew he wasn't praying with his flock but watching the curious newcomers making a stir.

As Lucy and Haniel's whispers and slapping hands echoed around the church hall, more eyes opened to see what fuss was distracting them from their conversation with God, but instead of shushing them into silence, they sniggered and smirked, making sounds which only served to encourage Lucy's cheeky behaviour.

"Lucy, you know the rules. Put your hands down, or we are leaving."

"I do prayer."

"I don't believe you."

"Why?" Lucy asked, bringing her hands back together.

"I just don't," Haniel said, slapping her hands apart again."

"But why?"

"Because of the cheeky smile on your face, that is why," Haniel answered, remembering what Ms Makewell had said about indulging her inquisitive mind.

Lucy snorted, knowing she had been found out, but enjoying the attention, she continued floundering with Haniel's hands. But when the pastor sighed and raised a single and softly judgemental brow in their direction, Michael intervened, pulling Lucy's arms into her lap.

"I suppose there's no harm in conducting prayer at the end when the little ones do not have quite so much energy," the pastor said. "Besides, I am giddied with excitement for the sermon I have for you today. So much so I am sure I will have developed an additional wrinkle by the time I am finished speaking. But believe me, it will be a wrinkle I will never forget. A wrinkle I will be happy to have. A wrinkle I will take with me into the next life."

The church fell silent, and although Lucy fidgeted, even she quietened. Though rarely was that a good sign.

"I have heard whispers amongst my congregation in the recent days. Whispers of divine and devilry. I must admit, even I have felt the presence of," the pastor paused for dramatic effect, "something otherworldly." Lucy bounced on Haniel's lap as the pastor spoke, knowing all too well that the pastor was talking about her, even if he didn't. "But was it good or evil that I felt? At first, I wasn't sure, but how can any of us be when evil so often disguises itself as good, and good too often gets confused with evil? But when word came to me of three miracles, I took these frail legs on a pilgrimage."

Haniel and Michael looked at one another to confirm they shared their suspicions, and when they saw they did, they turned their gaze to Lucy.

"Do you know what the pastor is talking about?" Michael whispered accusingly to his little sister.

"I don't know," Lucy said with an overexaggerated tone of innocence.

The pastor continued his sermon as his parishioners slid to the edges of their pews, muttering amens under their breath after each sentence. A fire burned in his heavy-set eyes, making him look ten years younger. They were alight with a reverence that Haniel and Michael had seen in human eyes many times over the millennia. Whatever the pastor had seen on his pilgrimage had reaffirmed his faith. Not that such a devout man ever needed it to be.

"My old bones ached, and my body grew tired," the pastor

continued, "yet even when I had doubts, I did not stop to feed the birds, as many of you know I like to do. It was my duty to keep going. I had to. To put your fears at ease. To find out if it was our glorious God who had cast his light upon our humble, ever-faithful community, or if it was the Devil's poison seeping through the cracks that lead to Hell." As the pastor paused to catch his breath, everyone held onto theirs until he continued. "It took me until sundown to investigate the claims of the three miracles, and I can tell you now that what I saw with these two very tired eyes was life where there was none before." The pastor paused again to let what he had said sink in, then he put his hands together and shouted as loud as his raspy voice allowed. "Life where there was none before."

The church erupted into applauding roars of wonder and speculation. Everyone brought their hands together, promising God to make the pilgrimage to the proclaimed holy sights themselves. With the parishioners distracted, Michael took this moment to retake control of his family. To put an end to the game that he had allowed his brother to play with their lives.

"That is it, Lucy. We said what would happen if you cast miracles. It is time to take you home whilst we fix your mess once again," Michael said, but as he reached out to snatch Lucy off his brother's lap, the pastor resumed his monologue with a sentence that caused Michael to pause.

"With all these miracles, I am reminded of the first," the pastor said.

Michael tensed and looked up at Haniel, who was already looking back at him with the same nervous expression. 'Why did it always have to be this story,' they thought.

With a nod of agreement to get Lucy out of the church

as quickly as possible, they both moved to gather up Lucy and her wings, but when they looked down, their little sister was gone, and in her place was Albert, coiled up and hissing with a smile stretched across his face.

"When Jesus turned water into wine at the wedding in Cana, he said to his mother, Mary, the virgin saint, 'My hour has not yet come.' But it was his hour, and on that day, he revealed his glory and his disciples believed." The pastor paused to let a murmur of amen ripple across the hall, not realising Lucy was lurking in the shadows behind him with a scowl distorting her face demonic. "There have been many interpretations of this miracle. Many reasonings for why Jesus decided to show himself then and there. When I recount this story, I think of all of you. Just as he laid his bounty on the wedding, bringing everyone together, we are here together now. His first miracle was not just a show of his connection to God but of our relationships with each other. It was the coming together of all people," the pastor said, waving his hand across the room, "the coming together of family," the pastor waved his hand again towards a couple and their newborn in the front row, "and the coming together of strangers, who we invite into our arms in hopes of one day calling friends," the pastor added, waving his hand over to Haniel, Michael, and the peculiarly missing girl the pastor was sure they had struggled in with, though he couldn't be certain, he was old after all. "Love. That is what I think the first miracle was about. We do not know how long we have together in his beautiful garden, but as long as we have love in our hearts, for one another, and for the heavenly Father, whatever time we do have will be cherished."

Another amen rippled out across the hall, but before it

could echo back to them, a clatter and crash of fortunately unlit candelabra silenced it.

"Lies, lies, lies," Lucy shouted, stomping to the front of the stage, fists clenched, face scrunched, her big, black bow waving as she furiously shook her head. "Jesus was not a nice man," Lucy exclaimed, ripping the amen's from every open mouth, striking them silent with her blasphemy.

The parishioners looked between the pastor and Lucy, wondering if he would chastise and expel her from his church, but the old man only smiled at the grumpy child. He had stood on this stage before his flock many times, he had told many stories, and, if he were lucky, he would tell many more, and so he saw no harm in sharing it with a passionate albeit impious child, just this once.

"Once upon time there was a man named Jesus." This was one of the longest sentences Lucy could say, but she had said it many times, so she was well-practised in its cadence. "Father say he a nice man. Father say he look after me. Then I get to go wedding." Lucy paused to make sure everyone was listening to her, and when she was sure they were, she added, "I was going to throw flowers." Lucy bunched the skirt of her dress in her angry fists, the same white dress she was going to wear to the wedding, the only dress she had worn since. "White flowers. Blue flowers. Pink flowers. And yellow flowers." Lucy huffed, stomping across the stage as she tossed miraculously plucked petals into the air for each colour shouted. "Then Jesus turn water into wine." Lucy sighed, and for a second, her anger settled as she kicked a pile of petals into an impossible breeze that carried them over the parishioners, who were too torn between shock and awe to question the multi-coloured miracles of a child's broken dream. "Jesus supposed to look after me,"

Lucy shouted. "Wine is not for little girls. Time to go home. That what Father say. I didn't want to go home. Jesus did it on purpose. He did. I know it. I was there. It not fair. I don't get to throw flowers, and…and…and…" Lucy held her breath until the red from her forever-fat cheeks spread over her entire face. If the parishioners hadn't been so scared of the devilish little girl, they might have laughed, but they were afraid, or at least they thought they should be, so they stayed silent and waited for Lucy to finish her story. "And now I'm not in painting," she wailed.

Lucy fell cross-legged to the floor, and if she hadn't already cried all she could for this woeful transgression committed by the human's favourite person, she would have wept sniffling and snotty tears. Instead, she sulked and pouted, and then, all tuckered out from her tantrum and tale, she collapsed backwards into the floral bed like a star into snow.

"Well, there you have it," the pastor said. "The truth of what happened at the wedding in Cana, as told by our newest little tike. Lucy, is it?" The pastor asked, but when Lucy rolled away from him, defeated and downhearted, he looked out into the crowd to get a nod of confirmation from Ms Makewell, who had already told him so much about the young morning star sprawled before him. "Apparently, Jesus wanted some time off his duties as a childminder. Something I'm sure many here can relate to. Though I am very sorry to hear you didn't make it into the painting, Lucy, as from what I hear—."

Haniel, having miraculously escaped his tight squeeze in the pews without being seen, bound down the aisle wildly waving his hands to cut the pastor short before he made Lucy aware that the artist of said painting had placed himself amongst the crowd despite, like Lucy, not having been there. A terrible truth that would undoubtedly set Lucy off for another century of tantrums and torment. Something Haniel was sure all would agree they could do without.

"Sorry," Haniel mouthed to the pastor as he gathered Lucy's limp, half-asleep body from the pile of fresh petals she had collapsed in.

The pastor gave an understanding nod, which was surprising for a man of God since stories like this often resulted in outcries of blasphemy. Though not wanting to outstay their welcome and risk the lighting of fires and gathering of pitchforks, Haniel ferried Lucy out of the church, followed closely by Michael, who, having just found out Lucy had been casting miracles, looked about as mad and self-righteous as Haniel expected him to. Another problem Haniel would have to deal with when they got home.

16

Haniel and Michael had argued all day and night about what to do with Lucy and the miracles she had been accused of performing. It felt to Haniel as if they were back in Hell, arguing in circles about the rights and wrongs of casting a child into the infernal depths. Worse, Michael couldn't seem to grasp why Haniel wasn't furious like he was, which only made his sentencing of Lucy's misdeeds more irrational every time he attempted to put his foot down. It wasn't that Haniel wasn't cross with Lucy for breaking the rules, but if he was being honest with himself, he had expected her to, so if anything, it was on him for not keeping a better eye on her.

He had hoped the arguing would stop when Lucy rose with sleep in her eyes, giddy with excitement to start her second week at kindergarten, but the moment the words, back to Hell, slipped from Michael's mouth, the screaming started.

The house they had miraculously commandeered was now in tatters from Lucy's tantrums and tripping. If she wasn't falling over her wings, crashing headfirst into walls as she ran around like, as the humans say, a bull in a china shop, she was throwing things about, determined to make herself heard over her equally stubborn brother's threats and accusations.

It was chaos. Lucy had strewn pillows across the floor, smacking them until their feathered fillings, duck not angel, exploded into the air. She had ripped books from their shelves, turned the coffee table on its side, and tossed the remote at the TV that they had never used, which now had a pixelated crack running through its centre as it flickered between channels, perfectly clipping news reporters' sentences into horrific threats of death and demise. When the living room curtains had been torn from their rungs, the shouting and screaming moved to the kitchen. Here, the floor was covered in cutlery from the drawers forced from their runners. Cupboard doors hung from their hinges, two mugs were shattered with their murky contents spilt, and the glass oven door was cracked from the repeated slamming that had taken both brothers to undo their little sister's firm grip. It was the most destruction Lucy had ever caused without having performed a miracle to do so, and with no signs of her rage abating, things would only get worse.

Lucy was out of control, though it was not her that Haniel felt the need to calm, but Michael. He, stubborn as he ever was, met every one of Lucy's transgressions with a transgression of his own. A tête-à-tête that only antagonised Lucy further. If it weren't for their night of endless arguing, Haniel might have believed his brother to be truly angry, but he now realised that, like most of Michael's emotions, his anger was but an act. He had learnt his wrath from their father, but wrath was not his sin. Not that it excused how he spoke to their little sister, who wanted nothing more than to stay on Earth where she had been born.

"Whyyy?" Lucy screamed at Michael, the only thing she

had said for the last hour.

"We do not want to take you back to Hell, Lucy," Haniel said in yet another attempt to placate her.

"Oh, we are taking her back to Hell," Michael said as if the decision was his alone to make.

"Why, why, whyyy?"

"You know why," Michael shouted back. "Now tell us where you performed the miracles so we can fix your mess once again."

"Michael," Haniel snapped.

"What?" Michael snapped back, a bulging vein pumping in his temple as he tried and failed not to let his frustration get the better of him. "We told her what would happen if she broke the rules. It is time we stopped playing this silly game. We are all going to go back to where we belong. Heaven and Hell."

"Noooooo, I not going Hell. I going school," Lucy wailed, fleeing from the kitchen at full speed, shaking the house as she tripped on her wings and took another chunk from the wall with her impervious head.

The vein in Michael's temple pulsed as Lucy picked herself up and punched her fist through the wall as if it were its fault for being there and not her wings for always finding their way beneath her feet, and then like a demon on all fours, she darted up the stairs to the safety of her bedroom, far, far away from her grumpy and mean brothers.

When her door slammed, and Haniel was sure he could hear her gathering up her school bag and whatever trinket she had planned to present for Monday morning's show-and-tell, he turned to Michael, determined to end this fight before Lucy returned.

"I think it is time you calmed down, Brother."

Michael puffed his chest out but caught himself before he roared at Haniel and proved him right. "You think it is I who should calm down?" he said, his nostrils flaring as he vented out the rage he was trying to keep in check.

"If you keep this up, Lucy will bring the house down upon us before we get her on her way to kindergarten."

"You cannot be serious? We are going home, to Heaven, and returning Lucy to Hell as we should have done when we found her here."

"No, we are not. Lucy was always going to break the rules. It is in her nature."

"Sowing chaos? Doing the exact opposite of what she is told?"

"Let us call that mischief and mayhem," Haniel said, hoping to lighten the very real damage their little sister had done in the past. "But no, Brother, I meant performing miracles. She is an angel, and an angel's duty is to spread God's light."

"Only when Father commands it."

"And what does that mean for us now that Father is gone? What does that mean for Lucy?" Michael tried to answer with something clever, but it was a thought that had been plaguing him also, so he remained silent and let Haniel continue, hoping he could provide the answers he had been seeking since the day they had said their goodbyes. "Father tried the firm hand. It is time we try something else."

"We did try, Brother."

"For a week," Haniel snapped, his words sharp and biting as he kept his voice lowered to keep his aggressive tone from travelling upstairs to a likely listening Lucy. "That is nothing compared to the millennia she spent alone in Hell." Michael, again, had no response, but Haniel was not yet done reprimanding his brother. "I thought you saw that. I thought we had an agreement on what was best for her. You need to stop talking to Lucy as if every bad thing that has happened in this world is her fault. You need to take some responsibility."

The accusation was harsh, but it had the desired effect of unstopping his brother's rage, allowing him to quickly repent for every terrible thing he had said to Lucy this morning.

"I do not think every bad thing that has happened is her fault," Michael said.

Haniel stole the tension from his brother's body with an understanding hand on his shoulder. "I know, Brother."

"Then what are we to do?" Michael asked.

"I think you are tired. I think you need to rest."

"Eternity is a long time," Michael admitted.

"You could go back to Heaven?"

"Are you trying to get rid of me?"

"You do not want to be here, and I can handle Lucy."

"And yet—."

"You are here," Haniel said, finishing for his brother. A touch of guilt weighed on Haniel's heart for not seeing how hard Michael was trying to fulfil his interpretation of their Father's final command to keep their little sister out of trouble. "And I would like for you to stay here, and I know Lucy does too, but you have to be better. Lest she destroys everything," Haniel said, gesturing to their ruined home.

"That is my worry," Michael said, gazing not at the house but out the kitchen window at the world their father had created.

In the spirit of peace and understanding, Haniel waved his hand and restored the shattered mugs of coffee and tea, refilling and warming the caffeinated morning beverages that were long overdue. "I know," Haniel said, offering the coffee to Michael. "But it won't happen. All will be fine. I promise."

17

There was something wrong with kindergarten today. Lucy wasn't quite sure what it was, but something was definitely not right. As she stood on the edge of the playground, six whole steps away from Haniel so that he didn't try to hold her hand like the big meanie he was, she watched her classmates filter into the schoolhouse. She couldn't see anything out of place, but Lucy trusted her feelings. They were never wrong. But something here definitely was.

Lucy assumed these feelings were a part of being an angel. It was like being tickled all over, but not in a way that made you laugh, but instead made you grumpy, kind of like her brothers always were. The grumpy, tickly, but not tickly feeling started in the tips of her feathers, and it shivered down her spine until all she wanted to do was frown. She had been getting these tickly, not tickly feelings a lot more since her last time on her father's garden. Earth was sick. Probably because there were too many people, and those people were building too many houses and other buildings that looked like houses but were not houses. The places where adults went to be sad. Or maybe that wasn't what was causing all the tickly, not tickly feelings. Lucy didn't know. It was hard to tell, and no one wanted to explain things to her. No one except Ms Makewell, of course. Maybe Lucy would have all the answers when she was a big angel, but that seemed like a long, long way away.

Not being big made Lucy sad sometimes, but only sometimes. Being small was fun. Being big was boring. It seemed that way, at least. But if she was big, then she might be able to know all the things her brothers knew and maybe even all the things they didn't know. Then she could make the tickly, not tickly feelings go away instead of making them worse like she sometimes accidentally did. However, doing the wrong things wouldn't stop Lucy from trying.

The garden, or Earth, as the human people called it, was her favourite place, and humans who weren't in Hell were quite nice. They smiled and waved at her. They played games and told her smart things; some even laughed at her jokes. The demons also thought Lucy was funny, but they were always too busy with demon things, just like big people were busy with big people things. Not Ms Makewell, though. She always had time to laugh and play with her, and that's why Ms Makewell was her favourite human and favourite big person. Especially now that her brothers were being loud and angry and saying not nice things to her. Things like she would go back to Hell just for trying to make the tickly, not tickly feelings go away with miracles, and how she was a bad angel, a bad angel who never listens.

Lucy was not happy with her brothers. Not one bit. So, when Haniel tried to say goodbye to her, she stomped off and didn't look back. Not even a little peek. Albert poked his head out from her hair and hissed goodbye for her because Albert was a good snake. He knew she really wanted to say goodbye but was too angry to look at her brother in his grumpy, big man's eyes.

Being angry wasn't Lucy's favourite thing. It wasn't even something she liked. Being angry was like being full from eating too much. It also made her do things she knew were wrong. But if she didn't do the wrong things like ripping down the curtains or pushing over the TV they didn't use, because TVs were boring, unlike trees, she would have miracled her brother into a chicken. She could do that. Lucy was pretty sure of it. But that would be really bad because if her brother was a chicken, a human might come and chop his head off and turn him into a sandwich. And then she would deserve to go to Hell. Which Lucy did not want and definitely did not deserve. Also, Lucy really did like her brother, all of her brothers, but that was a secret because if they knew she liked them, they might think she wasn't angry, and Lucy was most definitely angry.

Albert really was a good snake. The best friend she ever had. He understood Lucy all the time. She was glad he said goodbye to her brother for her because even though she was mad, she could feel that her brother was sad. Lucy didn't have time to say goodbye anyway. There was something wrong with kindergarten. Something deeply and terribly wrong. Lucy was the best angel of them all. The only angel who really cared about their father's garden. Whatever was wrong here, Lucy would fix it. Even if it meant she got punished just like she always did.

The feeling of wrongness inside the kindergarten schoolhouse was deeply disconcerting. Disconcerting. Lucy knew a lot of big words, but saying them wasn't as easy as thinking them. Saying long words in long sentences was even harder. It was hard to practice speaking in Hell when the demons were busy doing their secret demon things in the circles.

She sometimes spoke to Lilith, but mostly Lucy spoke to Albert. But Albert only spoke in hisses, which didn't help her learn how to speak human words. It was a good job she could speak hiss, or she would have been very, very, very bored. Which was more bored than very, very, bored, but not as bored as very, very, very, very bored, which is what she would have been if she had to spend one more millennium in Hell all alone.

The wrongness was getting bigger. The tickly, not tickly feeling was making her sadder. It really was most disconcerting. Disconcerting indeed. What was wrong here, Lucy wondered. The children were playing. The cubbies were full of bags. Not her cubby, though. That was empty because her bag was still on her back. It was a bit uncomfortable over her wings, but everyone else had bags, so she wanted one too. She was already different enough without a bag, and from what Lucy could tell, being different made it harder to make friends. So, it only made sense that having a bag would help her make lots and lots of friends.

Food went inside your bag, too. That was another thing that made Lucy different to everyone else. She didn't eat the same foods her friends ate. She didn't need to eat foods at all. She supposed that was why they cut chicken's heads off and put them between bread. That was not what Lucy ate, though. She didn't want to be too different, but she also wanted to be herself, and Lucy couldn't bear the thought of eating a clucking, clacking chicken, or any other animal for that matter, so she ate fruits and vegetables. Carrots, lettuce, tomatoes, peppers, the sweetest sweetcorns, and cutest cucumbers. That was today's lunch. They called it a salad. Her brothers did it different for her every day. They were quite nice when they weren't being big grumpy man babies.

As Lucy pushed her bag into the cubby at the very bottom, the one with her name on, the one Ms Makewell said was perfect for her because she was so small and could put it in all by herself, she realised what was off with the kindergarten and it had something to do with the way the children were playing, but it wasn't the lack of mess that surrounded them, because she had only just arrived, and Lucy knew she was the cause of most of the messes, no, what was wrong, was something else. It wasn't Lucy's fault she was clumsy. When she was big like her brothers were, she would be able to wrap her wings around her body just like they did, but right now, her wings were too big and too heavy for her to lift, and even if she could lift her wings off the ground, they were far too long to turn into a cosy coat.

What was she thinking about, Lucy thought. Why did she always get distracted? She knew the answer to that one. There was lots to think about. Lots of questions that needed to be asked. When that tickly, not tickly feeling hit her again, Lucy remembered that she had deduced something was wrong with how the other children were playing. It didn't take her long to see what was different because she was smart, a lot smarter than her brothers thought she was. Not all the children were playing, that's what was wrong. Some were tucked into the corners of the room, hiding in the shadows, trying not to be seen. But Lucy hadn't done anything naughty yet, nothing that would make them want to hide from her, not that she didn't have a funny plan planned. Ms Makewell was on to her, and she had replaced the crosses with statues of Jesus, but Jesus had eyes, and those eyes could bleed. But Lucy had definitely not done that naughty plan yet, so if the children weren't hiding from that, then what were they hiding from? Or who?

Boom. Big, heavy man footsteps slapped the floor behind her. Lucy span around. She wasn't scared. Nothing scared Lucy, except maybe going back to Hell and not having anyone to talk to. The booming footsteps belonged to a strange man. A strange man with a white beard and big fluffy eyebrows that must have made it hard for him to see. He was holding Ms Makewell's clipboard. The one with all the names on that she liked to read at the start of the day. She always kept it with her, so why did this strange, strange man have it? Very disconcerting, indeed.

"You're not Ms Makewell." Lucy crossed her arms and demanded an answer to her questionless statement.

"And you must be Lucy Morningstar, who I have heard so much about."

The man smiled at Lucy. But she did not trust his smile. It wasn't Ms Makewell's smile. "No," Lucy huffed, tightening her crossed arms further, still waiting for an answer to who he was and why Ms Makewell was not saying hello to her instead.

"It's the morning star," Sandy said, scuttling up behind Lucy, sticking her tongue out at the strange man, an impish act made only possible by her proximity to her new, but now not so new, best friend.

"The morning star," Lucy repeated, with extra emphasis on 'the,' because she knew for a fact that Ms Makewell had made a new list of names with hers written correctly six names from the top. That wasn't where Lucy's name was originally, but Lucy changed it with a little miracle because six was a funny number, because six, six, six, was scary to human people, and six was one part of six, six, six.

"I'm sorry. You're both right. It does say that right here," the man who was not Ms Makewell said, chuckling and turning the clipboard to Lucy and Sandy, but being so tall and not crouching down, probably because of his fat belly and wobbly knees, neither of them could see any of the words, even when they squinted.

Lucy stomped her foot and scowled. She would have to be more clear with this stupid, silly man. "Where Ms Makewell?"

"I'm afraid Ms Makewell is feeling a little under the weather."

Lucy gasped. That was what the tickly, not tickly feeling had been. That's what was wrong. Ms Makewell, the best big person ever, was gone. Who knows where? Somewhere that wasn't here.

"I'll be taking over her classes for a short while," the strange man continued, "but don't worry. I'm not as scary as I look, and Ms Makewell will be back before you know it. Now, I think it's time for a role call, don't you?"

The man who wasn't Ms Makewell called the register, and then the day went on not too dissimilarly to usual. They did things in the exact same order, and the man even seemed as interested in their toys and trinkets that they all presented for show-and-tell as Ms Makewell would have been. He seemed quite nice. Not as strange as Lucy first thought. He was jolly, and his belly jiggled when he laughed, but he still wasn't Ms Makewell. No matter how many times she or the other children asked, he refused to say what was wrong with her, but after a long, boring lesson on maths, Lucy eventually discovered the truth.

"Ms Makewell in hospital," Lucy said to Sandy and the other kindergarteners who had gathered at the cubbies for a super-secret meeting whilst the new teacher man was busy cleaning up Lucy's mess, some of which she had made on purpose.

"Hospital is bad," Sandy said.

"People get dead in hospitals," another kindergartener said.

"Not all peoples," another said.

"My grandma died in a hospital."

"Mine didn't," another said. "She still alive. I saw her yesterday. We had biscuits and cake."

All the kindergarteners were confused. Hospitals were either good or bad. You either died or you didn't, and death was bad, and not dying was good. Unable to decide what was what, they all looked to Lucy for an answer. She might be the smallest, and they might have known her for only one whole week, but she always had a plan, even if it was a naughty plan.

"We need to go hospital," Lucy said.

"Outside?" Sandy gasped, wondering if this suggestion was a little too naughty for her.

"Without adults?" a couple of kindergarteners said together, whispering so that the new teacher man couldn't hear them talking about breaking the main rule of them all.

"Ms Makewell needs us," Lucy said. "What if hospitals are bad?"

"But how do we get out?" Sandy asked.

The question had everyone fidgeting, but despite their nerves, they wanted to be brave for Ms Makewell, so when Lucy said, "I have a plan," all the children leaned in closer to hear what Lucy had to say.

Smiling wide and malevolently, Lucy pulled Albert from her hair and stroked his head as she prepared to enact a cunning plan, a plan that broke all three of her brothers' silly rules. No scaring humans with Albert. Stay with adults. And the last, silliest rule of them all, no true miracles.

18

Haniel returned to the house after dropping Lucy off at kindergarten and was thankful that calm had replaced the morning's chaos. Michael had set right everything broken by Lucy's rampage, though the TV had been placed by miracle in the house of someone in more need of it than they. Its purpose was only to make them appear more human if someone came to visit, but as Lucy preferred the outdoors, he decided it would be better off with someone else. In its place, there now sat a sprawling cheese plant that they had no doubt Lucy would love to sit beneath after a long day at kindergarten.

Calm or not, Haniel wanted to make clear what he expected of Michael going forward, so he joined his brother in the kitchen, where he found him perched at the counter with his head in his hands.

"I expect you to apologise to Lucy when she returns home," Haniel said.

"I will. I was out of order."

"There will be no more blame put upon her for acts of cataclysm that have been and gone. The past is in the past. We only move forward. We do not need our little sister developing a complex."

"I understand, Brother."

Haniel watched as Michael rubbed his temples, unable to hide how the strain of a life without duty was breaking down his rigid façade of certainty. He hated seeing his brother weary and defeated, and although he still thought he would find peace in Heaven, Haniel was glad that he had decided to stay.

"However, you are right about one thing. There does need to be consequences for Lucy's actions," Haniel said. "We cannot have her breaking things whenever she does not get her way."

"I agree."

"Do you know how humans punish their offspring?"

Michael mused. How do you punish an angel with the power to overrule them and the conviction to do so like their little sister could? "And we have decided we are not putting her on time out in Hell?"

"We have."

"Then I am not sure."

"I wonder what Father did when we were rebellious?" Haniel asked.

"Were we ever?"

"No. I do not think so," Haniel said. "Lucy is one of a kind."

A question parted Michael's lips like Moses had parted the seas. It was a question no angel had ever wanted to ask, but all had contemplated at least once. "Do you ever wonder if we came out like this?"

"Fully formed?"

Michael nodded. He thought he could remember learning to fly, but maybe it was only Lucy he was picturing.

"I do not think it bodes well to think that far back," Haniel said. "Sometimes I still fear to close my eyes. Without Heaven and the stars, the darkness was encompassing. Imagine what it would have been like had we not been gifted Father's light upon our backs."

"I dare not, Brother. I dare not."

The angel brothers sat in silence, both trying hard to keep their minds focused on the safety they felt when their father gave them Heaven. The eons of creation that followed were long and hard, but it wasn't dark, and they weren't alone, and best of all, it was worthy work.

"I think it is time we tell Lucy that Father has left to create another universe."

Haniel grumbled his agreement, knowing they could not put it off forever.

"Our little sister is strong," Michael said. "She can handle it."

Silent contemplation took over again as both brothers thought about how they would broach with Lucy the subject of their father's emigration to another reality, but before either could find an answer, the phone that never rang, rang.

19

The hospital's stark white lights meant for keeping the doctors awake served only to rile the runaway kindergarteners up. Haniel and Michael followed the trail of crying children, gently nudging them with their wings into the arms of the orderlies and nurses who were trying to corral them. Lucy had led her classmates on an adventure which, according to the frantic wails of the substitute teacher over the phone, had started with a snake and the blood tears of Jesus Christ and had ended with an empty classroom and a renewed sense of terror for Hell which he now believed he was destined for. It was an adventure that had unsurprisingly descended into chaos.

The other parents were on their way, but without wings to carry them, they were still far from arriving. As Haniel and Michael walked the corridors, the ill and infirmed placed their hands together in prayer as they passed. They believed that the inexplicably glowing men were here for them, to cure them of their ailments or, at the very least, carry them to Heaven in their arms. Sadly, because life and death were essential in maintaining balance, which was a fragile and fickle thing, divine intervention was not commonplace. Besides, it was not the residents of Lakeville Hospital they were here for, but their little sister.

Lucy had broken two of the three rules in getting the kindergarteners here. Rule one, no scaring people with Albert, and rule two, no running away, to always stay with an adult. From what they gathered from Sunday service, Lucy had already broken rule three: no true miracles. She had performed three miracles so far, though the reach of their influence was still yet to be discovered. Haniel and Michael felt foolish for not having noticed them sooner, but taking care of Lucy was a full-time job that neither of them had been prepared for.

Fortunately, or unfortunately, the rumblings of this fourth miracle readying itself to be performed were unmissable. It echoed through the hospital, through the unseen fabric that bound all things together. It was the beginning of something powerful, and the will that guided it charged the air like static. The hairs on the arms of those unaware stood tall, but to those not caught up in the trials and tribulations of the hospital's chaotic bustle, time appeared to slow. Then there were the good and pure in deep slumber, who were sung to by a child choir in their dreams on the footsteps of the realm that awaited them if they stayed the course.

Even to Haniel and Michael, the warm hum of Lucy's looming miracle was, well, to put it simply, miraculous. There was no other word for it. It gave them a sense of purpose that was hard to ignore, and it had them want to perform miracles of their own, but the powers of creation were not a toy, and when rewoven, the great tapestry of life had to be put back together just right. If one thread were pulled too tightly or another left too loose, creation could unravel.

Haniel and Michael had been arguing about what to do with Lucy all morning, but this needed no discussion. They had seen their little sister cause floods, famine, pests, and pestilence, and they had no desire to see what other evil her innocence might wreak upon their father's creation.

Ignoring the no-running signs, as the runaway kindergarteners were, Haniel and Michael meandered through the hospital's maze of corridors and stairwells towards the beating heart of power that was about to alter something with no concern for the consequences. The rumblings of change grew deeper. A shimmering mirage of what could be flickered across reality. They didn't have long. The threads hadn't yet been pulled. The ends had been found, but the knots were yet to be untied. They barrelled out of the fourth-floor stairwell and slammed together through a double door into yet another twist of corridors. Left and right they turned until the maze hit a dead end.

A gathering of wet-eyed kindergarteners whose spirit for adventure had been dashed by despondence sat beneath a single window that spanned from floor to ceiling. All but Lucy's best friend Sandy peered into the car park, admiring the bird's eye view of the single oak tree planted at its centre, which added a splash of colour to the otherwise bleak, grey campus. Lucy was not amongst them, but they only had to follow Sandy's gaze of sorrow and wonder to know where she was.

Michael charged ahead. "She's here," Michael shouted to Haniel, a contraction slipping into his forever formal speech as he launched into the last open door on the left.

Lucy was straddled on Ms Makewell's weary body with her hands pressed together in prayer, one eye shut, the other wide open. Unlike the other children, Lucy was not yet crying, but judging by the wobble in her bottom lip, she was not far from doing so. The only thing keeping her from crying now was knowing that if she wanted, she could perform one not-so-simple miracle and make everything all better, or so she thought because before Lucy could do the one thing she had been asked not to, Michael pushed on the doorway with his wings, leapt forward, and snatched her up.

"She's lying, she's lying," Lucy screamed. "She dying. I make better. Stop. Let me make better. Don't take me away. I do miracle."

Lucy writhed in Michael's arms, desperate to be free. Her screams tore at her throat, and her words broke into fractured syllables as she began to sob. She was still furious at Michael for his threats of banishment, and when she wasn't reaching back for Ms Makewell, she punched and kicked him, letting him know her hate. Michael took his beating, knowing he deserved every bit of her anger, and he was happy to do so, knowing it might lessen her pain, as even for an angel, death was no easy thing to accept. Just because you knew where a soul was destined for after its time on Earth, it did nothing to make the transition any easier for those it left behind. Michael supposed it was even harder for Lucy, who had no desire to go back to Heaven and constantly feared she might be sent back to Hell. It was a gut-wrenching realisation that filled Michael with guilt. His little sister may have broken the rules, but he wasn't going to shout at her, not now, not ever again, not now that he was beginning to understand the depths of her loneliness for which he was partly responsible.

As Michael gathered Lucy's limp wings, which still twinkled with light from the miracle she was about to perform, he wrapped his own around her like a blanket as she bawled and screamed. She hated him, she loved him, and as he carried her out of the room, Michael held his little sister tight as he knew she needed to be.

20

Now that the other parents were arriving to take their runaway children home and likely straight to bed after a long and tiring unapproved adventure, Haniel pulled up a chair and sat beside Ms Makewell. Her eyes were dark, and, like the children, she looked as if she could do with some rest, but as much as Ms Makewell loved every second with her kindergarteners, it was clear she wanted some adult company before she closed her eyes for the evening.

Haniel already knew what was wrong with her, as it was he who had suggested she see a doctor instead of a priest. However, it always saddened him how fast humans deteriorated when death decided it was time to eat away at their mortal bodies.

"Cancer," Ms Makewell said, her tight skin sweating as she shivered beneath her blankets. "Stomach," she added as she leaned over for the glass of water on the side table, allowing Haniel to help it into her hand when she couldn't reach it. As she took a moment to take a soothing sip of water, she thought back to the hellish visions she had witnessed in the weeks leading up to the rickety bed she now lay in. The demonic, hellish expressions of a child. The miraculous wonders at the lake. The violent spinning of the world as Hell tried to drag her below. "It explains so much," she said. "The doctors say it has been spreading for years without me knowing. They're surprised it got this far without symptoms presenting themselves. Doesn't matter now, I suppose. The doctors say I don't have long. Days, weeks, definitely not months."

Haniel could have given her all the answers the doctors couldn't. How long the cancer had gone undetected, the exact number of days she had left, and even where she was heading after. Heaven, obviously. Ms Makewell was too good for Hell. But answers were not what she was after now. Her gaze was stoic, like that of an angel. She had accepted her fate. Not an easy thing to do, though a lot easier for those with faith.

"I only wish I had a little more time with the children," Ms Makewell continued. "A little more time with Lucy. How she needs us."

They both looked out into the corridor, where Michael held Lucy in his arms, who was still crying but at least no longer screaming. Haniel could see his little sister's blonde head peeking out from the blanket of Michael's wings she was snuggled inside of, but to Ms Makewell, to whom their wings were invisible, she saw Lucy's whole body trembling in her brother's massive arms as she struggled to make peace with her favourite teacher's untimely and impending departure.

Ms Makewell exhaled a weary breath, and then, after a slow, pained inhale, she let out another, which crackled at the back of her throat as it threatened to be her last. "Lucy means well," she said. "I'm just glad none of the children got hurt on the way here. It's quite the journey for the little ones to have made on their own."

"Lucy always means well, but that is so often the problem," Haniel said. "She never listens because she never considers the consequences. I do not want Michael to be right. I do not want to send her away."

"Rules are ever so hard for children to follow, especially when they don't understand them."

Haniel wondered what Ms Makewell knew or thought she knew. It wasn't clear what Ms Makewell had felt of the miracle that was about to be performed for her or what she believed of the frantic ramblings of a four-eon-year-old child angel, but faith, as it always did, kept her from asking for the truth. Haniel wasn't sure if he wanted her to ask or not. He had a lot on his chest that he feared, if he didn't speak, would weigh him down forever. But was it right to drag a mortal into the worries of an eternal being, especially one who had a hand in their creation?

"I am not sure I could explain the rules. At least not in a way she would understand," Haniel said, opening up despite knowing that, without knowing everything, the teacher's advice might be vague at best. "I do not understand the rules myself. It is just what has to be. It is how things have always been. Reality, life, all that we see and feel, it is fragile. A butterfly's wings could unravel it. Lucy is a storm. Yet she is forever determined to weave things to her whims."

Haniel paused. He knew he must sound mad to a human who, through design or happenstance, could not ask the big questions. Ms Makewell's eyes rattled as she tried to work through the celestial deluge of thoughts. It wasn't clear if she would ever come up with something worth saying or if her mind was even capable of wrapping itself around the inner workings of reality, but the quiet, backed by Lucy's sniffling in the corridor, caused Haniel to fumble through another cluster of half repressed thoughts, saving Ms Makewell from having to consider the vastness of what she did not know.

"Our father made mistakes with Lucy. Too many of them. I know that now—. I knew it before," Haniel corrected, ashamed of his complicity in his little sister's banishment to Hell, "but I never said anything. But none of that matters now. Father is gone, and all is left to us. However, that is what scares me. Father was always there to put things right in a way that I am not sure we are capable of."

This Ms Makewell understood. She may not have been a parent, but as a teacher, she often worried she would not live up to the ideal version of herself. That somewhere along the way she would make a mistake she could not correct, a mistake that someone else might not have made had they been allowed to stand where she stood.

"It's normal to feel like an imposter. We can never know for sure if we are up to the task that our children require of us. Not even at the end." Ms Makewell paused to take another ragged breath and another sip of water to soothe the burn that breath caused. "I judged you too harshly to begin with."

"Not harsh enough."

"Maybe so." Ms Makewell laughed, but when that began to hurt too, she forced herself to stop and simply smiled weakly back at him. "You are doing your best. I can see that now."

"And yet, something always goes wrong."

"That is life. His trials make us strong," Ms Makewell said, nodding to a cross which hung above her head, which, in Lucy's agony, had been left right-side up. "Faith in his plan is what prepares us for the end."

Haniel had heard this speech countless times, but he would never tell Ms Makewell the truth. That there was no grand plan. There was no fate. Life was not preordained but a series of random events. That his father, in all his glory, had created her world with nothing more than hopes and dreams. It sounded nice on paper, but hopes and dreams could often appear inadequate when you believed there was something more.

Knowing the truth of Heaven and Hell, of angels and devils, or devil, singular, one which was not a devil at all but a mischievous handful of a child, faith had always seemed too human. Unlike Lucy, who always tried to make things better, Haniel looked upon Earth and the stars that lit it in the same way a human might gaze upon a fishbowl. From a distance, caring but unattached. In hindsight, it seemed like a cold way to live.

Haniel had never needed faith before, but now that his father was no longer here to bestow commands upon him, faith could be exactly what he needed to help Lucy become the angel she wanted to be. Faith that all would be right in spite of all that may go wrong, faith in that whatever must be endured whilst raising Lucy would be worth it, and faith in himself that no matter how hard things got, he would do right by her.

Haniel allowed faith to overwhelm him, becoming porous so that it could seep into every fibre of his being. It was warmer than he expected. It tingled like laughter, daring his stoic smile to curl at the edges into something childish and free; it filled him to the brim with possibility, glazing his eyes with tears as it tried to spill out of him. Even his feathers ruffled, illuminating his back as the desire to do good consumed him.

Haniel wondered if faith felt this good for humans because now that he had it, he couldn't imagine letting it go.

"You are right," Haniel said, his gentle tone softened further by the contentedness faith had brought him. "There is only forwards. What is, must be, and will always be."

Ms Makewell snorted as her sleeping tongue involuntarily flicked to the roof of her mouth. How long had he been sat contemplating her words of wisdom, Haniel wondered. Had Ms Makewell been watching him think the entire time, letting him mull over her words like one of her kindergarteners, or had she closed her eyes and allowed herself to drift off, knowing that he needed more than a moment to come to terms with what it meant to have faith? However it was Ms Makewell came to be asleep, it was rest she needed and rest she deserved, and so Haniel returned to his siblings waiting for him in the hall, though not before he placed his hands together in prayer and filled her room with flowers whose meadow scent stirred dreams of peace and infinity in the sleeping saint who had already done so much right by him and his family.

21

Michael's chest was drenched with tears, so much so that you could smell the salt over the antiseptic scent that hung thick in the air, and with Lucy still crying into him, the damp patch only continued to grow. Fortunately, the chaos his little sister had caused was over, and the hospital corridor was now empty, except for the lone nurse doing the last of her evening rounds. She looked twice as tired as she would have been had the kindergarteners not forced her to give chase, yet still, the nurse found the energy to flash a comforting smile to Michael as he attempted to soothe the instigator of her trying day.

"Come, Brother, let us leave," Haniel said as he emerged from Ms Makewell's room. "We have much to discuss."

Lucy stirred in Michael's arms, and although it wasn't he who had suggested they go home, it was still him who she was most mad at. Having broken out of both her brother's holds now, Lucy was getting good at it. It was the landing, however, that she struggled with. As she pushed off her brother's chest, her wings snagged on his arms, causing her to roll through the air like a falling trapeze artist.

The sole nurse stopped what she was doing and winced

as Lucy hit the floor with a thud. Although she couldn't see her wings, they flopped atop her crooked and ruffled, which might have made the sight amusing if it weren't for the rage palpitating between her clenched fists that signalled to the nurse that her day of screaming children was not yet over. Mouthing a sympathetic and unneeded apology to Haniel and Michael, she ducked stealthily into Ms Makewell's room, shutting the door quietly behind her, shielding herself and her sleeping ward from the incoming and wholly inevitable shouting match.

"We not go," Lucy roared, huffing as she crawled out from beneath her wings. "I make Ms Makewell better."

With difficulty, Lucy pushed herself up from the floor, gathered her wings, and threw them behind her. Her eyes were raw, and although she had stopped crying, it was only because she had tensed her face into such a ferocious scowl that it had put a stopper on her sorrow.

Remembering his promise not to shout at Lucy and wanting to prove to Haniel and his little sister he was willing to change, Michael took the lead and crouched in front of Lucy in the same way Ms Makewell did when she spoke to the kindergarteners. He didn't understand why Ms Makewell did this because until now, he had never thought it important enough to ask, but she always did it when talking with the children, especially when it was one-on-one like this, so that was what he did, too.

"I know you are very sad, Lucy, but you know the rules. No true miracles."

Michael hated that he still had to say no to his little sister, but it didn't mean the rules suddenly changed because he wasn't shouting. Lucy, however, didn't see the difference. Shouting or not, he was still the mean brother telling her no.

"No rules," Lucy said, her wings twitching as she pulled herself up as straight as possible. "Stupid rules. I hate rules."

"Your brother is right," Haniel said, joining Michael closer to the floor, hoping he might offer some aid. "It is too dangerous."

"No. You both wrong. I make Ms Makewell better."

Haniel and Michael looked at one another, unsure how best to handle the situation. To each other, their expressions were full of mourning and empathy, both of which, to Lucy, were signs she had said enough to convince them she was big enough to perform a miracle for Ms Makewell.

"You see. I can do it," Lucy said, unclenching her fists, daring to let go of her anger as she turned to the closed door barring her from her favourite human.

Before Lucy could open the door with a little miracle because she was not nearly tall enough to reach the handle, Michael placed his hand on her shoulder and pulled her back towards them.

"Let Ms Makewell sleep, Lucy," Michael said.

"No. I going to make her better."

"She needs her rest."

Lucy knew this was true. Everything needed to sleep. When you slept, you dreamt, and most of the time, dreams were nice. Lucy wondered if Ms Makewell dreamt of flying like she did. One flap and you were above the clouds. Another flap and you were spinning and looping, looking down on everything green and blue. Lucy shook the thought away. Whatever it was Ms Makewell was dreaming of, it could wait. For now, the only thing that mattered was making her better so that they could walk hand-in-hand back to kindergarten to do math, English, story time, and, if they were lucky, more adventures at the lake. They could check on the miracle fish Lucy had created, maybe even see if the buried apple in the field had started growing too, because despite what her brothers thought, Lucy could do miracles now. Or maybe her brothers did know but just didn't care?

Lucy gasped and clenched her fists as rage returned with a terrible thought. "You want Ms Makewell to die."

"No one wants that, Lucy."

"Yes, you do. You both do." Lucy pointed a provoking finger at her brothers. "You want her to die."

"Death is a part of life. It is unavoidable."

Lucy snarled, affronted by the statement. It all made sense now why they didn't want her performing miracles. She was just a silly girl. A silly little girl who should have known better.

"You don't care about Ms Makewell."

"We do care, Lucy," Haniel said, stepping in for Michael, who was at a loss for words as he stared blankly at their little sister, not knowing what to do as her mood spiralled out of his control.

"No, you don't," Lucy said matter-of-factly, though with a tremble in her voice that showed she was only keeping it together so that she could tell her brothers exactly what she thought. "You don't care about Ms Makewell. You don't care about Earth, either. Never have. Never, never, ever. "And..." Lucy's lip quivered as heartbreak tempered her rage, but before she could break out into tears, she scrunched her face up and screamed. "You don't care about me."

"We do care, Lucy," Michael said, but overwhelmed by regret for allowing his little sister to think such terrible things, he trailed off and looked to his brother for help.

Haniel, as penitent as Michael was, stared blankly at Lucy with his mouth wide open, hoping the words to make everything alright would come to him before he closed it again. But no words came, at least not before Lucy took their stunned silence as a sign that she was right.

"You don't care about me because I'm a stupid, silly mistake," Lucy wailed.

It was probably the longest sentence their little sister had ever said, and if it wasn't so horrible to hear, Haniel and Michael might have praised her for it. Instead, they wanted to cry.

"I am wrong. Wrong things go to Hell. But I'm not going," Lucy added.

The stopper that had kept Lucy from crying had been opened. Tears streamed down her cheeks. Her eyes glowed red, bright and burning with anguish, appearing not too dissimilar to depictions of the Devil in tapestries generations old. Her whole body shook, tremors rolling out from her fists. Even her wings, which usually were too heavy to manage, twitched as if trying to open in a mighty display of defiance. Another four-eon-year-old feat that would have warranted wonder and praise had the ache of regret not kept Haniel and Michael silent.

Both brothers wanted forgiveness, but mostly, they wanted to see Lucy's cheeky and always mischievous smile again. Not knowing who should be the one to take her into their arms, they both reached out for her, but assuming they were trying to drag her back to Hell, Lucy slapped their hands away and bolted for the window at the end of the corridor.

"You can't make me go back," Lucy screamed, her feathers ruffling as she forced her trailing wings to part. "I don't want to be alone."

The windowed wall was the last stop in the maze of corridors, and there were no more stairwells left for her to climb higher. There was nowhere for Lucy to run. At least, that was what Haniel and Michael thought before she threw herself out the window, leaving a comical impression of her body in the glass for her brothers to gawk at before it cracked and crumbled from its frame.

Haniel and Michael leapt to their feet, jostling with one another as they gave chase, feeling foolish for not spotting the signs of her plan sooner. Michael charged ahead and readied his wings for flight, but before he could leap after their little sister, Haniel held him back.

"She is flying," Haniel exclaimed. "Brother, Lucy is flying. Our little sister is flying."

Lucy initially fell, but with an unbelievable show of strength, her heavenly-white wings parted, and as she slapped them against the air in unison, she pushed herself high above the hospital car park. It was not the most graceful of flights, with her arms flailing and her feet kicking the air behind her, but it was her first. Each drop and subsequent bounce higher had Haniel and Michael gasping with joy, and if it weren't for the sounds of her sobs that could be heard over the boom of her wings, they might have forgotten that Lucy was fleeing from them and not flying for fun.

When Haniel and Michael shared the same thought that their little sister might fly too far away for them to catch her, one of her wings hit the air light, and the other didn't come down hard enough to compensate for the difference. The encumbrance of her oversized wings quickly became too much for Lucy's tired and tiny body, and the moment she began to spiral, she dropped like a rock.

"Brother, the tree," Michael said, gesturing toward the solitary oak at the centre of the car park.

"Wait. She might steady herself."

"I can still catch her."

"No, Michael," Haniel said, holding his brother's arm, forcing him to stay where he stood. "How can she learn if we never let her try?"

Michael knew Haniel wasn't only talking about flying. That his brief time sat with Ms Makewell had caused him to rethink his stance on their little sister performing miracles. Though it concerned him deeply, and the end of the world was not to be taken lightly, especially with three unaccounted for and as of yet undeterminably dangerous miracles tampering with existence, the sight of his little sister soaring, though now falling through the air, did have him wonder what else she might be capable of if they were only to let her try. Regardless, his desire to catch Lucy was not for her benefit.

"I really think I should catch her."

"Lucy will be fine, Brother," Haniel said, waving away Michael's concern. "You fret far too much."

"Of course Lucy will be fine, but what of the tree?"

"Oh..."

Haniel realised his mistake, but like everything he had done wrong leading to this moment, he realised it too late.

The angel brothers grimaced as their little sister disappeared into the rich, green canopy, but fortunately for the tree, it was old and strong, and as Lucy tumbled through its branches, the great monolith did not flinch as it knocked the falling angel to the ground.

Not bothering to remove the twigs and leaves from her hair, Lucy fled from the hospital, bawling her eyes out, but fortunately leaving her usual trail of tripped-over destruction for her brothers to follow.

Not realising they were being watched by the nurse who

had poked her head out of Ms Makewell's room to see what all the smashing and crashing was all about, Haniel and Michael put a foot each over the ledge. She couldn't be sure, but it looked as if the two giant men were about to jump, but as she reached out to stop them, she blinked, and they were gone, and the broken window pieced together as if it had never been broken at all.

22

Thanks to the trail of destruction, it didn't take long to find Lucy. At first, the angel brothers assumed she was running back to Little Woods Kindergarten, the place she first met Ms Makewell, but when they were led through the suburbs, past upturned bins, scattered mail, and broken topiaries, to a gate that opened onto a winding path between two houses, they realised they were heading back to the park where they had first made the decision to stay.

An experienced parent would know that when their child ran away to places known, it was because they wanted to be found, but when Haniel and Michael saw Lucy hiding between the two swings, huddled inside a tent made from her wings, they almost collapsed with relief, which in truth was how any parent would react, experienced or otherwise.

"Lucy," Haniel said, soft and unassuming. "Do you want to come out from behind your wings?"

"No," Lucy said with a sniffle.

"That is okay. I am sure it is very cosy in there," Haniel said. "Michael and I will sit out here, though, if that is alright with you?"

Lucy didn't reply, but by the slight ruffle in her feathers, they guessed she either shrugged or nodded. Whichever it was, they took it as a good sign, a better one than her running away again.

As they sat together in the park, enjoying the warmth of being with family, the trees rustled, and the empty swings creaked as the wind moved gently through leaves and chains alike. It was calm. It was not quite quiet but predictable and soothing, enough so that the muffled sounds of Lucy's crying eventually ended.

"You know, Lucy. What you said earlier is very, very wrong," Haniel said.

Lucy sniffled again, curious but silent.

"You are not a mistake."

"Yes, I am."

"Why would you say such a terrible thing."

"Because I am accident. Accident is a mistake."

Lucy's voice wobbled as if each word were getting harder and harder to say. She was past crying, though, and past being angry. She was far too tired for any of that. It was hard for her to remember what anger felt like now that it had passed. Only its ache remained like a shadow clinging to the underside of her skin.

"An accident is not the same thing as a mistake, Lucy," Michael said.

"Yes, it is. It is me," Lucy grumbled back. "Father made the garden, and oops, there is me. Mistake."

There it was again, another long sentence that would have been worthy of a pat on the back and a cheer of approval, but just as before, Lucy's words hurt too much to hear for either Michael or Haniel to want to bring attention to them.

"A mistake is wrong, but an accident can sometimes be happy. It can be the most amazing thing you have ever known, and when you see it, you wonder why you did not make it freely." Lucy didn't argue that. She was amazing. She knew it, even if she was too sad to figure out why. "Do you know how I know for certain you are not a mistake?"

Lucy's wings wobbled as she nodded, wondering what made Michael so certain, especially after he shouted at her like a big meanie this morning. She wasn't ready to open her wings to the world yet, but she wanted to see her brother's face if he was going to say something nice about her, so she made a small opening between two feathers and peeped out.

Michael pretended not to see Lucy opening herself up to him, afraid that if she noticed that he had spotted her, she might hide away again. With her arms wrapped around her knees, Lucy looked smaller than ever, which was no easy feat for someone so tiny. He wanted her to know he wasn't as serious and unforgiving as their father. That he wasn't Mean Michael, a nickname he worried he would end up with if he didn't step away from his self-righteous path. Michael wanted to be seen as someone fun who his little sister could laugh and play with. Someone like Haniel. And so, Michael decided to try something new. He smiled.

Lucy looked at him like something was wrong and recoiled deeper into herself. Michael hated that. He did not hate his smile, though. It felt strange on his face, but only because it was working hard to break through the mask of stoicism and certainty he had been wearing since before he could remember. Why had no one told him smiling could make you feel so free? In all of eternity, how had it taken him so long to feel one pressing upon his cheeks? It ached, but it was a nice ache that made you want to endure more, and endure it he would so that his little sister grew to know it.

"Father was always far too serious, don't you think?"

Michael said, scrunching his face, imitating the grumpy expression their father wore whilst he worked, which, now that Michael thought about it, was far too often for someone with children.

Lucy giggled, a sound often reserved for anyone but him.

Her laugh had always been beautiful, but there was something special about being the one to cause it.

"When Father first saw you, he glowed more radiantly than any of us had ever witnessed," Michael said. "He created darkness, then worlds and stars to fill it; he created Heaven, Hell, and a garden in between, but nothing made him smile quite as much as he did when he accidentally made you."

Lucy opened her wings wider, no longer pretending not to be watching and listening.

"Father might have made a few mistakes, but you were not one of them, Lucy," Michael said. Then, hoping to coax her fully from her wings, he said, "And if you look around, you might be able to see why."

Lucy took the bait and allowed her wings to flop to the floor so that she could better look around the park.

"Where I look?" Lucy asked, looking left and right but seeing nothing that could make her believe she was nothing but a silly mistake.

"Do you not see?"

Lucy sniffled and shook her head. "I don't see."

"Look up," Michael said, and Lucy did just that. "Do you see the sky? Do you see what colour it is?"

"Blue."

"Exactly the same colour as someone special's eyes."

Lucy gasped. "My eyes."

"And what about the sun? What colour is that?"

"Yellow."

"Exactly like your hair."

Lucy studied her hair, and when she deduced that her brother was right and that it was the exact same shade of yellow, she gasped again.

"And do you see your brother and I?" Michael said. "We look different, do we not?"

"You're boys."

"We are. We were made in his image, but Father loved you so much that he made Eve, who looked just like you," Michael said, playfully poking Lucy on the nose, causing that wonderful, loving giggle again. "And why would Father do that if he thought you were a mistake?"

Lucy shrugged. Michael knew she knew the answer, but having lived for eons believing the opposite, she didn't dare say it on the chance that she was wrong.

"It is because you are not a mistake."

"I'm not?"

"Absolutely not. You're perfect, isn't that right, Haniel."

Haniel put his arm around his brother, showing his little sister that he and Michael were a unit and that they loved her with all their hearts. "Michael is right, Lucy. Not only could you never have been a mistake, but you are also the best angel little sister any brother could ask for."

Lucy thought about this, and after a short six seconds of deliberation, she wiped the tears from her eyes and smiled. Glad to see the familiar cheeky grin that was both feared and loved, Haniel and Michael opened their arms wide for their little sister as she unhooked her knees from her tight grasp and crawled into their arms.

This was the first group hug they had shared since reuniting on Earth. Now that they were in each other's arms, it seemed silly that they hadn't done this sooner. Wasn't this a normal family experience? Thinking back, Haniel and Michael couldn't recall ever sharing a hug, just the three of them, and so not wanting to let go and not knowing when was appropriate to do so, they held each other for six whole minutes until Lucy decided it was time to release them.

"Did you see me fly?" Lucy asked, her eyes dry but burnt red, weary and exhausted.

"We did," both the angel brothers said together, beaming at Lucy as they recalled her first flight.

"I didn't fall," Lucy said, referring not to her crash landing but the brief moment she rose through the air. "I did six whole flaps."

"That is impressive," Michael said.

"Soon, you will be able to fly all the way to Heaven and back," Haniel added.

"Only on some days, though," Lucy said, yawning as the day of great sadness finally took its toll on her.

"Only on some days," Michael said, agreeing with Lucy, for which Haniel nodded in approval, grateful his brother had finally come around to the idea of them staying. "But for now, I think it is time to get you home and tucked into bed. You have had a long day."

"House home?" Lucy asked hopefully.

"Yes, Lucy, house home."

Happy, Lucy pulled herself to her feet using Michael's white shawl of feathers for leverage. "Fly?" she asked, holding her arms up, waiting to be lifted.

"How else do you think we were going to get there?" Michael said, scooping up his little sister, as excited as she was for a short, shared flight together into the sky.

23

When they returned to the house, Lucy had another cry about Ms Makewell being ill, but with no energy left to cause a stir, she cuddled up with Albert on the sofa, wetting his scales until Michael gathered them both up in his arms and tucked them, together, into bed.

"Starting tomorrow, we are going to check on all of your miracles and put right what is wrong," Michael said, putting a tissue to Lucy's blocked nose. "Blow."

Lucy scrunched her eyes tight shut and blew into the tissue, smiling sleepily as she cleared her head. "Nothing's wrong. I do good miracles now."

"Do you not feel it?"

"Feel what?" Lucy asked, wiggling her button nose, now free of the day's sadness that had blocked it.

"The wrongness?" Michael said, having taken a moment during their flight home to listen to the world below, feeling out any changes made by Lucy's miraculous hands.

"Something always feels wrong," Lucy said.

Michael nodded, softening his grim expression as he agreed with his little sister.

Since their father created humanity, Earth had always

been in a state of turbulence. Michael supposed that was a part of their charm, though he had not spent enough time here to say for sure. Whatever it was about humanity that had their father insistent on creating them, it was impossible not to notice the lack of harmony between species that had taken root in the thousands of years since their conception. Though Michael felt Lucy was not talking about the dire present state of things but resonating with a deeper connection to Earth that no matter how hard they might try, Michael, Haniel, and their brothers in Heaven could never understand.

"You were created here. This is your home. And I think you know you made a couple of mistakes, however miraculous they may be," Michael said, adding a sense of wonder to his voice so as not to sound like he was one bad word away from shouting.

Lucy shrugged and then nodded, knowing deep down something was wrong but not yet understanding what that was. "I don't mean to do bad miracles."

"I know. You only want to do the best miracles."

"Only good ones," Lucy agreed.

"Then, whilst you, me, and Haniel are out checking up on what went wrong, we will teach you how to perform miracles properly."

Lucy's eyes sparkled, and she lifted her head, hoping they could leave and learn right away. However, being far too sleepy to maintain that energy, her eyelids flickered, and her head sank deeper into her pillow.

"Then we can fix Ms Makewell?"

"I am not sure, Lucy. It might be for the best we do not tamper with what is done."

"Why?" Lucy asked, sadness returning with a croak to her

voice as if it had been waiting in the back of her throat for Michael to say something she didn't like.

"It is not how we do things," Michael said.

"But why?"

Michael saw where this was going. A week ago, he would have immediately shut Lucy's incessant questioning down, but that would inevitably backfire, and she would either start screaming or, worse, ask 'why' for a millennium without pause. Michael didn't like the sound of either of those outcomes. Besides, he wanted to do better, so he thought of Ms Makewell lying in her hospital bed, ruminating on all the good years she had spent educating and enriching young minds. She would remind him that if he answered Lucy's questions, he might learn something himself, and so that was what he did.

"It is not an angel's place to alter the course of life and death."

"Why?"

"We only ever do as Father commands."

"Why?"

"It is how things have always been."

"But why?" Lucy asked, her inquisitive mind now the only thing keeping her awake.

Michael thought on this for a second. He had always assumed that Lucy's questions were easily answered, which was partly why he never bothered, but now that he was forcing himself to do so, Michael found they were far more testing than he presumed them to be.

"Earth, Father's garden, it is a fragile thing," Michael said slowly, making sure every word he spoke was exactly the right one. "And nothing in this garden is more fragile than the balance between life and death. Your big brothers all decided it would be best not to tamper with this world without Father's permission," Michael finished, not feeling as satisfied with his answer as he had hoped because as hard as he tried, he could not recall their father saying this was what he wanted of them.

Lucy slapped her lips together, tasting the mellow bedtime air which, unlike the morning brace of dew and waking heat, had the peculiar quality of making one's eyes heavy. It also had a calming effect on excitable children that parents never took for granted once they noticed it taking hold of their offspring. Michael recalled helping his father create the many hidden qualities of the breathable air. He hadn't seen the point of them at the time, but now, as he watched his little sister doze off, he understood why so much care had gone into it.

"Then why Father go? Why he leave power in wings?" Lucy said, blinking her eyes awake, fighting the irresistible urge to sleep.

Michael opened his mouth to answer, but as he scrambled for a response, he realised he did not have one. Was this the learning experience that Ms Makewell spoke about, he wondered? It was a good question. Why would Father leave them alone in this reality and not take his power with him if they were not meant to use it? What if Lucy had been right all along? What if they had never needed his permission to perform miracles? What if their father wanted them to make their own decisions?

Michael's questions kept growing, and as their weight squashed the last of his arrogance, he realised a truth that should have occurred to him sooner.

"Lucy, did Father let you out of Hell?"

"He said goodbye and opened gates."

"He did?"

Lucy yawned and looked up at Michael through squinted eyes, now too heavy with sleep to force open. "He said you look after me."

Michael wondered why his father hadn't told him and Haniel that he had gone to see Lucy and why he hadn't let them know he was letting her loose of the play gates that kept her in Hell. He wondered what else his little sister knew that he had not been informed of, but when he turned his attention back to her, she was fast asleep with Albert, yellow-skinned and sleepy too, coiling up into a halo above her head.

"I wonder what Father would say if he could see you now," Haniel said softly from the open bedroom door, watching as Michael tucked Lucy in.

Satisfied his little sister was comfortable, Michael trod lightly over to his brother. "He would say that I have been stubborn. Brash."

"You have been like Father."

"Which is no excuse," Michael said.

"Have you been humbled, Brother?"

"I hear the humans have that effect."

"Maybe that was why he created them."

"We shall never know," Michael said.

There was a quiet pause as the angel brothers watched over Lucy together. In the silence, Michael wondered how his little sister had slept in Hell. Did she curl up in the blood-soaked dirt with nothing and no one to hold her tight, or did she keep herself awake, driven crazy like the tormented lost souls that once wandered there? He was afraid to find out.

"I know you think I should return to Heaven," Michael said, breaking the silence with hushed tones so as not to wake their sleeping angel, "but I cannot go back, and not for duty or obligation, but for our little sister, for Lucy. I want to be involved. I want to be better. I want her to have a home she loves, with a real bed and a real family. I want to be a part of that family. I want to stay."

Haniel smiled as if this was his hope all along. "Then we stay, together."

"Thank you for your patience, Haniel. Will you pray with me?"

"Of course, Brother."

The two angel brothers knelt at the foot of Lucy's bed, placed their hands together, and bowed their heads.

"I do not know if you are listening, Father. I do not know how long it has been for you since you left us. The humans think you have a plan, but I am glad you do not. If you did, Lucy might not ever have come to be."

Haniel nodded along, agreeing silently with his brother's words.

"In Heaven, we did as you commanded, set our own rules based on what we thought you wanted, but we never stopped to ask why."

Both smirked at the word, why, hearing their inquisitive little sister's voice in their own.

"Why you commanded what you did," Michael continued. "Why you asked so much of us." Michael paused again, thinking back on his long, long life. "Maybe that was our test. To realise you wanted us to make our own decisions. If it was, then we failed time and time again, but Lucy helped us see—. Helped me see," Michael corrected, "that it is time we, and Lucy, forge our own path. And I know she is still young, that there are risks, but you asked us to keep her out of trouble, and that is what we shall do, but if anyone knows what is right for Earth, your beautiful garden, it is our morning star."

Michael paused again to reflect on all he had said, hoping his father could hear his words. Satisfied with his message, he finished with one final sentiment.

"We love you, Father, all three of us, and all our brothers in Heaven. You will be missed for eternity, however long that may be. I hope we do you proud, and I pray that happiness follows you into all of your realities. Thank you for everything, Father. Thank you for Lucy. Amen."

"Amen," Haniel repeated.

21

Though Lucy was vibrating with excitement to be taught how to perform miracles, she had no desire to undo the ones she had already brought into this world. She told Haniel and Michael that there was no way her miracles could be bad because if you looked around, everything looked normal. Everything except for the forest that had seemingly popped up overnight in the field behind her kindergarten, which Lucy shamelessly attempted to veer her brother's attention away from by pointing to clouds shaped suspiciously like snakes every time they looked toward it. It was an obvious miracle, but they agreed to deal with it the next day because, despite Lucy's insistence, everything in Lakeville wasn't as normal as it seemed.

There was a stench of death in the air, and after a circuitous route from one body of water to the next, the angels eventually came to its source. A small lake that might have been called a pond if it were six feet shallower and six feet shorter in all six of its directions worth noting. Lucy hadn't wanted to believe her miracles were wrong, but as they drew closer to the lake, even she couldn't ignore the darkness she had wrought upon this once vibrant grove.

Flies buzzed close to the ground; their numbers so great they appeared as an ominous black cloud flitting from fish to fish. The water's edge had an unnatural red froth, and the lake's surface had a silver sheen made from fish scales lost to rot. The stench of ammonia was sharp and discomforting, though thanks to the steady breeze that blew through the quiet trees, there were intermittent respites from the stink. Pilgrims who had travelled to this presumed holy site had not stayed long, but all had returned at least once to stab signs into the ground, hailing this grove a hellscape. Signs that read, 'Devil's Work,' 'Hell is Here,' and 'God Forgive our Sins.' Fortunately, whoever had placed them here was long gone, for the angels had work to do if they were to set this wrong right.

Lucy leapt from Michael's arms before his feet touched the ground. For the first time ever, she didn't fall flat on her face, sticking the landing despite her wing's attempt to off-balance her as they unravelled and fell at her back. The shock of not falling took Lucy by surprise, and her face lit up with pride as she looked up to Michael and Haniel as if to say, look what I just did, but she quickly remembered why they were here, and she bunched up her dress to keep it from the mud and ran to the lake to look upon the damage her miracle had caused.

"The fishies are all dead," Lucy said, picking up a fresh corpse from the muddy shoreline and tossing it back into the lake, hoping that being back in the water might return its soul to its body. "Why they dead?"

Lucy grabbed another fish, thankfully avoiding all the ones taken over by rot, and tossed it back into the lake to join the other that was already floating back towards her. She eyed another fish, tail twitching as its body decomposed, but before she could grab it, Haniel stepped between them.

"They are dead, Lucy," Haniel said. "There is nothing to be done."

"I do miracle. You said I could. I bring them back."

"And steal them away from the pristine lakes in Heaven?"

Lucy mused on the thought. It had been millennia since she had been to Heaven, but her brother was right. The lakes there were much nicer than the murky, festering pools here. It would take a lot of effort to make them nice and clear like they were supposed to be, but that didn't mean things couldn't improve with time.

"Maybe fishies like it here. Like me?" Lucy said.

"We should not bring the dead back," Michael said, tightening his feathered shawl, falling back into his tried and tested serious demeanour now that it was time to impart lessons upon his little sister.

Lucy eyed Michael up, recognising the return of his stiff, wooden, boring self, hoping it didn't mean she would get shouted at again. She liked the new Michael. He was fun, and he liked to fly. "Jesus came back." Lucy pouted, unable to mention his name without doing so. She would never ever forgive Jesus for making her miss the party of the century, especially since she hadn't been invited to another party since. There was time for that, too, however, now that her brothers had said she could stay.

"Jesus was a special case."

"Why?"

Lucy's tone was standoffish, and Michael realised that was his doing, and so he tried to channel Ms Makewell's energy. He relaxed his wings so that they fell loose around his shoulders, let his stern brow raise to its natural position on his face, and turned the corners of his mouth upwards, not to a full smile but to something other than a frown. This felt right. Serious, but with the glow of approachability. Lucy seemed to think so too, as her shoulders dropped and her trailing wings fell flat to the ground, no longer preparing to fight – because flight was not yet an option for her from a standing start.

"Jesus was a symbol," Michael said. "A necessity for a people who had lost their way. Without his return, the humans would not believe, and as too many humans require faith to remain upon the righteous path, Hell would have become overcrowded without a sign from God." Michael paused, and Lucy lingered on his words as if he had left the gap between them for dramatic effect, but this was not the case. The pause was there because Michael realised that Hell had become overpopulated. The ever-increasing circles to house untold sin were proof of that. And if a symbol was needed back then, was another required now?

The pause went on a little too long, and Lucy's attention dwindled. "Why?" she asked.

"Like this lake needs balance," Michael said, gesturing to the hundreds of dead fish bobbing on its surface, "so do the higher realms."

"Okay, I make better."

Lucy turned to the lake, spread her arms wide, and looked up to Heaven as if God were still there looking down upon her, and in one swift motion, she brought her hands together.

"Not yet," Haniel said, almost slipping in the mud as he dashed his hand between Lucy's closing palms.

"But you said I do miracle."

"You will."

"When? Now? I do it now?"

"Remember, patience is a virtue, Lucy," Michael said,

nodding along with his words, sure he had said something wise like a teacher might.

Lucy blew hot air at the saying. Hadn't she already been patient, she thought? If anything, patience was a sin, especially if inaction only made things worse. The lake needed fixing right now, this very second. It was of utmost importance. The sin would be to wait, to allow it to get worse.

"If you listen to Michael for a little bit longer and then promise to do exactly what he says, you can put your hands back together," Haniel said.

"Promise?" Lucy asked.

"If you do, too."

"Okay, I promise."

"Then I promise too," Haniel said.

Lucy's eyes lit up, and a cheesy and still somehow mischievous grin spread across her face, an expression made slightly unsettling by how her whole body continued to shake with excitement. As Lucy looked up at Michael and waited for him to tell her exactly what to do, Haniel couldn't help but laugh as he admired both his siblings doing impressions of the person that they thought they needed to be, one of a teacher, specifically and eerily so of Ms Makewell, and the other, of a good little girl who couldn't and wouldn't possibly do anything wrong.

"What do you see?" Michael said, gesturing towards the lake.

"Dead fishies."

"Now close your eyes."

Lucy closed one of her eyes, the one furthest away from Michael, so he couldn't see her trying to take a peek.

"Both of them," Michael said, not fooled. "Properly," he added when Lucy closed them both to a squint. "Now, what do you feel?"

Powerful energies rushed through Lucy as she opened herself up to the fabric of reality. The upset and anguish of spoilt nature was heavy and overwhelming, in the same way finding out Ms Makewell was dying was. Lucy didn't like that. She didn't like that one bit.

"Sad," Lucy said.

"Do you know why?"

Lucy thought about it for a second. She wanted to answer, but dead fishies didn't seem like what her brother wanted to hear, because if it were, he would have said, 'Well done, Lucy,' when she said it the first time, but he didn't say that, so the correct answer must be something smart that only and adult would know, and so Lucy shook her head.

"Because there is no balance," Michael said. "You created a lake full to the brim with fish. More fish than there was room to swim. They fought for their place; they ate all the food, and when there was nothing left for them, they died." Lucy gasped at such a terrible chain of events. She wanted her brother to stop speaking, but the darkness was not yet over. "Their bodies decayed," he continued, "their rot poisoned the water, and all that drank from it suffered the same sad fate as the fish you created."

"Not everything," Lucy said hopefully, wanting her brother to agree that as sad as the sight of the sick lake was, it was only confined to its waters.

"Did you not notice how quiet it was?

Michael swished his hand through the air, performing a little miracle to wash away the ceaseless buzz of hovering flies. Other than the wind whistling through the trees, there was no twittering of birds, no rustle of leaves or crack of twigs from wandering squirrels or curious mice, nor was there any laughter and joy from children and their parents who had come to enjoy the evening sun by the water.

Lucy did not like the silence. It reminded her of the plains of Hell. Eerie. Lonely. Isolating.

"Death, it spreads," Michael said. "To the skaters atop the water and the birds in the trees. Eventually, even the flies buzzing around the dead will have nothing left to do but leave. Everything must be in balance."

"I didn't mean to," Lucy said, returning the stolen sound-scape from her brother's grasp with little more than a twitch of her wings.

"We know," Haniel said. "You are not in trouble. We are going to help you fix it."

"How?"

"Keep listening to Michael, and he will show you."

Over a morning cup of tea, a delightful, belly-warming beverage that Haniel had taken to drinking in the downtime whilst Lucy had been at kindergarten, Haniel had offered to be the one to teach Lucy the fine intricacies of performing miracles, but Michael had insisted it be him. Michael was still desperate to prove his devotion to his new cause, not just to Lucy but to himself, and Haniel had no desire to take that away from him. So long as Lucy was happy, Haniel would be too.

"When you cast a true miracle," Michael said, "you must keep your eyes closed."

"Why?"

"Your eyes can deceive you, but your angel instincts never will. You must feel for the spot directly in the middle where everything is just right because, like too little of something can cause an imbalance, too much of something can, too."

"Like the fishies."

"Exactly."

"And like the flood?"

"Yes, Lucy, but that was an accident."

"It was an accident," Lucy said honestly.

"Then it is in the past," Haniel said.

With everyone in agreement on what constituted a poorly performed miracle and where they should remain, Michael asked Lucy if she was ready.

"Yes, yes, yes, I do miracle," Lucy said.

With a nod from her brother, they all closed their eyes. Lucy swung her arms wide and slapped her hands together, a little too dramatically for Michael's taste, but he wanted Lucy to be herself, so he let it slide. As Lucy listened to her clap echo around the sadly lifeless grove, she tried extremely hard to pay attention to each leaf it rustled, each droplet in the lake it rippled, and every buzzing fly it disturbed. It was hard to pay attention for a long time; there was far too much going on that needed inspecting, especially when some things required a second or third glance to decide whether they were interesting or not, but when the crack of her hands finally faded, repeating only in her memory, Lucy had woven her mind into the fabric of reality.

There was a lot wrong with the tapestry before her. As she untethered the strings that bound it together, Lucy felt for all the life that should have been here and all the life that could have been had she not tampered with it so carelessly. Death in excess had corrupted the picture before her, and when Lucy found all the colour it had desaturated and poisoned, she pulled at the threads, removing them one by one, leaving space for life to be woven in between.

It was a wonder for Haniel and Michael to feel Lucy work her miracle. Though they could not intervene, for two angels could not perform the same miracle together, they could sense the changes being worked. The grove pulsed with intention as if a warm, beating heart were at its centre. Lives were being born anew, the lake made fresh, the birds, the bees, and all manner of scuttering, fluttering, and crawling creatures were ushered into new homes, and the stains of all that was wrong were being scrubbed away. All mistakes were corrected, but they hoped they would not be forgotten and their lessons would remain.

The eerie silence and the unsettling buzz of flies consuming decay were pushed aside to make way for the wonderful chipper of birdsong, but instead of settling into a chorus, the grove exploded with a deafening cacophony of sound.

Michael opened an eye, knowing that Lucy was doing the same. "Close your eyes," he said to her. "Do not allow abundance to breed destruction once again."

Lucy snapped her eyes shut and squeezed so tight that multicoloured speckles fuzzed in the darkness. She hadn't meant to open her eyes. She had just wanted to see things working. Wasn't it wonderful seeing all the little changes come to life, she thought? Plus, she had to be sure things were going exactly as she envisioned. Making things just right was a complicated process. Just right didn't mean okay. Just right meant perfect. The perfect number of birds. The perfect number of fishies. The perfect number of seeds floating on the wind. That was always the plan. It was not her fault that it never worked that way. Or maybe it was. She just had to keep trying.

"Do not look for the change," Michael said, knowing Lucy still sensed his single, serious eye upon her. "Feel it."

With her eyes tight shut, like she was told, Lucy felt for everything the grove needed to thrive. When Lucy came here with Ms Makewell and all her new friends, the lake was nice to splash and play in, but there weren't enough fishies to catch, and if there weren't enough fishies to catch, then there probably weren't enough little things for fishies to eat. And if there weren't enough little things for the fishies to eat, then there probably weren't enough plants and microscopic things for those even smaller things to eat. There was so much to do, and now that her eyes were closed, she could see that.

Lucy worked hard to make the lake sparkle. She wanted to open her eyes to see all she could feel, but she wanted to prove to her brothers that she could be a good angel and perform good miracles. If she could do this, maybe they would let her fix Ms Makewell's cancer.

Haniel and Michael opened their eyes. They had told their sister not to open hers, to feel for the change, not to see it, but they couldn't help themselves. Time, it ran differently for an angel. At least it felt that way. Eternity was a force much like gravity. It had a way of warping your perspective. A gift from their father to keep them from losing their minds as time took its toll on everything but them. Acts like performing a miracle could feel like a human lifetime, when in reality, only seconds had passed, yet still, Lucy had been working on the grove for a while longer than what seemed normal, even for a child.

The grove was not as they expected. Nor was it as they ever could have imagined. It reminded them of the beginning. Before man and woman came to be. When all around was green. When the air tasted sweet like honey and blossom, and songs of woodland and sea were carried on the breeze. Their little sister had not stopped when she found balance but had looked back to a time when all was as good as could be. Death hadn't been tossed into the ether to drift until time could use it for parts. It had been given purpose in the here and now. Death turned warm and humid. Decay made rich and mossy. These were scents befitting a well-aged forest, not those that belonged to a grove or a lake once on the brink of collapse. All that had been wrong was reworked and rewoven into the tapestry of life in a way neither Haniel nor Michael could have done themselves. However, that wasn't entirely true. They probably could have performed this miracle exactly as Lucy did, but both were ashamed to say they did not love Earth quite like their little sister did.

Seeing the garden as it had been from the start, neither could put a finger on a reason as to why they had not fallen in love with Earth or why they had not come down to play with their little sister more often before her exile into Hell. Maybe it was because Heaven was made for them, and Earth was a product of her. Whatever the reason, it did nothing to excuse their absence in her life. Fortunately, eternity was long, and there would be plenty of time to amend for their mistakes.

An elated gasp pulled Haniel and Michael from their memories and rapture.

"I do good miracle?" Lucy asked, staring up at them both, shoulders hunched, half smiling, eyes squinting, as the expression of amazement on their faces told her everything she needed to know.

"You tell us, Lucy. Is there balance?" Michael said.

Lucy brought her hands back together, softly this time, a gentle pat as she trembled at the possibility of having performed her first true miracle, and one which didn't make everyone mad at her. She double-checked, and then she triple-checked, only because she thought that's what her brothers would do, and when she decided all was as it should be, that balance, as precarious as it always was, had been achieved, Lucy threw her arms apart and squealed.

"I'm a good angel, Lucy said, bunching up her pristine white dress, spinning and dancing across the muddy shoreline, leaping high with a flap of her strengthening wings onto the freshly grown grass that hadn't been there when they had flown down. She bounced around, laughing and pleased, careful with every step to avoid all the new critters coming in two by two to the gorgeous grove she had created for them.

With a hop and a skip, Lucy lifted her wings wide, and with a pirouette, a would-be graceful move had she not almost sent herself helicoptering into the air, she felled every wooden sign planted in the earth that proclaimed this place touched by the Devil. Which, technically, it was, both now and before.

Dizzy, Lucy stumbled, laughed, and fell to the floor. She rolled around in the grass surrounded by the broken signs, her laugh switching from angelic to demonic with each blink of an eye. Her pristine white dress, now dirtied, cried to be clean, but like her laugh, with every blink, there was a girl of pure white, shining and radiant, and one made of hellfire, comically evil in all her mischief.

"Now we go fix Ms Makewell," Lucy said, fumbling on all fours toward them like a demon out of Hell.

Michael didn't have the heart to tell her no. Especially not now when she was happier than she had been in days.

"How about we go fix one more miracle first? You can fly there yourself and show us how strong you are getting."

Lucy was still not strong enough to propel herself higher than a few feet without help, so she lifted her hands high, ready to be carried into the air. "Then we fix Ms Makewell."

"And then we can go see Ms Makewell," Michael said, choosing his words carefully as he scooped his little sister into his arms.

25

Ms Makewell's eyes were sunken black pits, and her lips were chapped and dry. She was clinging to life the way humans so often do, with fierce determination. She should have been sleeping, but having had so many parents and children come to see their favourite kindergarten teacher, she had forced herself to stay awake on the chance that it might be the last time she saw them. And now, with Lucy here, her final visitor of the day, Ms Makewell took up the challenge of keeping her eyes open a little longer.

"I can do six whole flaps," Lucy said, tiptoeing at the side of Ms Makewell's bed as Haniel and Michael miraculously returned forgotten toys to their homes so that the nurses had one less thing to do at the end of the day. "Soon, I fly on my own."

"That's amazing, Lucy," Ms Makewell said. "And are you being good for your new substitute teacher?"

"I'm not going kindergarten," Lucy said as she scrambled onto the bed.

"You're not?" Ms Makewell asked, looking disapprovingly at Haniel and Michael over her glasses as she used what little strength she had left to help Lucy up to her side.

Lucy playfully swung her legs back and forth over the edge of the bed, not picking up on the serious tone of Ms Makewell's voice that had her brothers hiding in the corners of the room fiddling with flowers, awkwardly rearranging them in hopes that they would not get a telling off.

"Nope. Brothers teach me angel things. When I make you better, I go back."

Everyone winced at Lucy's comment. Ms Makewell could see that Haniel and Michael had been avoiding a serious conversation about her health with their little sister, but with not long left, the talk was as inevitable as her death.

"And I wonder, what 'angel things' are more important than math and English?"

"We fixing miracles."

Ms Makewell had heard a lot of these supposed miracles since the last Sunday service, both bad and good. She would have loved to have seen a few of them herself, but bed-bound, the best she could hope for now was to hear about them from her friends, family, and students. She wasn't sure how much of the stories she believed; some sounded truly horrendous, and others were magical beyond words. However, faith was becoming much easier now that her next big journey was upon her. Faith that, despite how little energy she had left, allowed her to suspend her disbelief and see Lucy as the angel she claimed to be.

"Angel things do sound very important."

"Very important," Lucy said, glad Ms Makewell agreed. "Did you know too much good is bad?"

"I think I have heard that before, but maybe you would like to explain it to me one more time."

Lucy shuffled up the bed and whispered, "Balance," to Ms Makewell as if it were secret knowledge meant only for exalted powers. "Too many fishies in lake is bad," Lucy said, showing her left hand to Ms Makewell. "Not enough fishies is bad, too," she said, this time showing Ms Makewell her right hand.

Ms Makewell took in every detail of Lucy's face as she spoke. The way her eyes sparkled, and her cheeks grew fat and full as she smiled, the way she wobbled her head side to side as she explained the intricacies of her angel lessons, and how her yellow hair floated around her waist as if a breeze were caught inside her waves. It was not hard to believe that someone so perfect might be an angel, especially when the fish being described were the ones she herself witnessed being spawned, flipping and flopping as if from nowhere, bursting from the lake to assault her children. Was it so hard to believe that instead of a hellish hallucination, she might have been front and centre stage to the work of God or, as she was being led to believe, the poorly performed miracle of his inexperienced angel daughter?

"Then what is the right number of fish for a lake?" Ms Makewell asked.

"In the middle fishies," Lucy said, bringing her hands together at her centre. "That is balance."

"That's very wise, Lucy. I think you will make a very good angel one day."

"I think so too." Lucy nodded, pleased with herself for teaching Ms Makewell about balance. "The best angel."

"Better than your brothers?"

Lucy smirked. "Probably."

Ms Makewell coughed as she laughed at Lucy's smile and sneaky look back at her brothers as if it were foolish to think she would be anything other than better than them. Haniel, rolling his eyes, secretly agreeing with Lucy's deduction, appeared at their side with a glass of water, which he had miraculously pulled from nowhere, a family feat Ms Makewell continued to be amazed by.

Taking a soothing sip of water, Ms Makewell cleared her throat and turned the conversation back to Lucy, wanting the attention placed on someone who needed it more than she did. "And are you fixing all of your miracles? I hear one of them happened right on our kindergarten's doorstep."

"I don't know what you talking about," Lucy said sweetly, still trying to keep her brother's attention away from her first miracle. "But we not fix all of them," Lucy said with a happy nod. "I made Sandy a real rabbit."

"Did you now?"

"We go her house to make it gone. But, but, but—." Lucy stammered, tripping over her words with excitement. "Michael said it was a good rabbit. I did a good miracle. All on my own."

"I bet Sandy was thrilled to be able to keep her new rabbit, especially seeing as she had been so very sad for such a long time."

"She very happy. Very happy indeed."

"But do you know what I think made Sandy happier?"

"The tea party we had in her garden?"

"That sounds lovely, but no, I think something made her even happier than that."

"What make Sandy happier than tea party or rabbit?"

"You did."

Lucy gasped. "Me?"

"Your friendship is the real miracle, Lucy."

"I'm a miracle?"

"You are." Ms Makewell ran her hand through Lucy's hair, no longer afraid as to whether Albert was or wasn't hiding within it, only wanting to remember every detail about this child who, like the miracle she was, appeared from nowhere. "I'm glad I got to meet you, Lucy."

Forgetting Lucy was more intuitive than she seemed, Ms Makewell immediately regretted her choice of words.

"Don't say that." Lucy snapped. "Tomorrow, we fix last miracle. Then I am good angel. Then I fix you."

Everyone winced again, and with a single shared solemn look, the adults in the room decided it was time to have a sit-down conversation with Lucy.

"I'm not going to get better, Lucy," Ms Makewell said as Haniel and Michael pulled up two miraculously materialised chairs to the side of her bed.

"I can make you better."

"Everyone dies eventually," Ms Makewell said, her voice weighed down by a sadness she couldn't hide. "Even me."

"Not Jesus."

"Even Jesus, Lucy."

"But why? I have angel power. I can make you better. I know I can."

"It is a part of the human journey," Ms Makewell said. "It is the journey of all life," she corrected.

"Why?"

"We live hopefully long and happy lives on God's green Earth, and if we have been good and deserving, we get to go to Heaven."

"But why?"

Ms Makewell placed a hand on Lucy's chubby cheek, hoping her warmth would be enough to quell the tears pooling in her eyes. "So that we can be with the angels."

"You already with angels. I don't want you to die."

"Do you not want Ms Makewell to go to Heaven?" Michael asked.

"I think she would like it there, don't you?" Haniel added.

Lucy shook her head without letting her cheek leave Ms Makewell's comforting palm. "Not die yet. Don't go Heaven."

"Do you not think Ms Makewell deserves to be in Heaven?" Michael asked. "Where she can rest. Where she can be at peace in the light?"

"Yes, no, yes." Lucy jumped between answers, confused about what she was meant to say when all she wanted was for Ms Makewell to stay. "It's better here. With me. Together. Friends."

Ms Makewell stroked Lucy's cheek, wiping away her tears with her thumb. "We are friends, Lucy. The best of friends."

"Then I make you better?"

"Even if you could, how long would you give me?"

Lucy shrugged. "Forever?"

"Now that doesn't seem very fair for everyone else, does it?" Ms Makewell said. "What about all the other sick people? Will you give them forever, too?"

Lucy nodded. "Forever with me."

"No one should live forever," Michael said.

"Ms Makewell can?"

"I thought you were a good angel?" Ms Makewell said.

Lucy averted her gaze from Ms Makewell and her brothers, not wanting them to see her lie. "I am a good angel."

"Because what was it you said about balance?"

Lucy refused to answer. Adults liked to ask questions they knew she knew the answer to. It was an adult trick. They always did it. She wasn't sure why they did, but she wished she hadn't shared so much about her angel lessons with Ms Makewell. Maybe then she wouldn't know to ask such a mean thing. Because Lucy knew that Ms Makewell knew that she knew that if all things lived forever, Earth, her father's garden, would become too crowded like the lake had. Then everything would die, not just Ms Makewell, which would be bad. Very bad.

Ms Makewell could see Lucy wouldn't answer, so she did so for her. "You said too much of a good thing was bad."

"But I don't want you to die," Lucy said, wailing as she threw herself across Ms Makewell's chest, holding her arms out expectantly, wanting to be held for as long as humanly and angelically possible.

"I don't want to die either, but you're a good angel and a good girl," Ms Makewell said, still unashamedly feeling for Lucy's wings as she held her.

Even though she had yet to feel Lucy's wings or even get a glimpse of the heavenly light Lucy had told her glowed so bright it could blind, Ms Makewell believed. When she first met Lucy, when her cancerous symptoms first started to show, she believed Lucy was evil incarnate, and if she could believe that, then she could just as easily believe that Lucy was the angel sent here to see her off.

"We will see each other again."

Lucy sniffled. "When I can fly on own?"

"Exactly," Ms Makewell said. "When you can do six more flaps of those big, beautiful wings," she assumed, she imagined, she believed.

"Plus one more six."

"If that's how many flaps it takes to get to Heaven."

"I think so. Three sixes."

"Which is?"

"I don't know."

"When you can do eighteen flaps, then we can see each other whenever you want."

"Eighteen flaps," Lucy said, committing the number to memory. "Six. Six. Six. Then I see you every day?"

"I'd like that."

"Me too," Lucy said, crying until she fell asleep in Ms Makewell's arms.

26

The hospital called early in the morning to let Haniel and Michael know that Ms Makewell was not doing well and that they should visit as it would likely be their last. With little family of her own, Ms Makewell had decided to make them their first contact, and whilst it was mainly for Lucy's sake, having not been taking the news of her illness well, she had also grown fond of Haniel and Michael's company. Whether that was despite their initial shortcomings as caregivers to Lucy or deep respect for their continued attempts to be better, they didn't know. Regardless, they were glad to spend much time with her. She had become a human they, too, were fond of, and they were sure that when her story was over, she would be someone they would remember for eternity.

Lucy was strangely unfazed by Ms Makewell's worsened condition. In fact, she had reverted to her usual mischievous self, clumsily darting about the house as she pestered them to leave for her final angel lesson. It was an odd change, especially considering how late she had kept them both up the previous night crying. As they rubbed the bags beneath their eyes, bags neither were aware they could get until they had started taking care of their little sister, they reminded Lucy that whether or not she was able to fix the last miracle and become what she was happily referring to as a 'good angel', she was not allowed to upset the balance and make Ms Makewell better.

The brothers were glad they didn't need to argue with Lucy for once because the final miracle, which had been easily ignored a day ago, was now in desperate need of attention. Its power was rampantly spreading, and even before the hospital called, they were awoken by a deafening roar of life that hadn't been there the previous day. Had the miracle not been causing such a disturbance, Haniel might have questioned how quickly Lucy complied. Michael might even have been suspicious of the adorable sparkle in her eyes, which seemed to be twinkling for him and him alone. A trick which could have only been learned from a demon. Instead, they took her compliance as a sign that their little sister was, at long last, listening to them.

Whilst they were drawn to the first miracle by the putrid stench of death, an abundance of life guided their flight toward the last. They had chosen to leave this miracle for Lucy's final lesson, as unlike the lake whose disease risked spreading, or Sandy's stuffed rabbit made real, which posed no threat at all, this last miracle appeared to be causing no harm. But that had changed.

Their flight to the miracle took them to Little Woods Kindergarten, where their recent time together on Earth had begun. As Lucy waved to the blurry children running around the playground, Haniel and Michael thought how strange it was to see the kindergarten from this perspective again. Not just because there was now a thick and deciduous forest growing in the once-empty field behind it but because it reminded them of how much they had changed. For Lucy, it was the friends she had made, the first friends she had made after millennia spent alone, but for Haniel and Michael, it was the gaining of a new perspective, a closer one. Because instead of surveying this world from the comfort of Heaven, this humble building of laughter and learning had forced them to try something new. It would forever be their anchor on Earth. A reminder that whether you were four eons old or forty, there was always room to grow.

"Hello, friends," Lucy called out.

Michael tightened his grip on his little sister as she struggled to be free of his arms. Lucy had already done her six successful flaps of the wings today, and if she escaped him, she would plummet into the playground like a falling meteor, which was not something this world needed again.

"Hellooo," Lucy squealed, giggling as she spread her wings, making herself too big for her brother to contain.

"Can you not do that," Michael said with a mouth full of his little sister's feathers.

With Michael too focused on keeping Lucy from launching herself into the playground, it was Haniel who spotted the hordes of journalists and their TV crews below.

"Can you tell us more?" one of the interviewers asked the local pastor.

"Do you really think an angel is living here, in Lakeville?" another interviewer asked.

"Miracles from Heaven or curses from Hell?" another exclaimed, clearly trying to get a rise from the elderly man for the entertainment of their viewers.

The pastor smiled gently. He was as composed with the outsiders barraging him with questions as he had been this Sunday gone when Lucy interrupted his service. It was a patience that could only have been grown from years of service to the church and the myriads of people he had happily helped along the way.

"I'm afraid I could not say more than I already have," the pastor said. "It wouldn't be right. If God wanted the angel to be revealed to us, our own Little Miss Morning Star would be here now, talking in my place."

"Up here," Lucy wailed, the second of the angel siblings to spot the camera crews below.

Everyone looked up to an impossible sight of heavenly wings and blinding light, but by the time the cameras found their mark, there was nothing but clouds and a flock of birds swirling through the sky.

"That was close," Haniel said, pulling his still-fighting brother and sister down to the opposite side of the miraculously grown forest. "You must pay more attention, Brother. The last thing we need is to be caught, wings ablaze, on camera."

"Yes, me not paying attention is the problem," Michael said, fumbling with Lucy's crooked wings, struggling to untangle them and tuck them together behind her back. "I swear to Father that her wings are getting bigger."

Haniel pushed Michael aside and ran his hands down the leading edge of each of Lucy's wings, effortlessly straightening out the kinks and tucking them out of the way in one smooth motion.

"They are the same size they have always been," Haniel said.

"Far too big."

"Exactly."

The rewilded sounds of the forest called to the angels, tempting them in, but before Haniel and Michael could fully take in their surroundings and enjoy the majesty of what Lucy had created, she bolted.

"Let's go," Lucy screamed, tripping twice before disappearing between two trees.

Haniel and Michael followed after their little sister into the shaded forest, lit only by the diffused glow of the sun through verdant leaves. They were hit by the rich and humid scent of moss and decay as they crossed the threshold. It was a hungry, revitalising smell usually found in ancient forests left to their own devices, and yet here, the young trees had worked fast to encourage diversity.

Like the lake repaired at Lucy's miraculous hands, the forest reminded them of the beginning. Untouched and unrestrained, free to grow as it wished. Birds flew between trees, testing the strength of every free branch before they built their nest. Bees were buzzing, butterflies were fluttering, and squirrels and magpies rustled together in the undergrowth, unperturbed by the angel's presence as they searched for food to store for the winter.

As Lucy ducked and weaved between low branches and fruiting shrubs, birds flew circles above her head, tweeting words of thanks that only she could understand. Haniel and Michael struggled to keep up with her as she followed the paw-trodden paths calved out by foxes and felines that had found their way here from their concrete homes. If it weren't for her wings snagging on every prickle bush and tangle of ivy, they would have lost her, but as it was, they could walk at a leisurely pace and take in the sights, even the ones Lucy tried to ignore because despite how perfect the forest seemed, it was not a miracle for all animals.

There was one animal's need that this forest paid no heed to. Humans. The seed that had created it had one purpose, a singular goal, and that was to grow. Whilst in the beginning, this would have been exactly what humankind needed, a sanctuary from the harsh light of the midday sun and a perpetual harvest of meat and fruit, it was now at odds with the multifaceted ideals and desires of the modern man.

"What have you done," Michael uttered under his breath as he gazed upon the abandoned homes destroyed by single-ringed trees.

From above, they thought the forest had only grown to the edges of the field, but in the darkest shadows lay bare the memories of once happy families. Trees burst through roofs, roots enveloped cars, roads were sunk, and wildflowers and fungi replaced the flowerbeds of ornamental roses. Eden claimed all that had once belonged to the curated hand of man, and whilst flying and four-legged creatures enjoyed this sanctuary, there were no humans in sight. Miracle from Heaven, or curse from Hell. Michael supposed it was all a matter of perspective.

According to modern faith, there were two trees of note in the fabled garden: the tree of life and the tree of good and evil. The truth was they were one and the same. This seemed fitting under the circumstances, as it gave more evidence to the lesson they hoped to ingrain in Lucy that too much good could be bad. Because if even the Tree of Life could cause death, their little sister should surely understand how careful she must be with her power.

"Lucy," Haniel said, pausing to hold back a sigh that would have made his little sister think he was about to get mad. "Did you plant one of Albert's apples in the kindergarten's field?"

"Yes," Lucy said, miraculously plucking an apple from thin air.

Albert lunged out from Lucy's hair to swallow the apple in one bite before quickly curling back into his hiding home.

The brothers shook their heads in dismay as their little sister led them deeper into the forest in the direction which they now knew was toward the first tree. None of Lucy's siblings had any idea how Lucy came to be able to summon the Eden apple. They had once thought it due to her being the only angel foolish enough to taste the tree's fruit, but Eve, who did very little of anything now that she possessed all there was to know, liked to remind them that she had seen Lucy perform the miracle long before she and Adam had been tricked into tasting it.

It was hard to know what the truth was. Lucy was too young to remember, and since eating the apple, Adam and Eve had gained a predisposition to tell tall tales of fancy and whim. Whilst this penchant for lies was entertaining at best and mildly annoying at its worst, it never did answer the eternal question of what came first, the apple or the tree.

"Father told you not to plant another Eden apple," Michael said, a waver in his voice as he forced himself to stay calm.

"No, he didn't."

"You know full well he did," Michael snapped.

"Nope," Lucy said, sniggering behind her hand as she ducked beneath a low-hanging branch.

Before Michael started shouting, he caught his rage in a deep and heavy breath and used the sounds of the wandering winds moving through the trees to help guide him back to inner peace. Being patient was not as easy as Michael had hoped, but he would keep at it until it was normal.

"It will all be fine, Brother," Haniel said. "Its roots have not yet spread so far that it cannot be undone."

"So, you agree all must be returned to as it once was?"

"I do."

"Then let us find a way to explain that to Lucy in a way she can understand."

"She is smart."

"A good angel." Michael rolled his eyes but couldn't help but smirk as Lucy looked back at him with a cheeky grin as if to say, 'are you talking about me?' "Lucy, can you come here, please," Michael said.

Haniel and Michael blinked, and Lucy was already between them, looking innocently up at them with her hands tucked into theirs. This was it, she thought, the final lesson to be a good angel. All she had to do was listen and do exactly what they said. Well, not exactly what they said because Lucy had a plan. She knew her brothers would ask her to get rid of the forest, but she wasn't going to do it, and she knew what she would say when they asked her to. Six little words that she had been practising all morning, six little words that would make her brothers see she wasn't a pushover, that she knew who she was and what she wanted, but her brothers didn't need to know what those six words were until the time was right. Until it was time to say her six practised words, Lucy would listen, be a good angel, take in all the knowledge they had to share with her, and then when all was done, she would be something else, something better than a good angel.

Lucy had practised these six words after waking up this morning with a thought that didn't end with a why. The thought had spawned from a dream. A relatively normal dream that had begun with a memory.

In this dream, Lucy was in kindergarten with all her new friends. Sandy was talking to her rabbit. Which was strange because, at this point, Lucy hadn't made the rabbit real, but mostly, it was strange because the rabbit was talking back with human words. Which rabbits couldn't do.

Ms Makewell was telling all of them, including Sandy's rabbit, that it was important to listen to adults. That adults were smart and wise and wanted their children to learn everything they knew. Lucy had scoffed at this and then followed it with a grumpy impression of her brother Michael, who at the time was especially grumpy. Not like he had been lately. Quite nice. Quite fun. And quite friendly. Like a friend. A friendly friend who was also family. Kind of like Haniel but just a little bit different.

"I'm so grumpy. I know everything. Grumpy, grumpy, grump," Lucy had said, straightening her back and pulling her shoulders high, the perfect impression of her brother.

This made her new kindergarten friends, who all had a grumpy adult like Michael in their lives, laugh. It made Ms Makewell laugh, too. Maybe she also had a grumpy adult in her life or did once, a long time ago. Or perhaps she was a grumpy adult sometimes, but Lucy didn't think so. Ms Makewell always seemed happy, except now she was sad and in hospital.

After Lucy did the impression of her brother, the really, really, really good impression of her brother, Ms Makewell said that she was right. Lucy didn't believe it at first, but then Ms Makewell told all the kindergarteners that adults can sometimes be grumpy and that being wise didn't mean they were always right. It was good to challenge them, but only sometimes and only if it was safe to do so. That they should always be true to themselves as long as it didn't hurt others or themselves. Don't just be good, she had said. Be you.

It was quite confusing, and most of the other children shrugged and started looking around the classroom for something more interesting to do, but Lucy knew Ms Makewell was super, super smart and that one day she would understand what it meant to be you, or to be her, to be Lucy. Then, suddenly, she forgot where they were, and without reason, they were flying through the sky, running their fingers through the clouds, as if they had always been there and not in the kindergarten classroom at all.

Ms Makewell and the other children didn't have wings like Lucy; instead, they held onto giant angel-shaped kites. It was funny but so weird and out of place that her sleeping smile woke her up. It was annoying that dreams always stopped at the best part, Lucy had thought to herself, but as she wiped the sleep from her eyes, she realised it was the first time she had thought about Ms Makewell without crying since all the bad things had started happening to her.

It was nice to smile again, and as Lucy wondered what it must feel like to fly like a kite, her inner head voice whispered to her, 'Don't be a good angel, be a you angel.'

Lucy knew this thought had nothing to do with kites. It was a big angel thought that had metastasized in the forgotten part of her dream. It was a good thought. A happy thought. A thought that made her feel like herself again after so long of being sad. And even though the thought came from a blurry part of her dream, Lucy knew she had Ms Makewell, her favourite adult human, to thank for it.

When the dream started to fade, leaving all but the message it had imparted to her, Lucy coaxed Albert from her hair and tickled him awake. 'There is no need to be sad anymore, Albert. Everything on Earth will be just right for everyone and everything,' she had said to him, though with fewer words and also not in the proper order. Long sentences were still hard when said out loud, especially when she was still sleepy.

"Why did you plant one of the Eden apples?" Michael asked Lucy.

"The birds needed a home." Lucy pouted as if the answer were obvious.

"And what about the humans whose homes are being destroyed?"

Lucy tugged on her brother's hands as she noticed a parting in the trees with enough room to spread her wings. "Swing."

"Answer the question first."

"What question?" Lucy asked, having forgotten thanks to the idea of flying taking over her thoughts.

"Why did you not think about the humans when performing this miracle?"

"I don't know," Lucy said, though not with words, just a mumbling sound and a shrug because she did know, and she knew it was wrong because since then, she had learnt about balance, and this forest did not have it.

"I think you do."

"They have loads of houses," Lucy said, though this time with words. "It's not fair." Then, trying her luck again, she demanded, "Swing."

Now that she had answered, Lucy's brothers did as they were told and lifted her into the air. She held tight to their hands and used all her strength to pull her wings off the ground so they could swing her backwards with all their might. It was strenuous, but she did it. She was definitely getting stronger every day.

As they swung her forwards, Lucy squealed happily as the g-force wobbled her insides like wibbly, wobbly jelly. When she hit her peak, Lucy shouted, "Fly." And as she had hoped they would, her brothers let her go.

Lucy soared through the air. She tried with all her might to open her wings, but no matter how hard she bunched her fists or how furiously she scrunched her face, Lucy couldn't get them to open. Her wings were tired, but that did not mean she couldn't pretend, so instead of flapping them, she flapped her arms instead, imagining they were taking her higher and not the momentum of her brother's strong arms.

Without her wings open to control her ascent, Lucy rose higher and higher into the thick of the trees, where squirrels bound along branches that grew miraculously beneath their feet. Lucy waved at all the animals that squawked and squeaked, amazed and awed by an abundance they had never known. It was a happy place up in the trees, but as Lucy was about to breach the canopy and glimpse the bright blue sky above, a thick branch from a magnificently tall tree grew before her eyes.

"Uh-oh. Sorry, tree," Lucy said before she smashed face-first into its new appendage, ripping it with a splintering snap from the trunk.

Lucy tumbled back to Earth, splayed like a star, and laughed, knowing one of her brothers would be waiting to catch her.

"Again, again," Lucy said as she landed in Haniel's open arms, and the broken branch crashed beside them.

"I think Albert wants you to keep your feet firmly on the ground for now," Haniel said.

Albert slithered out of Lucy's hair and hissed in agreement as Haniel placed her down. He wasn't sick of her antics; Albert never could be. He and Lucy were kindred spirits. That being said, it had been a long time since he had seen a forest as beautiful as this one, so, for now, he was quite happy to slither circles in the dirt. Besides, Lucy had come crashing down at their final destination, the Eden tree, and Albert wanted to eat as many apples as he could reasonably fit in his belly before Lucy and her brothers uprooted it and everything else in sight.

"Oh, we are here," Lucy said, giving the Eden tree a swift punch, knocking a whole bushel of apples to the ground for her salivating snake.

27

The Eden tree was neither the tallest nor the widest tree, and whilst all of its leaves were an unblemished, shimmering green, they were no more resplendent than the leaves of all the trees that grew around it. In the thick of the forest, it would have been an otherwise innocuous addition to the surroundings if it had not been for the sun's glorious light shining down directly upon it through a break in the canopy. That, and the perfectly round, shiny, red apples growing temptingly from its branches. To all eyes, this tree was of no danger to the world, but Haniel and Michael knew that the imbalance it caused happened beneath the earth, where eyes could not see.

Using the heat from Hell below and the light from Heaven above, the tree's roots spread far and wide. They connected to all which grew around them, sharing the nutrients of the two realms to create abundance. It was harmony in the purest form, but it was not balance for the modern man. The tree had only been growing a few days and had already created an entire forest where there was once nothing but grass and a hedgerow to keep it hidden from the world. In another day, the street it had already begun to stake its claim on would be gone completely. Two days more, and it would envelop the entire community. A week after that, the continent would be nothing but forest. Eventually, the Eden tree's roots would spread beneath the deep oceans, reaching out for new lands to reclaim from the humans who had once thought this world was theirs and theirs alone.

It was a nice idea, a world covered in nothing but trees, but that was balance for a different time.

"We should put things right. Before it is too late," Michael said.

"Why we have to make it go?" Lucy asked.

"You know why."

"Balance?"

"Exactly."

There was silence. A familiar pause, which was usually followed by a 'why.' Instead, Lucy said, "I'm confused."

"There's nothing to be confused about," Michael said abruptly.

Haniel slapped his brother on the arm. "What are you confused about, Lucy?" Haniel said, asking his little sister the question Michael realised he should have asked instead.

"Make it go isn't balance."

"But it is. Do you not see the harm the Eden tree has already caused the humans? The harm it will continue to cause if we allow it to keep growing?"

"What about birds and bees?" Lucy asked.

Haniel and Michael looked at each other in shock. They were sure this wasn't a conversation they were supposed to have for at least ten more eons, nine at the very least, eleven or twelve if they were lucky.

"Where birds and bees live?" Lucy asked again, bored of waiting for her brothers to stop looking at each other all funny. "Don't they get miracles too?"

"Thank Father," Haniel said to Michael, glad the big talk wasn't upon them already.

"Thank Father for what?" Lucy said, eyeing them both with suspicion.

"This is the human era," Michael said, quickly answering Lucy's previous question before they got dragged into a conversation they were in no way prepared for. "One day, like all things do, the time of humans will end, but until that day comes, balance must be preserved with them in mind."

"But I like all animals."

"I do too," Michael said. He really did. Though not with the same passion as Lucy. Not with the same fervour he was sure his father wished of him. "But you know that all animals go to Heaven," he said, knowing he didn't need to specify non-human animals to his little sister, who had spent too long in a place filled only with human sin. "As sad as it may seem, it is up to humans to realise their mistakes. It is up to them to make the right choices and earn their place in Heaven."

Lucy pouted and hummed a noise Michael assumed was approval.

"It is time to put things right. Remove the forest. Restore the homes. Uproot all the Eden tree has touched."

Lucy was still pouting, and she hummed again much louder, this time with her arms tightly crossed. It was time for those six words she had been practising. "I do not agree with you, brothers," she said, giving an affirmative nod, proud of how adult her stern and serious voice sounded.

'Oh dear, that was seven words, not six,' Lucy thought as she counted up with her fingers. Why were numbers so hard? At least it was only one mistake. Lucy didn't intend to make another by taking away the homes of so many happy little animals. She kept a straight face, swearing never to tell anyone of her numeric miscalculation, and waited to see what her brothers said next.

Haniel and Michael shared a discreet smile as they tried their hardest not to laugh at Lucy's oh-so-serious face. This was not the response either of them had expected, but in the spirit of development and learning, they didn't demand she do as she was told but instead did as Ms Makewell would have done and asked their little sister why she felt this way.

"Nothing isn't balance," Lucy responded, flailing her arms about, hoping excessive movement would aid her point. "Lots of people in Hell because of nothing. They all go to Hell because of nothing. We can help them not go there. Make Earth better for everyone and everything. Why have power if we do nothing? Always nothing. Never something."

Lucy was impressed with herself. That was a lot of words said all at once. She was sure it was easy to understand, too. She didn't even practice those words. They were all new, conjured from her passionately beating heart. And by the looks on her brother's thoughtful faces, she had made them think like a tricky kindergarten lesson made her do. She had done it, she thought. Lucy had been not just a good angel but a you angel. The best angel she could be.

"Sometimes doing nothing is what is best," Michael said, but his voice did not carry the same stoic certainty it usually did.

Lucy refolded her arms like Michael did when he wanted others to know how serious he was. "You are wrong," she said.

Michael had no answer because all of his thoughts ended with a why. He wondered if he had spent too long on Earth and if he needed to go back to Heaven to find his certainty again, but in his silent contemplation, Michael realised it was the opposite. It wasn't that he had spent too much time on Earth. It was that he had finally spent enough. Maybe it was because of the humans, perhaps it was his little sister, it might even have been the fresh, albeit slightly polluted, Earth air, but an idea was forming in the back of his mind, one he did not yet have all the words to describe, but it was an idea he was sure his little sister would approve of when it came together in a way that could be spoke aloud.

"You are right, Lucy, and I am wrong," Michael said, looking up to Heaven, wondering if his absent father's final task for him had been to lead him to this moment of self-discovery.

Haniel turned aghast to his brother. "You are?"

"He is," Lucy confirmed.

"I am," Michael said, relaxing as a weight that he didn't know he had been carrying for eons lifted from his shoulders.

"You cannot mean to say you think the Eden tree should stay?" And almost worried he would have to become the serious angel of the two, Haniel added, "This isn't like Sandy's rabbit, Mr Fluffywuffy Bunnykins the Second." Haniel was glad he made it through that name without breaking his composure, but he certainly couldn't end his point there. "This tree will wipe out civilisation."

"Of course not, that would be ridiculous."

"No it is not," Lucy said.

"It is, and you know it," Michael said, playfully nudging his little sister off balance with a tap of his wing to break the stern pose she had regrettably learnt from him.

"I don't know it," Lucy said, laughing as her brother tickled her back into mischief.

Michael turned to his brother as their distracted little

sister leapt onto his wing.

"Hell is full," Michael said. "You remember what Lilith told me. There are more circles than the demons can count. While we have watched from Heaven, humans have found new ways to sin. Some are simply evil and deserve their fate, but I cannot believe that more of them deserve to be down in Hell than up in Heaven. What if Lucy is right? What if she has always been right? There is faith here in Lakeville, but life is hard, too hard. Should we not be using our father's power to make life on Earth better, for them and for everything else that lives here? Maybe what this world needs of us now is to be caretakers, not the distant, apathetic watchers we have been."

"I hear you, Brother, but there is more you are not telling me," Haniel said, noticing a buzz of energy that could almost be described as excitement, ruffling Michael's feathers in the wing that their little sister was not attacking.

"I think—. I'm not sure yet," Michael said, stumbling over his words like a child who didn't know how to order their thoughts. "I might have an idea of how to help all those lost to the wrongs of our inaction, but I need more time to think, to ruminate, and process what I believe needs to be done."

"Well, until then, are we getting rid of the Eden tree or not?" Haniel said. "We do still have this little devil to teach before you change the world."

"No," Lucy said, growling as Michael flailed her about, trying to remove her from his wing now that she was gnawing on it like a hungry demon.

"The Eden tree can be placed in Heaven where it has room to grow into infinity, but the forest it has created can stay."

The shock of being mostly agreed with was enough to loosen Lucy's grip on her brother's wing. "Forest can stay?"

she said as she was tossed into the air, this time falling flat on her face in the dirt where Albert waited, fat and full of apples, to slither back into her hair.

"A compromise," Michael said.

"Compromise," Lucy repeated.

Lucy knew what the word meant. It meant they would both get something they liked and something they didn't like. It was a middle. Just like balance. She couldn't say it, though. It always came out as com-pro-pro-promise. It was too many syllables in one word. Syllables was another word Lucy couldn't say. That always sounded like silly-ables when she said it. Lucy knew it was wrong, but her tongue didn't always do what she wanted it to. However, Lucy knew she would get both of these words right one day, probably after six more English lessons with Ms Makewell.

"We pull the growth," Michael continued. "Fix the houses. Rehome the birds and the bees who thought they might get to live out their lives in a cosy attic. Then, who knows, maybe we can plant a few more apples in a few more fields. Do in a day what humans cannot do themselves in a lifetime."

Haniel was surprised by the change of pace thrust upon him by his brother, but he was also happy, and so with the deal made, Michael instructed Lucy to put her hands together.

Whilst the Eden tree had a greater potential for devastation than the death and decimation Lucy had brought to the lake, this miracle wouldn't be half as difficult to fix. Step one was to remove the tree and place it in Heaven; next would be to rein in the growth; finally, Lucy would have to restore the homes to how they once were.

Each task required a different focus. The Eden tree needed Lucy's full attention to reach all of its winding roots, making this the most difficult of steps because getting Lucy to hold her attention on one thing was known to be a near impossibility. The reining in of the forest was simple. All Lucy had to do was add a touch of death to everything new and let nature take its course. The earth would reclaim and reuse what was left, and life, in its unyielding persistence, would stop that death from spreading too far. The homes that needed restoring meant looking into the past, seeing things as they once were, and recreating them now. It was a shame it was not within their power to rewind time, as it would be to no one's surprise that Lucy would take creative liberties with the homes she fixed, and so it would be up to Haniel and Michael to put the finishing touches on her work after she was done.

It took Lucy a while to find all the roots of the Eden tree. There were many, and they were connected to everything that had grown here. It was a lengthy task, and even with her eyes closed, Lucy could feel the cool shadows shifting as the sun moved through the sky. The morning had long since passed, and with the afternoon waning, Lucy worried that she didn't have long left before Ms Makewell took her final breath. It was hard not to get distracted with that thought rattling in her head, but this was her final lesson before she visited Ms Makewell, so Lucy had to prove to her brothers she could do this. If she could hold her focus and do what was right and find balance with her miracle, then they would surely not get mad when they found out what she planned to do at the hospital.

Once Lucy had a hold of the Eden tree, getting it to Heaven was easy. Heaven was obnoxiously loud with its perfection. There was no turmoil, no fight, nothing pushing back in the way which gave Earth the unique charm Lucy adored. Life in Heaven was too easy, and Lucy often wondered how her brothers and the souls that lived there didn't get bored. She supposed humans did deserve a break after the hardships that they had to put up with. Especially those who didn't have jobs that they enjoyed like Ms Makewell did.

In the infinity of goodness, Lucy found an empty field waiting for something to take root. It was there that she planted the Eden tree, but uninterested in what became of it next, Lucy returned her focus to Earth and the miracle between her hands. She let her mind drift to the edges of what she could hear the local pastor dubbing Godswood Forest. It was an okay name but not the best. Lucy would let the pastor know next Sunday that Lucywood Forest would be more fitting, and if he disagreed, she would keep changing the sign until it was all anyone could remember.

With a touch of death, Lucy pulled the forest back until all the homes it had destroyed were revealed. Now that she knew about balance, the pain that she had caused all the humans who had been forced to flee was impossible to ignore, and Lucy felt a little bad, but only a little, because it was humans who cut all the trees down to begin with. But knowing those families needed homes to sleep, eat, and feel safe in, Lucy looked back to how it was before and put their homes together again, but because she knew her brothers expected her to change something, Lucy did just that.

"Done," Lucy said.

"What did you change?" Haniel and Michael said together.

"Nothing," Lucy said, doing her best to hide her mischievous grin with her practised bright, white smile.

Not believing their little sister for a second, Haniel and Michael put their hands together and checked the remade houses for anything amiss. Fortunately for Lucy, they didn't check the numbers on the doors, which all now read six-six-six.

Six-six-six was so funny, Lucy thought, but not nearly as funny as the handwritten letters of apology penned in the blood of the damned, signed and sealed by the Devil herself, and tucked discreetly inside each letterbox for when the families returned.

"You see," Lucy said, grabbing her prairie dress and swishing it innocently. "I'm a good angel."

With the final miracle set right and her brothers unable to find her acts of mischief, Lucy skipped into the space where the tree once stood and sang a song sung by demons to torture those in a very specific circle of Hell.

"Remorseless tree choppers, chop, chop, chop, how many rings do you got, got, got. One ring, two ring, three rings, four, what do you think of my saw, saw, saw."

28

Haniel, Michael, and Lucy arrived at the hospital to find Sandy and her family at Ms Makewell's side. Their legs still stung from the imagined blades of Lucy's demonic rhyme, but fortunately, they had got their little sister to stop singing long before they arrived because no one in the room, not Sandy, her parents, Ms Makewell, or the flitting nurses deserved to suffer from her hellsong.

It was a tight squeeze with the two families packed into the tiny room filled to the brim with flowers and home comforts to keep the visiting children occupied once they had finished crying. Usually, the nurses would have encouraged one family to move along as another came to visit, but as Ms Makewell had taught many of the nurses and their children, they gave her a familial wink and tapped their noses as they obliged her request to be crowded for her final hours.

"I've lived a long life," Ms Makewell said. "I may not have a family of my own, but I'm glad I got to meet one final class of children, especially you two," she said to Lucy and Sandy. "Try not to be too sad. I am happy, and I am sure we will all meet again in Heaven one day."

Ms Makewell's voice was a tired croak, and the adults in the room knew she was leaving out important details in each sentence to spare the children from further heartache. Details like she wished she could finish the year with her new class of children, to see them as they took their first steps into education, where they would grow to become strong, brave, and smart adults like she knew they would all be. And because of these omitted details, the adults knew that whilst Ms Makewell was happy because she couldn't not be when surrounded by so much love, she wasn't ready for what came next.

Whilst these omissions were mainly for Lucy and Sandy's sake, children not yet familiar with death, it was also for the benefit of the adults. No matter how many times you have been forced to go through loss, death is never easy. Age and experience can never truly prepare you for lost time, but Ms Makewell was tired, and everyone had shed enough tears over her, even a couple by the ever-stoic angel brothers. Strangely, none of these tears were shed by Lucy, not today at least. She had kept her eyes dry, and whilst Haniel and Michael were keeping a close watch on their little sister, suspicious of what she might be planning, they took her at her word that she was being brave for Sandy's sake, whose eyes were burnt red from all the tears she had cried.

"I'm tired," Ms Makewell said, each breath hoarser than the last. "Go get yourselves a drink whilst I close my eyes."

The adults looked at Ms Makewell, concerned as her eyes fluttered closed. Her skin was grey now, but for the soft blue bruises where the frames of her glasses pressed into the sides of her face. Whilst the nurses had been good to her and had bathed and washed her one last time before everyone arrived to see her off, the fight she was battling with death had drenched her in a sweat that matted her hair. None of them wanted to leave her, not like this.

"I promise I won't die," Ms Makewell said, a white lie disguised with a weak but no less sincere laugh. "I just need one last nap before we say goodbye."

When Lucy and Sandy were made comfortable on the rug that one of Ms Makewell's visitors had brought in to add some homeliness to the otherwise bleak room, Sandy's mother asked which unlucky soul was staying behind to keep an eye on the budding miscreants whilst they went to get a coffee.

"I will stay," Michael said. "So long as you bring me back one of those delightfully stimulating beverages when you are done."

"Sure thing, and a juice box for the girls," Sandy's father said.

Whilst Haniel was a tea angel, Michael was undoubtedly a coffee angel. Each cup hit differently. Some had hidden floral notes, others spice. His favourites had notes of chocolate, the kind that had mixed nuts crushed within it. However, seeing as this would be a brew from the hospital vending machine poured into a precarious paper-thin polystyrene cup and not the kind that came in an oversized mug with a delicious decorative froth atop it, Michael wouldn't hold his breath for anything other than bitterness. It was of no mind, though. Right now, he wanted the coffee for one reason, the same reason all the rushing nurses wanted one. He was tired.

Michael took a seat and pointed it so that he could keep one eye on Ms Makewell and another on Lucy. One who might leave without saying goodbye, and the other a risk of stopping her from ever doing so. The chair creaked as

Michael collapsed into it, putting his faith in the decades-old hospital furniture that was overdue for a replacement. He would see to refurnishing the hospital with freshly cushioned sofas and seats when he was less tired. The doctors and nurses certainly deserved something nice for all their hard work.

Yawning, Michael thought it strange how much energy was used when he wasn't sitting around brooding all day. Teaching Lucy to perform miracles was tiring enough, and then there were the flying lessons on top of that, but even those two things combined didn't come close to the energy it took attending to all the little things he had to do for her throughout the day. She needed to eat constantly, which for an angel was very unusual and completely unnecessary, but she got extremely grouchy if she didn't. Another thing that made her irritable was missing nap time, which was a task in and of itself. Lucy had boundless energy until the very last second, which made getting her down for at least an hour before she started screaming near impossible. Then, there was undoing all the chaos she had wrought upon the world as she tripped and crashed into everything in her path. It was all far more draining than he had anticipated, and Michael found himself wondering how human parents managed to look after their children without collapsing on the spot.

Any parent would have forewarned Michael that it was expected to feel this tired when looking after children. However, until now, he would not have believed them and wouldn't have thought to ask. Michael knew that if he had paid humans more attention when looking down on them from Heaven, he might have learnt a thing or two from them before he decided to be a better big brother to his little sister, but Michael tried not to let his mind stray too far into these thoughts of negativity, of the self-righteous, inconsiderate angel and brother he had been. Haniel would remind him that at least he was here for Lucy now, and he would be right, as Michael was beginning to realise that his brother so often was. However, none of this helped Michael keep his eyes open, and seeing as he was sure that his devil of a sister was up to something, it was imperative that Haniel get his coffee to him soon.

29

The beat of Ms Makewell's heart monitor pulsed rhythmically, as one would want it to do. The steady metronome tone weighed on Michael's eyes as he watched the girls mouth silent words to one another. Why did little girls always whisper, Michael wondered. They were always up to something. Always trying to get away with naughtiness and nonsense. Lucy was watching him, too. Not that he could prove it, as she had her back to him. Though, Michael was sure his little sister had her eyes on him somehow. He wouldn't be surprised if Albert were watching him from within her hair, hissing constant updates on his cognizance into her ears.

The heart monitor continued to beat, and as Michael's eyes dropped shut to its rhythm, he jumped alert. He couldn't fall asleep now. What would his brother and Sandy's parents think of him for being so careless? His eyes fell shut again. Michael was sure he opened them a second time, but if he had, then why was Sandy's backpack hopping across the floor in some peculiar attempt at escape? He was dreaming, wasn't he, Michael thought, the last thought he had before his head dropped.

"Come back here, Mr Fluffywuffy Bunnykins the Second,"

Sandy said, pulling her backpack into her crossed legs, being extra careful not to squeeze too hard and squish her secret rabbit that she had snuck in to see Ms Makewell one last time.

Sandy's uncle had told her rabbit feet were lucky. That made her mum mad. She told him not to talk about such evil, godless things in front of her. That didn't make sense as rabbit feet were fluffy and cute, certainly not evil. Regardless, this rabbit had four feet. That was four times the luck. Sandy only hoped it was enough luck to save Ms Makewell from the big, scary cancer that didn't want her to be alive anymore. If it wasn't, at least her best friend was an angel, a very naughty angel who was going to do what her brothers had explicitly told her not to do.

"Michael asleep?" Lucy whispered.

"Yeah. Your big brother is asleep now," Sandy said. "Can Mr Fluffywuffy Bunnykins the Second watch?"

Sandy unzipped her bag, and her rabbit poked his head out and wiggled his nose as he assessed his surroundings. Something was amiss. Sandy's mischievous friend was certainly up to something, but it wasn't that which had his floppy ears standing to attention. It was something deadly. A flash of yellow, ever-so-slightly darker than the naughty girl's hair, moved toward him and hissed.

"Don't be scared," Lucy said, speaking in rabbit language with sniffles and twitches of her nose. "Albert only eats apples."

This girl called Lucy may have created him, but Mr Fluffywuffy Bunnykins the Second didn't believe for one second that this snake wouldn't eat him. His rabbit instincts were telling him to hop, hop, hop away, but before he could, Sandy, his lovely little lady who had given him the best name a rabbit could hope for, smushed his head back down into her bag and zipped him inside. It wasn't a field of scrummy, yummy grass, but at least he was safe from that slippery, slithering snake. Nothing could eat him when he was with Sandy.

"Albert, don't be scary," Lucy said, scolding her snake with a series of serious hisses. "Mr Fluffywuffy Bunnykins the Second wanted to watch."

"Oh well. Maybe next time." Sandy's bottom lip wobbled. She couldn't believe what she had said. "I didn't mean that. I don't want more people to die," she said, snorting up snot as she tried to hold back tears that had, in the last hour, started to feel less like water and more like broken glass. "I don't want to cry anymore."

"No more crying," Lucy said, tucking Albert back into her hair. "I make Ms Makewell better. I do it now."

"But your brothers say it's bad for balance."

"They wrong."

"Then why did they say it?"

"War. Famine. I don't know." Lucy shrugged.

Sandy didn't know how making Ms Makewell not die would cause war or what being a girl had to do with it, but Lucy didn't seem too concerned, and so she wouldn't be either. Besides, the beat of Ms Makewell's heart monitor had slowed, and the two best friends knew that if they wanted to keep their kindergarten teacher from leaving them, they had to act now before the adults came to stop them with all their silly rules.

"It won't go wrong," Lucy said. "Promise, Sandy. No more crying."

As Lucy hopped away, kind of like a rabbit, Sandy opened a tiny peephole in her bag so that her bunny could watch

God's work unfold. Lucy was sneaky when she wanted to be. Her oversized wings didn't get in her way once, not even as she clambered onto the bed and scurried over Ms Makewell's sleeping body. It was only when Lucy's face was pressed right up against Ms Makewell's did their favouritest kindergarten teacher stir.

"I'm going to make you better," Lucy said to Ms Makewell, who was unsure if she were dead or alive as a bright, blazing, heavenly light blinded her from above. "I'll be a me angel. Like you taught."

30

Michael's heart stopped, something he wasn't aware it could do, when he heard, or for better words, didn't hear, the metronomic beat of Ms Makewell's vitals. She was gone, and it didn't matter that he could fly to Heaven and greet her eternal soul as it found its place in her afterlife. Michael had slept through Ms Makewell's death, and as he began to add not saying goodbye to a cherished friend to the ever-growing list of his wrongdoings, he heard Ms Makewell's gentle voice, her songlike laugh, loved by children's ears and adults alike, and the familiar sound of his little sister's name, which bore no tones of frustration, only love, as Lucy pestered her favourite and very much alive kindergarten teacher.

"You'll never believe how far away that coffee machine is," Haniel said.

"You allowed Lucy to do this?"

"It really was too late to intervene. Not that I am sure I would have stopped her had I arrived sooner. Besides, were you not the one who was supposed to be watching the girls?"

"Father, what have I done," Michael said, jumping to his feet. "Where is Sandy?"

"It is a new day, Brother," Haniel said, gesturing out the

window to the rising sun. "They left many, many hours ago, though I expect the good news will reach them soon, and you will have your chance to apologise for falling asleep whilst on watch."

Ms Makewell looked bright and healthy; she was even strong enough to sit herself up without any help from the nurses. There was a smile on everyone's face, and the only tears were happy ones. It was a joy that involved you, even when observing from a distance. It was contagious and provoking, making Michael wonder if his insistence on not letting Lucy give Ms Makewell more life was wrong. Or, more importantly, if he had been mistaken for not performing the miracle himself.

"How long has our little sister given her before we find ourselves here again?"

"A day. A week. A month. Who knows, maybe a year," Haniel said. "I have looked. It is impossible to know these things. Her touch is deft. You must have taught her well. It is not eternity, though. That much, I am certain."

It was strange being the one fretting. Having Haniel do all the busy work before he opened his eyes to know it needed doing. Whilst they had both learnt to relax, the change had affected each of them differently. Michael's relief came from no longer feeling the burden of pressure to be in control, whilst Haniel's relief appeared to come from his self-worth. Before they arrived on Earth, Haniel had beliefs but lacked the conviction to do anything with them. Refusing to take Lucy back to Hell was the first step in Haniel's journey; allowing Haniel to make that decision was Michael's. It was nice to rely on his brother. That did not mean that Michael intended to stop being an angel that Haniel could depend on because he, like his little sister, intended to be a good angel, the best angel he could be.

"It's nothing short of a miracle," the nurse said, doing her best to work around Lucy, who was bouncing at her side, saying silly, miraculous, and biblical things she wasn't sure whether or not to believe.

"I make her better. I am doctor like you. An angel doctor. Can I have your hat for show and tell?"

The nurse gave Lucy her cap and humoured her, telling the happy little girl she looked like a lovely angel doctor and that if she wanted, she could come back and help with her other patients, all of who deserved a miracle. Asking this, however, had the nurse recoil at herself with guilt because if Lucy were indeed an angel, was she asking too much of God, and was it right to ask a child for another miracle when one had undeniably happened before her eyes? When she managed to catch up on her sleep, she would head straight to the local pastor and run these thoughts by him, but for now, she had a job to do.

"We go kindergarten now. Come on, Ms Makewell. Get up. Time to get out of bed. Everyone want see you and my hat."

"I think you ought to stay on bed rest until next week at the very least," the nurse said. "Miracle or not, you nearly left us there, and as much as we have loved your company, I know we would all like to make sure you don't come back anytime soon."

"I don't think Lucy will stop hopping around unless I go back right away."

"Well, if Lucy is a good angel, then she will let you have a little more rest, isn't that right?"

Lucy knew this adult trick. They would say something good about her and then threaten to take away the compliment if she didn't do what they said. Normally, Lucy would do something nefarious and naughty, something downright dastardly, even maniacally mischievous, to punish the adults for thinking they were smarter than her just because they were at least six times bigger than she was, or maybe more, she wasn't sure. When Lucy returned to kindergarten, she would get those sticks with all the numbers on and see just how small she was compared to a big person, but for now, she had to deal with the nurse's adult trickery. Fortunately, Lucy was in a very good mood, and she supposed the nurse had helped Ms Makewell lots and lots, so Lucy decided, just this once, to be nice.

"Okay, Ms Makewell can rest," Lucy said. "But only until end of week."

"What a good angel you are," the nurse said, a compliment that sent Lucy dashing over to Haniel and Michael to share the good word.

"You hear. I am good angel," Lucy said, giddy with excitement.

Naturally, Lucy stumbled over her wings and the nurse, still not used to Lucy's clumsiness and angelic resilience, winced as her face hit the vinyl floor with a slap.

"I did hear," Michael said, waving away the nurse's concerns as he picked up his little sister.

"I do good miracle," Lucy said, both a statement of fact, refusing to accept anything other than what she knew to be the truth, but also a question because, despite her assuredness, Lucy still wanted her older brother's approval above all others.

Lucy had performed this miracle flawlessly, she thought, as Michael closed his eyes to check on the state in which she had left the fabric of reality. There was no way he wouldn't see how good she had done. Ms Makewell had briefly opened her eyes, and with her mind drifting between day and dream, she had seen Lucy's father's light erupting from her wings. Fortunately, Ms Makewell's eyes flickered shut as her imagination reclaimed her, allowing Lucy to focus entirely on her miracle, just as her brothers had taught her.

When she had told Sandy what she was going to do, Lucy's intention was to remove the cancer completely, but the moment her hands came together, she knew that was not going to be possible. The malicious growth had spread to all parts of Ms Makewell's body. The strands of death had knotted themselves not only to her physical form but to her soul, too. It was a tangle of mess that could not be undone no matter how hard Lucy pulled.

Ms Makewell's only salvation from her cancer was Heaven. It was brilliant and pure, and the journey there was the only way for Ms Makewell to escape the darkness that had claimed her. It seemed a cruel fate that the only cure for her cancer was death, but Ms Makewell wasn't ready for that yet, and neither was Lucy.

Lucy had contemplated removing death, to have Ms Makewell live here, on Earth, forever, but the thought didn't give Lucy the solace she had hoped it would. Now that she understood balance, Lucy could see how easy it was to upset. Besides, Lucy understood eternity, and it would be far too long for creatures to exist who were as dependent on time as humans. Loss would crush Ms Makewell, and eternity would take something from her more vital than her life. It would take her spirit. Eventually, nothing would be left of the woman she was, and what would happen then? Love would no longer be her motivation, only pain and despair. Eternity would make a monster of Ms Makewell and everyone else around her. But if eternity wasn't balance, then what was?

Lucy couldn't remove the cancer altogether; that much she had figured out all on her own, and she had also realised that time upset the balance as well. Again, she figured that out all on her own, too. Lucy was proud of herself for these deductions, but if eternity was too long, and to let her die now was too soon, then what was the perfect amount of time to give Ms Makewell?

As Lucy untangled what she could of death from Ms Makewell's body, she weighed each possibility up between the palms of her hands. How long could she give her without causing more pain, and not only to Ms Makewell but to all who loved her and beyond? How much time did Ms Makewell need to be ready for her final journey to Heaven? How much time did everyone else need? There were so many questions, but Lucy intended to answer them all by herself. Lucy was an angel. A good angel. A me angel. It was on her to decide Ms Makewell's fate. She had ensured that the moment she had brought her hands together.

It took Lucy a while to decide, but not as long as she had expected. Not long enough for Michael to wake or for Haniel to return and catch her in the act. She was getting better at miracles, Lucy thought, as she put the cancer into remission.

"Let me be good," Lucy said, speaking to her father, hoping he was listening wherever he was. "Don't be mad." And before she parted her hands, Lucy quickly added, "Love you, Father. Miss you, Father. Kiss, kiss, kiss."

Lucy looked up at Michael, waiting for him to tell her exactly what she knew she was. She had done everything right. He had to see that. Lucy didn't want to go back to Hell. She was happy here with him, Haniel and Ms Makewell, too, but if she had done this wrong and set another cataclysm in motion, her brother would certainly lock her back behind her play gates. There would be no running and hiding in the park this time, and her tears would not keep her where she wanted to be.

Michael opened his eyes.

Lucy held her breath.

Haniel smiled at them both.

"You did a good miracle," Michael said, lifting Lucy into his arms and letting his little sister know with a hug that there was nowhere she would ever be but here, with them, with family and friends. "You are a good angel, Lucy."

31

It was good to be back at kindergarten. To be around loud and laughing children once again. Most people didn't like the screaming, but to Ms Makewell, the noise was soothing. More so now, after having believed she might never hear it again.

It was show-and-tell, and Charlie Shaw and Kaylie May were running around with their fire engines and police cars, pretending to be heroes like their parents. Others were hiding something new, something interesting they wanted everyone else to see for the first time. Many of the girls carried dolls, and some of the boys, too. Sandy had nothing in her hands, but her school pack did have two curiously fluffy and floppy ears. Fortunately, Sandy's parents were getting wise to their daughter's recently learnt mischief and had provided Ms Makewell with a rabbit hutch in case things got out of control, and it would, because the cross she had decided to return to the kindergarten wall had fallen upside-down, and that meant only one thing. The angels had arrived.

It had been three weeks since Ms Makewell had met Lucy and her brothers, and in all that time, Ms Makewell had yet to learn their surnames. She couldn't call them the Morningstars without getting berated, and calling them the Lucies felt ignorant, especially since she had developed such a close bond with the brothers. So, despite being unsure whether she believed their claims, Ms Makewell had resorted to calling them the Angels. Besides, there was an image Ms Makewell could not shake. One of Lucy looking down upon her with a bright light spread at her back like wings. Whether it was a memory or a dream, it was beautiful in ways words could not describe, and if that was what death looked like, Ms Makewell wasn't afraid to greet her again.

Half expecting to see Lucy's heavenly visage once more, Ms Makewell hid behind her clipboard to shield her eyes from her divine glow, but the only light was that of Lucy's smile beaming up at her, happy to see her favourite kindergarten teacher back where she belonged, and that was a sight Ms Makewell never wanted to hide from Whatever the truth was surrounding her recovery, whether it was God or this little girl who had given her more time, Ms Makewell would learn it if she was meant to, but only when her time came. Being back at kindergarten with her rambunctious children was enough for now. This was all the excitement Ms Makewell needed.

"How's our little morning star today?" Ms Makewell said, putting a tick next to Lucy's name on the register to take note of her arrival before class began.

Lucy wailed hello, a greeting with at least six extra o's attached. As usual, Lucy tripped on nothing, falling flat on her face as she ran toward her, reminding Ms Makewell she needed to return the classroom to a more Lucy-proofed layout. The substitute teacher must not have noticed the various dents in the furniture that hadn't been there before

Lucy's arrival. That and the young rebel had been skipping class whilst Ms Makewell had been in hospital, so he hadn't got to experience the mess of a day spent in the Devil's company. Which was probably for the best because the last she heard, the substitute teacher was still shaken up from his brief encounter with Lucy's pet snake, Albert, and the blood tears of Christ.

"Silly little wings," Lucy said as Ms Makewell helped her to her feet.

"They are not little," Michael said, huffing, still a touch of sleep in his eyes, having not been able to find the time to spend a moment in front of a mirror before leaving the house. "It is all I can do not to step on them."

"Give it a few more eons, and she will be able to wear them as we can," Haniel said.

"If I have not broken both of my legs before then."

"I do not think you can break your legs, Brother."

"I am aware of that. It was supposed to be a joke."

"In a few more eons, you might be able to tell one of those, too."

Ms Makewell ruffled the hem of Lucy's white prairie dress, undoing the creases and curls that her fall had put into it. She straightened her bow, the very one that had given her a scare on their first meeting, and then gave Albert a pat on the head before tucking him away inside Lucy's golden curls.

"You are very smiley today, Lucy," Ms Makewell said, admiring Lucy's fat, rosy cheeks. "Not about to do anything naughty, I hope."

Lucy shook her head. Ms Makewell didn't believe her. Neither did her brothers. Lucy always had something naughty planned.

"Happy you back," Lucy said, opening herself up for a hug.

Ms Makewell hugged Lucy and, deciding it best not to overthink what antics were coming her way, sent her off to say hello to the other children who were unpacking their things at the cubbies. Besides, it seemed that the ones who needed her attention now were the bickering angel brothers arguing about who was better at telling jokes. Ms Makewell didn't have the heart to tell either of them that neither was particularly funny.

"It is good to see you on your feet," Michael said as Ms Makewell coughed, reminding him with a stare that the only petty squabbles in the classroom should be between the children, and even those were to be resolved immediately.

"Must be nice to be back in your element," Haniel said.

Ms Makewell pushed her glasses up her nose. She had lost quite a bit of weight during her stay in the hospital, but determined to get back into fighting, kid-wrangling shape as quickly as possible, she had packed herself a healthy, filling lunch to eat after some midday math. "It does feel nice to be back."

Haniel and Michael had spoken their minds since the day Ms Makewell had met them, so she was surprised when their morning greeting lulled into an awkward silence. Like the other parents, she knew they had one question on their minds, a question they were too afraid to ask. Ms Makewell took this as a sign they had all grown fond of each other and nothing more, but she was not scared of what the future held, and they had no need to be either.

"I have been given a couple of months, a year if I'm lucky," Ms Makewell said. "I can feel it inside me. The darkness. The cancer. Growing. Spreading. I am just thankful I have more time to say my final goodbyes. More time to turn the last pages of this life before I begin the eternal story, in Heaven, in his arms." Ms Makewell looked up through the wooden rafters to Heaven and beyond into what she believed were the eyes of God.

Like Ms Makewell didn't have the heart to tell Haniel and Michael that they weren't funny, the angel brothers didn't have it in them to let Ms Makewell know that God had left this reality and she was looking up at no one. Besides, it didn't matter either way. God's love was everlasting, and wherever he was, whichever reality their father called home, his love would reach them.

"We look forward to enjoying every moment more that we have here with you," Michael said.

"Then you have finally decided to stay," Ms Makewell said. "No more fighting with Lucy as to whether you are coming or going?"

"Lakeville, Earth, humanity, they have grown on me."

"The stability will be good for your little sister," Ms Makewell said, ignoring the usual odd references to humans as if they weren't ones themselves because they were angels, she supposed. Maybe faith wasn't as easy as it seemed, even for those in Lakeville.

"Though it may be Haniel doing the drop-offs from now on."

"Oh?" Ms Makewell said, pushing her falling glasses up her nose again.

"With Lucy staying on Earth, I intend to reopen Limbo and help the wrongly damned souls find their way to Heaven. Of course, we will have to improve things here, too, lest I be stuck in Hell for millennia." Michael realised the irony of that statement, and it still pained him to consider the loneliness of his little sister's existence locked away in a place she did not want to be. "Which also means we might have to pull Lucy out of class early some days for a miracle or two."

"Kindergarten ends at three. No earlier and no later," Ms Makewell said, again ignoring the biblical things they said. "The stability will be good for the two of you, too. I can see you have both grown since we first met, especially you, Michael."

"But there is always room to learn, no matter how old we are," Michael said.

"So, you do listen."

"Only to you."

Whether that was a joke or a lie, Haniel wasn't quite sure. It was hard to tell the difference between the two sometimes. He wished Michael hadn't said it because it was neither funny nor true. His brother had been listening to him and everyone else. Michael had more than grown. He had transformed. He was a new man, a better man, a better brother, and Haniel intended to support him with his plans for Limbo and Hell, as he had supported him with Lucy.

"Well, I suppose you have to start somewhere." Ms Makewell laughed, a false one, but no less convincing for it. They really weren't very funny, she thought. Unlike their little sister who, with Sandy, was stood beneath the upside-down cross, undressing all the dolls the other children had brought in for show-and-tell.

Ms Makewell wasn't quite sure how they had got their hands on all the other children's toys, but if she knew Lucy, which Ms Makewell believed she did, she had either used Albert to steal them or used trickery and deceit to get the others into giving them to her. That, or she had asked for them, and they obliged because everyone loved Lucy. However they came into possession of the dolls, one thing was certain. Albert looked great in a summer hat, and Mr

Fluffywuffy Bunnykins the Second looked phenomenal in a dress.

"Kindergarten or zoo?" Haniel asked, he, too, practised in the art of spotting Lucy's mischief from a mile away.

"Sometimes I wonder," Ms Makewell said, laughing, and this time genuinely. Maybe angels could learn to be funny, she thought. "Now do run along, you two. Things to do, names to call, little devils and their well-dressed pets to deal with."

"Good luck, Ms Makewell," Michael said. "We shall see you this afternoon at three o'clock."

"On the dot. And Michael..."

"Yes, Ms Makewell?"

"Do call me Mary."

EPILOGUE

On the sixth hour of the sixth day of a wonderous and perfect sixth month, Ms Makewell greeted the children earlier than she normally would. Each face was new, and whenever another soul entered her kindergarten, the walls spread out to accommodate them. Lucy rushed in to greet Ms Makewell, too, not looking a day older or an inch taller than when they first met the year before. She thought it strange that Lucy was still in her class when all the other children had moved on.

Ms Makewell looked at the cross on the wall, ready to right it, but oddly, it did not fall, unlike Lucy, who tripped and stumbled over her oversized wings as she rushed to play with all the other children, crashing without fuss into everything in her path.

"You really must be more careful," Ms Makewell said as she ran her hands down the leading edge of the mischievous girl's shining wings, tucking them neatly out of the way, ready for her to fall again. "Picking up after you is becoming a full-time job." But that was not true in this perfect place because when she turned to tidy Lucy's mess, her classroom was already as she wanted it, clean and tidy, as if by miracle.

'Good,' Ms Makewell thought, offering a quiet thanks to God, wherever he may be, because all her souls were here, and she was ready to start a new day.

AUTHOR'S NOTE

Just as time runs differently for an angel, so it
does, too, for those without a purpose.

Find yours.
Feel a little less sad.
Make sense of the messy world
we live in together.

Thank you for reading,

Ashley Anthony.

Printed in Great Britain
by Amazon